A TIGER WALKS

IAN NIALL

A TIGER WALKS

WILLIAM MORROW & COMPANY
NEW YORK, 1961

Published in Great Britain in 1960
Published in the United States in 1961

Printed in the United States of America.

Second Printing, April 1961

Library of Congress Catalog Card Number 60-13345

A TIGER WALKS

CHAPTER 1

Josef was tired, and sick. He was tired of the road, of the hum of the engine and the endless vibration that gave him such an acute headache. He was sick of fumes; sick of the smell of diesel oil and sick, much more sick, of the odor of tigers, for the odor had been with him a long time, and today, in the heat, it was unbearably strong. It was strong because the tigers were in a poorly ventilated transport and because they hadn't been cleaned out. Josef glanced at his companion as though accusing him of neglect and responsibility for the smell of the animals, and the Indian's strange dark eyes flickered as though he read the very thought.

"I am happy," Josef said, "if I never smelled tiger in my life. I am happy if I never had a job driving them from one place to another. Next time we stop I am shooting them all. Boom! Boom! Boom!"

His companion reached into the compartment in front of his knees and brought out an old, heavy revolver.

"Boom!" he said with a high-pitched laugh. He pulled the trigger and the gun clicked. He pulled it again with the same result.

"The tigers laugh," he said. "It is like everything else. No good!"

To prove it, he put the muzzle of the gun to his head and pulled the trigger again.

"No good!" he said with delight, but Josef knew that the gun was loaded and his face blanched as he applied the brakes and brought the big vehicle to a waltzing standstill.

"Are you mad?" he gasped. He pronounced the last word with a final "t".

Ram Singh took the revolver from against his brow and broke the weapon open to tip the bullets into his palm. "They are no good," he said. "I try them yesterday."

"If I am having to shoot one of the stinking brutes with these what is happening?" asked Josef.

He slapped his hand to his brow and seemed to be filled with gloom.

"What is happening?" said Ram Singh. "Nothing but the tigers feeding on your bones. That is all. Tigers are always hungry when they are not fed."

The logic of this remark was lost upon Josef who groaned as he thought of trying to defend himself with a useless gun.

"It is time," he said at length, "that they were cleaned out. The smell travels in front of us. It is all over us and my stommick is made to heave."

"It is time we were feeding them some meat," said Ram Singh heavily, "or they will be eating their way out. If inspectors stop us they are requiring to know when we are feeding them and who is responsible."

"Peterson is responsible!" said Josef vehemently. "Peterson is their owner. Peterson has not paid us for a month. We have two pounds left. Are we to starve while the tigers are stuffing themselves?"

"Starvation is difficult for anybody and very difficult for a tiger," remarked Ram Singh.

He put the useless bullets back in the revolver and replaced the weapon in the compartment.

"When I was in Poland," said Josef thoughtfully, "I starved. Once we ate dogs."

"If we are stopping at dusk and catching sheep that would be excellent feeding for the tigers," mused Ram Singh.

Josef considered the suggestion for a moment or two and then set the vehicle in motion, not because he was impatient to get on along the road, but because the stench from the trailer had become overpowering and the tigers in their cages were beginning to complain of their hunger.

"In Siberia," said Josef above the noise, "where I was for a time, there were wolves, but if they are smelling like these tigers they are keeping far enough away and we don't smell them. If these tigers were mine I would have no cages. I would train them as they should be trained. I would make them sit up and beg and jump through hoops. I would make them roll over on their backs and use no whips, no revolvers."

Ram Singh laughed his high-pitched laugh. "They would eat you. They would turn their backs and urinate on you. They would chase you up a tree! They know who is a trainer."

"To train tigers you have to have the mentality," said Josef proudly. "You have to be without fear. You have to have an aristocrat's dignity. You have to be bold!"

"You are bold," said Ram Singh, "chasing a woman round a bed, but tigers are not like women. They don't like to be caught. They do not like to be made to roll on their backs."

"How are you understanding such things?" demanded Josef. "You are a builder of dung heaps, a cleaner-out of mangy cats! You are an emptier of receptacles! An underling!"

Ram Singh brought the revolver out of the compartment again.

"You are welcome to shoot yourself," he said. "Try it to your head. You are bold. See if this time the little bullets are awakening themselves!"

Once again the Pole brought the vehicle to an abrupt stop. He grabbed the revolver and dramatically put it to his temple and pulled the trigger. Nothing happened. He pointed it at the Indian's foot and pulled again. Boom! The explosion in the confines of the cab was deafening.

Ram Singh's eyes rolled. He coughed. There was a neat hole in the metalwork of the floor six inches from where his foot had been. The engine still throbbed with life. Josef stared at the revolver and the thin wisp of smoke rising from its barrel.

"It is fortunate that I am not aiming it at my head when it fires," he said shakily.

"Fortunate that you are missing my foot," stormed his companion. "You are an unstable character. You are inconsiderate of human life! You are the son of parents unaware of your conception, forgetful that they ever met!"

Josef set the engine in gear, relieved that no vital part of it, or of his own skin, had been affected.

"I am sorry," he said, "but you must remember that you were the one who said the bullets were no good. Your foolishness might have ended my life!"

Ram Singh rolled his eyes heavenward and rubbed his slender hands together.

"If this was a tiger, it is dead, perhaps. If it was your head, you are dead. If it was Peterson, he is dead, I hope. Since it was my foot it is miracle I am not crippled, bleeding to death."

He licked his lips and seemed to fall asleep. The cabin filled with sound as they lurched round boulder-marked corners on their way through the Welsh hills. On the slopes about them, right to the skyline, it seemed, on the vertical faces of sheer cliffs, sheep grazed. A buzzard sailed over a tract of boggy ground where a stream tumbled among rocks. The big, blue trailer swung and swayed as Josef steered, braked and accelerated. The tires showered grit into the fine grass at the roadside. They were heading for a distant coast and a holiday town where the attractions billed included Peterson's Tigers from the Bengal Hills, and little stickers on telegraph poles and lamp standards told the riders of outlandish bicycles and the eaters of cotton candy that this was a show the like of which had never been seen before outside India.

The line to book seats at the agency depot was, however, not even two-deep. It was non-existent. Who wanted to see tigers in the summer's heat? A paper published that afternoon carried an item that would have turned away even a tiger enthusiast. It described events that had put Charlie Peterson, the tiger man, in hospital in London. His tigers were coming through the Welsh hills to an appointment that Peterson would not be able to keep. His brother, travelling with a circus in the south, and aware of Charlie's misfortune, was busy drafting a telegram which read, "Bring tigers to Boscombe immediately. Booking cancelled." It was addressed to Josef and Ram Singh. How was Charlie Peterson's brother to know that the two had next to no money to buy meat for the animals and no inclination to travel back without their long-promised wages?

At the booking office the trap was down and the seedy occupant of the three-by-four wooden coffin dozed.

Josef and Ram Singh were weary and aggrieved. They were also thirsty. They looked for the next inn or public house. They only thought of the tigers when the vehicle slowed and they could smell them. As the trailer swung round a particularly tight bend one of the big tires at the back rubbed itself across the surface of the road like a schoolboy's eraser and then burst with a loud sound of a gun being fired. Josef began to fight the wheel and say things in Polish. He braked, swung the vehicle over, righted it, and began to pull up. Inside the trailer the tigers snarled and lashed out, tumbling in their own dung, prevented from doing harm by the partitions that separated each one's cage from that of his neighbor.

"This is the work of evil spirits," said Ram Singh. "I am shooting myself if it continues."

Josef said nothing. He could see a little village ahead, a

garage with a petrol pump, and an inn, which meant, he hoped, that he could get a wheel changed while he had a drink, and Mr. Peterson would pay.

"You are knowing the great Peterson," he was saying in imagination. "The tamer of tigers? Mr. Peterson will pay."

At that particular moment Mr. Peterson was unconscious and quite incapable of paying or being paid.

The trailer bumped into Pentre Ddu. The tigers snarled and worked themselves into a frenzy. The flat tire spread itself out like a pancake as the wheels stopped turning. Ram Singh got down and laughed. The little man laughed at everything and anything. His laughter was a strange thing, for there was never an atom of mirth in it. When Ram Singh was amused he didn't laugh. He smiled and his eyes glowed, that was all. His laughter was expressive of quite different emotion.

"I am Josef Pietz," said the driver getting down. "My friend, Mr. Ram Singh. We are tiger trainers in the employ of Mr. Charles Peterson, the owner of Peterson's Tigers from Bengal. This is Mr. Peterson's trailer. It has just suffered an unfortunate accident. Please to change the wheel and to charge the expense to Mr. Peterson who will pay, have no doubt."

"Well aye," said Bill Watkins, garageman. "What you got in the trailer?"

"Tigers," said Josef. "This I have just been explaining."

"Tigers?" the man sniffed. "Smells worse than pigs."

Josef moved in the direction of the inn and Ram Singh followed.

"Are they safe?"

The Indian laughed. "Mister," he said, "in the compartment of the cab you are finding a revolver. Sometimes it is shooting and sometimes it is not shooting. If one of the tigers unhappily is escape shoot him once, twice, until sometime it is going boom and he is killed."

Josef said over his shoulder, "If you are needing help I am at your service after I have got rid of my thirstfulness. I am not afraid of tigers!"

"I'm not afraid of tigers either," said the garageman. "Only of getting my head chewed off by one, isn't it? I will change your wheel for you with pleasure when you are ready to stand by, and I hope you are not going to be long because the smell is worse than a pigsty, worse than old Davy Evans's cesspool on a hot afternoon!"

At that moment one of the tigers roared and the trailer shook with a fearful vibration that could only have been the beast venting its wrath upon the main structure of the cage.

"If these tigers is tigers," said the garageman, "they better be small ones, that's all. I'm not in the mood for bein' chased by them."

But Josef and Ram Singh were already inside the Horseshoe ordering drinks for themselves. They knew only too well that the tigers were tigers, for they carried the odor of the beasts with them.

"A peculiar smell," said Betty Collins, the barmaid.

"Tigers," said Josef. "Only tigers smell like tigers. I am not alarmed."

"It's an alarmin' smell," she said.

"It is the smell of tigers," said Ram Singh.

"Go on," said the barmaid. "Pull my other leg."

"If your legs are as beautiful as your busts," said Ram Singh, his eyes glowing, "I shall be delighted."

"That'll do from you!"

Josef shrugged his shoulders and swallowed his drink.

"Pay no attention to him," he said. "He is a builder of trash piles, a cleaner-out of tigers. I am the one who is responsible for the tigers. I am not a chicken-hearted little man of no consequence. I am bold."

"You are bold," said his companion, "but only with your

trousers down. The tigers roar, and your bowels give up. I come from the country of tigers."

He smiled at his reflection in the mirror behind the bar and turned his gleaming eyes upon the barmaid once more. Betty Collins glanced in the mirror, saw Ram Singh looking at her, and flushed. For some reason she felt quite naked and she pulled at her blouse and then adjusted her over-tight skirt. Ram Singh was not in the least put out.

"I am dreaming wonderful dreams, dear missie," he said. "I am floating in the clouds. Your beauty takes my breath away. I am sleeping with you on a bed of feathers or a single board of wood. It makes no difference. I am in heaven."

"You are a cockerel from a dung heap," said Josef. "You are lecherous, indecent."

"If you don't stop talking disgusting," said the barmaid, "I'll have you both turned out of here, see if I don't!"

Josef looked at his companion with great contempt.

"I apologize for him," he said. "He is burned up with indecent thoughts. He is like a fly that breeds and breeds. He is a sex-machine and no more, and yet his laugh is emasculated!"

"I don't know what you are on about," said the barmaid. "I don't get you at all."

"Nobody gets me," said Josef. "My genius is incomprehensible. I am unique."

"You are without equal," said Ram Singh. "There is nothing like you. You will burst with conceit."

He ordered another drink and attempted to stroke the barmaid's hand as she gave it to him, but he failed and she swiped at him with a wet cloth.

"I'm warning you," she said.

"She is warning you," said Josef, "and I am warning you. I am not a person who warns without acting. I am afraid of nobody. I am not afraid of tigers even."

Ram Singh laughed again. "You are so afraid of tigers that you foul yourself every time you go near them."

Josef pondered this insult for a moment and then turned to the barmaid.

"Look," he said, "just outside I have five wild tigers." He drew himself to his full height. "You can smell them from here. You can almost feel the hot breath. I have no revolver. I have no whip. I have only my brave heart, but I will go out there and make them jump through hoops in your honor. I will make them roll on their backs for you!"

He swayed, for, not having eaten, he was becoming very drunk, and clicked his heels and bowed. Betty Collins raised an eyebrow and shrugged with a gesture that made it quite plain that not only was she unimpressed, but she considered Josef insane.

"You shall see," said Josef as he staggered out.

"Is he right in the head?" she asked Ram Singh.

"He is full in the bladder," said the Indian. "When he is full in the bladder he talks."

"Where's he gone? To see the tigers?"

"To relieve himself in probability," said Ram Singh. "You are beautiful. Your body fills your clothes. I am dreaming that I am caressing you and you are fainting in my arms. I can see you, pink and beautiful with no clothes . . ."

"I can see you gettin' locked up! That's what I can see!" said the barmaid who had, nevertheless, allowed him to catch hold of her hand. "You think he's gone to get a tiger out?"

"He is leaning against the wall in the urinal," said Ram Singh. "He is wondering what he would do if I am not with him to look after the tigers. He sleeps with an ax by his hand in case the tigers get to him and the tigers are locked in their cages and the cages are locked in the trailer!"

He drew her arm across the counter and attempted to

fondle her in spite of the fact that a large glass case was in the way.

"Here!" she said at length. "You better cool off!"

"If you are coming round to me," said Ram Singh, "I show you the way to heaven. I am making you delirious with happiness. I marry you."

"I don't want to be married, thanks!" she told him. "You give over! You better roll into bed with somebody else!"

Josef appeared at the door. He had removed his jacket and stood in his shirt and trousers with his thumbs in his belt, his blond hair tousled, and a wild look in his eye.

"Can you hear how furious they are?" he demanded. "Can you hear them? I have unlocked the trailer. Come out and see them! Their ears are flat on their heads, their lips are curled up. Their eyes are like glowing cinders. Rage devours them and I am not afraid."

"Fancy that!" said Betty Collins.

To Ram Singh she gave a significant look. "He's gone round the bend. That's what!" she said.

The tiger in the cage at the end of the trailer had a mask to strike fear in the heart of any sort of man. Its body was lithe, long and lean. Its odor was nauseating. Had it been able to pace the cage it might have been a less enraged beast, but it could not. The cage was not large enough and the tiger sat hunched, its head at times lowered in a reptilian posture and at times raised to the top of the cage so that it looked down balefully. Its tail, when new fury surged in the animal, beat upon the bars of the cage at the back. It watched Josef, and the hair on its body stiffened, its ears slicked back until they were almost lost in its heavy skin.

Josef could see only the tiger. Perspiration trickled from his eyebrows and beaded on his upper lip. His breathing was heavy. He knew, in a strange way, that he had to stand unguarded before the beast even though he was afraid. His fear had gone quite beyond the shaking of limbs, the trembling of muscles, the beating of a pulse. His mind, scrambled with a thousand frantic thoughts, only vaguely guided his hands to the key, the lock and the drawbar of the cage.

"I am not afraid," he said.

The words, as he repeated them, became a hoarse shout.

"Come out! Come out! Come out, you stinking beast!" he yelled.

Along the village people stopped doing what they had been doing. Dogs pricked up their ears. Backyard hens ceased picking among the potato peelings. An old man in a chair on a porch stood up.

"Iss murder bein' done?" he asked.

"Somebody drunk at the Horseshoe," said his neighbor.

In the Horseshoe Betty Collins lifted the counter flap and made for the door. Ram Singh smiled and attempted to embrace her.

"Give over!" she exclaimed and pushed him so that he collided with a table.

Ten yards from the door, in the forecourt of the garage, Josef stood with his legs spread and his hands by his sides. He had opened the door of the tiger's cage. The tiger remained where it was, its tail moving gently, its eyes fixed on the man who stood between it and freedom.

"I am not afraid. I am not afraid."

Josef was whispering now. He was no longer in a mental turmoil. His mind was free and clear of fear. He stood looking at the beast, confident that he had only to speak for it to obey. Behind him the barmaid screamed. The tiger's tail stopped moving. At first Josef missed the change in the beast and then fear came surging back. Its head was set at a new angle. The tiny signals that a tiger trainer might have recognized passed from the tiger's brain to its extremities. It was about to spring. An age that was measurable in fleeting seconds passed. For Josef there was no retreating and no going on. The cage was open, the door swung back out of his reach now, his boots half buried in the granite chippings, his body as heavy and incapable of movement as the big white stones that marked the drive-in. Now his thoughts ran to recollections of childhood; to a carved church in the shelter of pine trees, to mountains dusted with snow and a remembrance of the sharp, lung-searing air of winter in his own country.

Ram Singh came out of the door and looked at Josef. His tongue licked his lip and his hands clenched and unclenched for an instant.

"Walk back, Josef!" he hissed. "Walk back!"

The world was suddenly still. Even the tigers in the other cages were silent and motionless. Far away on the mountain a sheep bleated, but it was a small sound, the song of a gnat at dusk and no more.

The tiger sprang.

"Ai . . . eeh!" Ram Singh gasped.

The great beast struck Josef in the chest and came down with him. It slashed him with its claws, bit his body across the lower ribs, dragged him suddenly in a half circle and disembowelled him with a fearful movement of a leg that might have been a casual kick but was intended to destroy him as the man might have struck down a fly. Josef died. He had made no sound throughout the attack. The tiger crouched over him.

Ram Singh turned swiftly on his feet and attempted to jump through the door but the door was closed! Betty Collins had thrown it to behind her, and for some reason it wouldn't open. Ram Singh beat upon it with the palm of one hand and struggled to open it with his other hand. He rolled his eyes and laughed again. Someone inside tried to open the door which seemed to have stuck. The granite chippings moved under the feet of the tiger. It stood now not twelve feet away. There was blood on its head and on its underbelly. It had walked through the blood of its victim. Part of his shirt trailed from a hind claw. Ram Singh began to say prayers in his own tongue. The door would not open. The more he pushed the more the person inside tried to help him, the more obstinately the thing stuck, and the tiger tensed and seemed to rock back on its heels. Inside the Horseshoe the barmaid screamed again. Outside it was as quiet as it had been since the tiger first sprang.

CHAPTER 2

Like all village dwellers, Jack Roberts was an incorrigible peeper at the window and the passing scene. There was no malice in him, but a great curiosity. His curiosity had increased a little with the years, but this was a natural thing in a man who had walked the streets of Cairo and seen the famous cities of Italy, fought in towns where tanks crouched amid shattered buildings and snipers lay behind parapets. Here in Pentre Ddu there was no excitement in life unless one looked for it and looked hard. Sometimes, even when one almost tipped over backwards tilting a chair too far, there was little to increase the pulse rate or make a man look again, except on a Saturday when blows were exchanged outside the Horseshoe, or a pair of lovers acted with indecent abandon, imagining themselves unobserved while on their impatient way to the shelter of the bushes.

It wasn't that Jack longed for a skirmish in the village and hoped for the chance to go clattering out with a Bren to set it up behind his own garden wall, but he found the bleating of sheep in the brackened hills and the noisy progress of the baker's van along the road unexciting markers of the passing of the hour and the day. Gradually, however, when he returned to his carpentry shop, to making gates and cupboards and bee-boxes, he found that the sound of a footstep on the otherwise quiet road was a welcome excuse for him to break off doing what he was doing, to rest on his elbow at the bench, to lower his newspaper or halt his spade. Now in the evening, he sat in the front room of his cottage reading the news, faintly aware that something was happening along at the Horseshoe and in the forecourt of Bill Watkins's garage.

"What's the big blue van at Watkins's, Jack?" his wife asked.

"A trailer of some kind," said Jack. He didn't need to look again. He had noticed the thing there earlier.

"What was all the shoutin' just now, Jack?"

Elsie Roberts was one of those women who love to name their husband every time they ask a question.

"Dunno," he said, and then, recalling that something out of the ordinary must have been going on, he sat up, tilted his chair and looked out, balancing with one hand on the window-sill. His mouth opened and stayed open.

"What is it, Jack?" his wife asked.

Jack replied in a whisper, a strangled, urgent whisper. "Where's Pat?" he asked.

"Here, Dad," said his small daughter.

"There's a tiger on the road at the Horseshoe!" Jack gasped. "There's blood on the stones! I think there's a man lyin' behind it an' it's walkin' towards another fella standin' in the door of the Shoe. He's a black man an' he can't get in! They've shut the door on him!"

Elsie Roberts didn't move for a moment. She looked at the round eyes of her daughter and looked at her husband again, wondering for a second whether all the things he had seen and done in the war had finally turned his mind. Faintly, and far away, it seemed, a woman screamed and she could hear the hollow sound that was Ram Singh beating a message of terror on the door.

"My God!" she exclaimed. "It can't be, Jack!"

"It bloody is!" said Jack, and at that instant his chair went over.

Before he could recover or even rub is head, Jack's wife and daughter were crowding in the window to see the tiger. Elsie Roberts saw the beast and the body of its victim. She put her hand to her throat and began to feel faint.

"Oh, Jack!" she said.

Jack came up from the floor shaking his head and muttering curses. He stood for a moment looking at the scene beyond the window and his mind began to race. He must do something; stop what was going to happen down there as once he had stopped an enemy poised to put a grenade into his patrol. A gun was what was needed. He scrambled across the room, picked up the shotgun that stood in the passage, dragged out a drawer in the kitchen and found a single cartridge. He loaded the gun as he ran and was on the road before his wife was aware of what he had done.

"Jack!" she shrieked, but it was too late.

Little Pat began to cry. The door remained open. As he ran, Jack remembered the door, but it was too late to turn back. He put up the gun and pulled the trigger when the moment came that he knew the tiger was about to spring. The shot cut leaves from the bush near the window of the Horseshoe. It spattered lime from the wall in several places and it clipped fur from the head of the tiger, nothing else. If Jack hadn't fired the tiger would have brought the little Indian down, but instead the beast sprang about, its great body swaying. Ram Singh stopped beating on the door and clutched at the wall to stay himself from falling. He looked with disbelief at the tiger and the man who had intervened. Jack Roberts stood still, aware that there was nothing he could do and that the tiger might at any second spring towards him. How long it was before the tiger moved no one could have said with certainty after the beast plunged off the road. Perhaps it was half a minute; perhaps minutes passed. Jack saw Ram Singh running towards him with his hands outstretched, but, before he could say a word, the Indian had the gun and was racing after the tiger.

"Come back! Come back! It's not loaded!" Jack yelled, but if the Indian heard he didn't understand.

Jack made to run after him and for the first time knew that his wife was not in the house where he had left her. She tugged at his arm and held him. He swung around to shake her off, and then the futility of chasing the Indian, who ran like a madman to the gully and the swaying bushes through which the tiger had passed, dawned upon him.

"He'll be killed for certain," he groaned and then he shouted, hopelessly, "Come back! Come back!"

Down the street doors began to open and people came onto the road. In the thicket, below the rock at the side of the gully, a crow flew up. The tiger stopped with its forefeet in the water of the stream. It could hear Ram Singh coming. It half turned and looked in his direction, hearing the swish of branches, the creak of a fence which he crossed, the sound of his small feet on the stones of a nearby dry ditch. It was a long time since the tiger had stood in the jungle or walked beyond the confines of a cage of one sort or another, but here, its oldest instincts told it, was the jungle and pursuit. Here was its enemy and the lesson that took no learning. The Indian had never stalked a tiger and needed to know how, but the tiger knew, without being taught, how to turn and kill. It sprang up onto a boulder, stepped across another and stood waiting for its pursuer to come. Midges spun above its head; an owl flew from a crumbling stump of a tree. Up in the hills a curlew, disturbed on the boggy ground by some passing animal, went beating off, crying the lonely cry of its kind. Ram Singh halted among the hazels. His hands, clutching the useless gun, were wet with perspiration. He cocked the hammers and stared ahead. Somehow he knew the tiger was there.

Mrs. Baker, mother of the landlord of the Horseshoe, came downstairs. She walked with great difficulty, plagued as she was by arthritis. She was a woman who was always being irritated by things large and small and this evening, it seemed, there had been more to annoy her than ever; more noise in the bar; too much banging outside, and then a car had backfired.

"Is there to be no peace here?" she demanded when almost at the foot of the stairs. "Have you no authority in this place, Frank? Am I to be disturbed by hooligans in the bar and Saturday-night brawls outside every night of the week?"

Betty Collins was lying on a couch in the back room. Old Mrs. Baker looked at her round the end of the stairs.

"What's the matter with you?" she demanded. "Got yourself pregnant?"

Her son, who was shaking in every limb, came through with a glass of water.

"She's fainted," he said. "There's been a tiger outside."

"You've been at the port!" accused the old woman. "I've warned you before. That's the way your last bout started! Port!"

Frank Baker ignored his mother as he tried to get control of himself. He needed a drink. How he needed one! A man had been shut outside at the mercy of a wild beast and how was he to pretend that he had tried to open the door? It had never stuck before. It wasn't sticking now, as people would soon find out. It was half ajar, in spite of what had happened, and anyone in the hall could see the awful thing strewn about the garage forecourt like the débris of a slaughter-house.

"A man has been killed, Mother," he said, putting the water to Betty Collins's lips as he raised her head.

"I've always said it would come to something like this! You've no control! No control at all! Even in the middle of a week two or three locals can do just as they please!"

"There was a tiger . . ."

What was the use? His mother never listened and heard only what she wanted to hear. Her mind was fixed, and she was incapable of being influenced or swayed except by her latest whim or the twinges of her complaint. Now she went to the door and looked out at the little group of people standing horrified at the sight of Josef's mangled body. Somehow she didn't understand what it meant.

"A disgusting sight!" she exclaimed.

Frank Baker put down the glass and let the barmaid fend for herself. He went to his mother and took her arm. She glared at him.

"A tiger got out and killed that man," he said loudly.

She began to grasp what he had said.

"A tiger? A tiger? God save us all!"

At that moment one of the tigers in the trailer growled. A concerted cry went up from the bystanders. They thought about the escaped beast and remembered those in the trailer. Mothers clutched at their children and the group moved back, shrinking from the scene, fearful that another tiger might spring out and throw itself upon them. No one had attempted to cover the corpse and a dog was sniffing at the fragments of clothing, its hackles up and its nostrils full of the smell of tiger.

"Shut the door!" ordered Mrs. Baker. "Ring for the police. Do something, you besotted idiot!"

She hobbled in and looked at the tearful barmaid. "You!" she shouted. "Gather yourself together and get the bar closed down. Look as if you had something more in your head than men and love-making!"

Betty Collins scowled. "You dried-up old battleax!" she said. "You sour old bitch!"

The old woman made a habit of never listening to any sort of retort her own remarks might produce. She banged her stick on the floor and asked, "If the tiger killed that man where has it gone?"

Her son shrugged his shoulders. He was jiggling the rest of the telephone, trying to distract the local operator at the exchange from his favorite pastime of listening-in. "Up the stream, I suppose. It's probably miles away now."

The significance of what he had said was slow to come upon Frank Baker. A tiger loose in the hills! How would they get it back? He had a vision of the beast padding through the Forestry rides, across the fire-breaks and through the ranks of young conifers. He could see it crossing ridges in the mist, on the trail of hikers, terrifying sheep, pulling down one of the store cattle up by the lake, sniffing at the doors of remote farms and bringing terror wherever it was seen. It would have to be shot and a rifle would be needed, but once it found its way into the rocks and the boulders, through the scrub-oaks, the alders, the blackthorn bushes and the tangles of dead birches, who would dare to stalk it? It would have to be caught at once! It would have to be found before dark. Already the heron was flying down the valley and the last of the crows had fallen silent. Dusk would soon be settling about the hillocks where nightjars hawked for moths and in places where owls would fly silently from one perch to the next.

"Hello! Hello!" he said urgently.

Someone was knocking at the door, but he ignored the summons and Betty Collins, who had got to her feet and smoothed her tight skirt, went to see who it was.

"Don't let them in!" said old Mrs. Baker.

"Who is it?" Betty asked.

"Bill Evans. I want to telephone."

"Bill Evans wants to telephone," she repeated.

"Let him telephone somewhere else!" spat the old woman and then she thought about Bill Evans who made pin-money for himself sending little bits to the local newspaper. Perhaps if he telephoned the news, reporters and photographers would be sent down. The bedrooms would be booked. Meals would be eaten and drinks bought.

"No," she said quickly, "let him in."

The door was opened to admit Bill Evans.

"Can I use your phone, Mrs. Baker?" he asked.

"You can," she said, "when Frank has done with it. If you're telling the newspapers, tell them I've six bedrooms and first come, first served."

"I will," said Bill. "Iss only fair to you, Mrs. Baker. Jack Hughes wouldn't let me use his phone. He was tryin' to get a doctor. A doctor! Imagine it, an' that poor chap's body all chewed up the way it is. I said a fine lot o' good a doctor'll be. What you want iss a undertaker, mate!"

"Get me the police," said Frank Baker suddenly. 'We've got a tiger loose in the village, Ted. A man's been killed by it."

"I know," said Ted. "I wouldn't like to be the bloke what goes after it, neither!"

A minute passed and then a gruff voice said, "Newydd Police Station."

"This is the Horseshoe at Pentre Ddu," Frank said hurriedly. "A man has been killed here by a tiger that escaped from a circus trailer."

"Don't tell 'em no more, Frank!" pleaded Bill Evans. "He'll only ring through to the newspapers an' do me in the eye, like!"

"Would you repeat that, please?" asked the policeman.

"A tiger loose in Pentre Ddu," said Frank. "A man killed."

"Look," said the policeman soberly, "I hope this isn't a joke."

"A man's been killed," said Frank, wishing he had had the drink he now needed so badly.

"Hurry up, mate!" urged Bill Evans.

"Where? How?"

"The tiger got out of a cage in a trailer in the forecourt of Watkins's garage. It killed one of the men who was in charge of it. It has gone off into the gully."

"One of the men? How many men were concerned?"

Frank Baker thought of the Indian. His head seemed filled with the sound of the frantic drumming on the door. "Where did the Indian go?" he asked over his shoulder.

"Took his hook," said Bill Evans. "Suppose he knew it was his fault."

"It wasn't his fault," said Betty Collins. "It was the other chap what let it out."

"There was an Indian bloke with it," said Bill Evans, talking over Frank's shoulder, "but he's gone."

"All right," said the policeman. "Hang up. I'll put a report through."

"He's putting a report through," said Frank. "If they don't act at once nobody will dare go out of doors tomorrow for miles around."

"They'll track it with dogs," said Bill Evans, grabbing the telephone. He had been busy composing what he had to say on the back of an envelope and now he was anxious to make his call.

"Hey, Ted!" he complained into the instrument. "Where the hell are ya, Ted?"

On the road Jack Roberts shepherded his wife back to their cottage.

"I gotta see what I can do here," he said. "There's more tigers in that thing an' somebody should cover the poor man's body an' keep the dog from sniffin' at it."

He had a great respect for the dead and he was troubled at the thought of a village dog wandering through the blood of the tiger man. When he had closed the door firmly he went back to the garage forecourt. He was alone on the road now. People watched from their doorways and windows.

"Get back inside, Jack!" someone shouted. "Kitty Price seen somethin' in the bushes up there. It's comin' back!"

Jack didn't know what to do. He looked at the bushes, at the pitiful remains of the dead man and at the trailer with its open door. If he closed the door and the tiger did come back of its own accord, it wouldn't be able to return to its cage, supposing it felt inclined to do such a thing. He went to the trailer and looked in. The other cages were evidently locked. The tigers were moving about restlessly. They could smell blood, he fancied, although he vaguely recalled having heard that tigers have little or no sense of smell. He was sure they could sense that one of their number was loose in the open and perhaps when they growled the escaped beast stopped in its tracks and listened to them. Picking up a piece of sacking he found on a wall nearby, Jack attempted to cover the body. He felt that he shouldn't disturb things and when he found a round stone at his feet he stepped carefully over it, but an instant later he swooped down, picked up the stone and hurled it with all his strength at the hovering dog. The dog put its tail between its legs and ran up the village.

"It's comin' back, Jack. It's comin' back," someone shouted again. They weren't talking about the dog. He stood still, his hands by his sides, peering at the bushes around the stream. It seemed that something watched him from cover, and he began to work out how far away it was, and how far he could run before a beast that might be more than nine feet in length bounded after him and pulled him down. The feeling of being in danger was familiar. He had known it many times before, but now there was a difference. A human enemy could be relied upon to act in a certain way. The moves were numbered and the reaction predictable, but a tiger was a jungle beast. It could wait to outlast the patience and nerve of the best of men. It could come out and kill while it was being killed and human strength was nothing to it. He had no way of defending himself and he was like the poor Indian, bait for the wild beast; as helpless before it as a sparrow nestling before a cat.

"Hey, black fella," he shouted on the spur of the moment. "Come an' take shelter in my house. There's nothin' in that gun!"

If the Indian heard he made no reply, and Jack began to walk backwards away from the trailer, fancying that he saw the bushes moving and the tiger's head emerging.

"He's goin' back," they whispered from door to door. "He was mad to go so close."

They had forgotten that their own curiosity had lured them out but a minute or two before, but now dusk was creeping out from walls and gables and the tiger walked everywhere, larger than life; as big as a pony, silent, ferocious; seeking, as the Prayer Book said, whom it might devour. It was a warm summer's evening and there was no breeze in the valley and yet, although the leaves of the creeper, the rose and the honeysuckle were motionless, people along the village street shivered.

At the telephone Bill Evans, prompted by an ambition to launch himself on a career as a newspaperman, said: "A tiger walks the village street of Pentre Ddu tonight and a dead man lies in the forecourt of the Horseshoe Inn."

He had varied the facts just a little to please Mrs. Baker, who was listening at his elbow, because she was giving him credit for a call to Fleet Street.

"Come off it," said a voice at the other end of the line. "Give us the straight facts. We'll do the descriptive touches."

This daunted Bill Evans, who had found it a great effort to compose what he felt was a grand introduction to a front-page story.

"A tiger escaped and mauled a circus man called Josef Pike here this evening," he said in his best English. "It killed him. There was an Indian chap with him. The tiger then went for him too and Jack Roberts, the carpenter here, shot at it with a shotgun and it made off into the hills."

"What happened to the Indian, brother?" asked the sub-editor.

"I never said nothing about the Indian's brother," said Bill testily.

"What happened to the Indian?" repeated the sub-editor. "Give me his name! How did the tiger get out? Who did it belong to? Has it attacked anyone else there? Have they started to hunt it down? Can you get a picture of the scene? Is there a picture of this Jack Roberts chap?"

Bill tried to answer these questions as best he could. "Can I get a picture?" he said finally. "It's nearly dark now. The tiger's gone and the police have been called, but so far nothing else has happened. Oh, you can put up here if you like to book. They got six bedrooms."

"Hold on a minute," said the man on the news table.

While Bill waited Ted, the switchboard operator, broke in.

"You better clear the line, Bill," he said. "The police want to talk to Frank Baker."

The phone crackled as someone in Fleet Street began to say something, and then the policeman's voice came through.

"I am to ask you to warn everyone in Pentre Ddu right away to lock their doors and stay in their homes," he said. "Police officers and military are on their way there now."

"They're gettin' the Army out to hunt the brute," said Bill, "an' not before time!"

The tigers in the trailer began to roar. In the gloom of the hall of the Horseshoe Frank Baker looked at Bill Evans and then at his mother.

"Somebody's got to go knockin' on doors," said Bill. "Maybe we better go and do it together."

"I need a drink first," said Frank. "I need a couple."

At that moment the tiger, which had watched Ram Singh

as the little man stood in the gloom holding the shotgun until his arms sagged, began to tense and prepare to spring. Its pads splayed on the mossy rock and it shot its body into the air in a single movement that propelled it through a screen of hazel branches, but the sound and the striking of the beast were one to its victim. Ram Singh's feet, protruding from beneath the tiger's body, kicked once or twice and dug into the loose earth as he died. The gun clattered into the roots and the beast dragged the man five or six yards, as a cat might have dragged a half-grown rabbit, and then it stopped, crunched an arm and abandoned the kill to drink in one of the pools close at hand. Some of the blood on its face was washed into the stream.

The telephone had rung again in the Horseshoe and Bill Evans, fortified with his glass of whisky but not yet ready to walk abroad to warn the village, picked up the instrument and tried again to impress a newspaper with a hastily improvised description of the events of the evening.

"Tonight, behind locked doors and lamplit windows," he said, "sit the villagers of Pentre Ddu, while a tiger, bloodied and savage, stalks in search of a new victim. In the forecourt of the centuries-old Horseshoe Inn lies the body of a tiger-keeper named Josef who was killed . . ."

"For God's sake, give it a rest!" said Frank Baker.

He could think of nothing else but the door and of the Indian beating to get in. He looked at Betty Collins and wondered what she would say when the time came, for he hadn't been trying to let the Indian in with his foot holding the door shut, although he had pretended to tug with all his strength at the latch and the handle.

She came over to him and nudged him.

"You won't say nothing about me shutting that Indian chap outside?" she asked quietly.

He looked her in the eye. "I tried to let him in, but the door stuck fast. A stone, I suppose," he said.

"I suppose so," she replied. "You say what you saw and I say what I saw. That's only fair and right, isn't it?"

She patted his arm and he looked at her again, noticing for the first time a swimmy look in her eyes and a certain voluptuous invitation that had never been there before.

"What you saw and what I saw," he whispered, "was the Indian going out and closing the door and the door sticking when I tried to let him in again."

"You got a wonderful memory, Frank," she said.

She had never used his first name before. He gulped down his drink and smiled at her.

"You better get cleared up. The place will soon be swarming with police. I'll talk to you later."

Old Mrs. Baker screwed up her eyes and regarded them both from the chair in which she was sitting. She had taken more gins than usual and her uncertain temper was even more uncertain. She sensed what she called hanky-panky. Betty Collins, the barmaid, was too buxom and far too sly, in her opinion, and Frank was as weak as the beer they sold at closing time, but let them hanky-panky. She was sure that the fat trollop would find Frank as useless at one thing as he was at another!

"Well," said Bill Evans, swaying just a little, "we got our duty to do. It's not everybody that would walk in the dark with a tiger at his heels!"

They went out at length, stepping nervously, listening to their own heartbeats and all the little sounds of the night. Slowly the moon had climbed up behind the eastern hills. They were knocking at the first of the doors when the police car came swishing through the village. Its headlights, traversing the shadowed wall, came to rest on the trailer and the dark lump that was the dead man's body. Doors clumped shut and heavy feet sounded on the garage forecourt. Someone whistled and said, "My God!"

Far away, in the deep shadows of the hills, a fox barked.

Betty Collins peered through one of the glass-whorl windows in the direction of the car and the shadows that moved around its lights. She patted her hair in place and began to hum to herself. Pentre Ddu was coming to life at last, with exciting prospects. Not the least of them was the light in Frank Baker's eye. She knew what that meant as surely as she knew a double bed from a garden hammock, and for as long as she liked to remember she had preferred sleeping in a double bed—with a bed-mate.

CHAPTER 3

There is a time, in the evening in summer, when the hills seem to brood. The sun leaves them, and the darkening hollows and lesser valleys belong only to the grazing sheep. The raven retires to the crags, calls once or twice and makes short flights preparatory to going to roost. There is no more sobering hour than the one that marks the departure of the day, when a breeze, no longer warm, passes through the bracken and on to press the water of the lake into a swell, without ripple, like a pool of heavy oil. In such an atmosphere a man needs a buoyant heart and a controlled imagination. If a bird flies across the hills it is a black bird. Sounds can be heard a long way off, but in the remoteness of the mountains they are small, plaintive sounds, sad and almost human as the bleat of a sheep can be at times. A light may show like a glow-worm on some distant slope, but the hill farms are on the fringe of more civilized places, and the wild mountain has no hospitality for the wanderer, even though, here and there, stout-hearted climbers or walkers may camp in the shelter of a rock.

Four miles above Pentre Ddu, beyond the edge of the fir

plantings and the forestry boundary, a green tent was pitched on a little plateau that overlooked the black lake and the stream running first through rocks and then through peat to come at length again to the rocks and the ridge above the village. The owners of the tent were four young students who had come to tramp the hill paths and scale the crags. They were formidable fellows dressed in the uniform of the mountaineering enthusiast. Their stockings were thick, their boots studded, their parkas fitted with a dozen pockets and zip fasteners. When they were in camp they sang songs ribald and profane but most of the day they travelled in line, like a flight of cormorants. At evening they had much to say. By day they saved their breath for the punishing slopes and grey cliffs up which they clambered one after another, no longer like wild birds, but more like insects. Johnnie Flynn, a medical student, was one of this party. He was known as the Quack, partly because of the profession to which he aspired, and partly because someone thought he had the characteristics of a duck, which he had, his walk being a sort of ungainly waddle. Flynn, however, didn't resent the nickname. He was a good-natured fellow who liked to lift his spirits and the spirits of those about him, if he could, by playing the mouth organ.

At dusk on this particular evening the Quack had been in the lead as the party of four made their way to the place in which they had pitched their tent, and rested with his hands on his hips while his slower companions toiled up the slope.

"Hurry up, you dragends!" he shouted as he waved them to come on.

His voice echoed back from the hill.

"Did you hear that?" he asked as they reached him.

"Hear what?" said the tallest of the party. "You bellowing like a sick bullock?"

"Damn me if I didn't hear something like a lion roaring!" said Flynn.

"Damn you then," replied his companion, "but get down for water and stop mooning about here. Are we to have nothing to eat because you want to make love calls to the bullocks over yonder?"

"It was a powerful sort of bullock," said Flynn.

"A powerful lot of old bull!" somebody said with a laugh, and Flynn shrugged his shoulders and went into the tent to get the collapsible bucket and go down to the lake with it for water.

"It could have been," mumbled Flynn as he came out into the open with the bucket.

"Watch a goblin or something doesn't get you, Quack," they said. "This is the witching hour and all that sort of stuff."

He went down the slope to the lake, swinging the bucket in his hand. He could see the outline of the water well enough, but the big boulders were in shadow and, in spite of himself, he felt nervous as he came through the smaller rocks and slipped and slithered to the water's edge. At first he was unaware of any but his own movement there, and then, as he saw the darkening of the water when he stooped to fill the bucket, he somehow knew he wasn't alone. The bucket hung in the water. He let it hang there as though he had been caught in the act of stealing, and looked slowly first to left and then to right. Every shadow along the lakeside seemed to have moved a little, but when he steadied himself and controlled his shaking arm and looked again, he knew the shadows hadn't moved, and yet something was there, something bigger than a sheep. He let the bucket sink and then pulled it out with water streaming from the saturated canvas. The sound should have comforted him, but instead it frightened him in an odd way. He felt that it might be covering the approach of something or somebody not so far away.

"You didn't run into any lions down there, did you, Quack?" he could hear them saying. He shrugged his shoulders and stepped away from the water with the bucket. It was then that he knew something was imposed on a long boulder that sat half in and half out of the lake. It was a black shadow. As he peered it changed shape. It could only be a man, he told himself at length, a man sprawling there waiting to carry on doing whatever he had been at when Flynn came down. He was tempted to say something, but instead he began to whistle softly to himself. From the far skyline someone shouted down to him.

"Hey, Flynn! Quack! Have you gone for a swim or something?"

The jumbled words were shout and echo. Flynn made nothing of it. The shadow on the boulder didn't move. He paused, suddenly emboldened, and stood looking directly at it long enough to leave no doubt that he was watching it, as it was watching him. There was no tune to his whistling as he went up the slope. He didn't like the silence. The hair on his neck was standing. His scalp tingled. He paused to shift the bucket from one hand to the other. He was perhaps a hundred and fifty yards from the lake. He could hear the shingle gritting under the weight of something crossing it. The silence that followed could have been the man trailing him up the grassy slope. Well, they would be four to one at the top. He wasn't afraid of physical violence, the thing that unnerved him was not seeing, waiting, wondering.

"There's something down there," he told them when he reached the tent and put down the bucket.

Jimmie Temple, his close friend, had lit the little storm lantern and was busy cooking something in a frying-pan over the stove.

"I know, Quack," he said. "I ask what, and you say, the flaming lake, and spend the rest of the evening laughing."

"That's right," he said, suddenly feeling foolish. After all, what had he seen but shadow among shadows? What had he heard but some small stones moving? Perhaps a sheep had moved the stones.

"Thought you had gone clean to hell," said Taffy Davies. "Steady now, boy, you'll bring on an attack of the banshees like last time!"

Flynn was listening again. He could hear far-away sounds that were like bullocks bellowing or dogs barking, and yet were deep and somehow stronger and more savage than any dogs.

"Shift it, Quack," said Willis. "What's up with you to-night? Got a bad attack of the Celtic twilight or whatever it is you get?"

A wood fire would be a fine thing, Flynn was thinking. He had the willies all right and to be truthful he hadn't been so disturbed in the dark since he had been a child. He looked at the dark outlines of his companions busying themselves around the tent. He could see the little lamp and Jimmie, crouched over the stove like a witch-doctor.

"I'll be glad to get into my bag," he said to no one in particular. "This day's had me and I've had it. If I weren't so hungry I'd turn in now."

No one answered. They were busy and he was talking to himself. Taffy Davies was peering at the map with a pencil torch. Willis was doing something with his boots and his socks. Over Jimmie's shoulder came the smell of frying meat out of a tin.

"There was something down there, you know," he said again at length. "I wonder what it could be."

At the edge of the black lake, Bob the Cough, as he had been known almost all his life by the natives of Pentre Ddu, listened to the sound of the mouth organ and cursed the campers. Bob hadn't worked for more than seven days in his life on account of his "consumption." His record of seven days had been achieved when the magistrates had simply insisted, for once, that he produce the fine in that period, for hitherto one offense had hardly been atoned for before he was being fined again, and all his crimes produced no more than a shilling a week to the coffers of authority. Nobody expected poor Bob to follow an honest calling. If he went off to the mountain and spent days there that was plainly because mountain air was good for his complaint. The unfortunate Bob couldn't work on a road gang, help make hay or gather flocks for shearing and dipping. That sort of exercise would bring on the spitting of blood that Bob talked about. Nevertheless, Bob could climb a steep slope with the best and could fish for eighteen hours when he liked, in rain, mist or cold wind. Now he was about one of his favorite games, ottering for trout. Most poachers who use an otter like to have a companion with them. It is a lonely occupation and a companion not only lends a hand when things go wrong with the gear, but he can stand on a look-out place and keep his eyes and ears open for the approach of an intruder, a bailiff, for instance. The otter board has lead to keep it submerged in the water, riding like the keel of a boat. It is rigged like a kite to a line which the poacher manipulates, working the board against the current until he has it drifting out and away from him carrying a long string of flies across the fish the lake holds. There is nothing to stop an otter board being used by day, but for various reasons it is generally manipulated at dusk and after dark. The best fish rise at this time and the poacher has a better chance of remaining undetected. Bob the Cough had never been anything but an individualist and he worked his otter board alone, trusting no one for the good reason that no one trusted him.

If he disliked labor of any sort Bob, when it came to unraveling tangled lines with eel-like ways and unfastening hooks that seemed to catch in everything but the mouths of trout, had great patience and industry. He swore and mumbled to himself, it is true, but he never gave up and usually by daybreak, whatever his misfortunes, he came away with what he had set out to get, rewarded by persistence near to living a prayer. As he moved about the rocks preparing his gear for the drift, Bob the Cough wondered whether he might not have been wiser to have packed it all up and carried it over the mountain to another lake where he could work in peace. It wasn't that he felt that the campers would be down to spy on him, or that even if they saw his board they would know it for what it was, but their presence meant that there might be sound and movement to cover the approach of bailiffs and he would have to consider, at every small sound, whether the time had come to dump his line and throw his catch into the first peat-hole he passed as he took himself off. There was no mystery about Bob the Cough's activities. The bailiffs knew him, and knew what he was in the habit of doing. When and where remained his secrets, so long as he stayed alert.

Bob had removed two fish from his line at the end of his second drift when he looked up and saw the shadow that briefly changed the skyline. He had looked too late to know whether a sheep had passed over, either coming or going, or whether it had been a man or men coming down. He was sure, from the direction, that if a man had started down the slope it was not one of the camping party. If more than one figure had crossed, both were on the slope now and probably one was moving to outflank him. He dropped the fish into his bag and kept the otter moored with the coil of line and flies lying on the rock.

"Bob knows you're there, mate," he whispered, "an' even if the moon comes round the corner you still won't see 'im sittin' 'ere, mate."

Two hundred yards lay between the skyline and the first of the big rocks. If the bailiff or bailiffs were on their way down he would hear them once they reached the loose stones.

They would try to trap him between the water and the cliff face in the corner where he couldn't climb out. They knew the lake and every rock about it as well as he did, and they would come steadily along, peering into every hiding place, probing, listening. There would be time enough to let the otter and the line go; time enough to slip off his boots and play a stealthy hide-and-seek through to the boggy grass and the peat slope beyond. Once there he could judge nicely where the skyline would expose him and steal away without being detected. He might even take his trout with him, although they would have to be hidden before he got home, for they would have somebody waiting at home, skulking in the garden beside the shed, sitting on the wall in the shelter of the privet bush. The moon was beginning to light the top end of the valley now. In a little while it would illuminate the slope and make his chances of getting away a great deal less, but he sat still, knowing that half the art of hunting and half the secret of escaping lies in being motionless. He could almost see in the dark and certainly no one could hear better than he could. He knew immediately that something had passed from the grass to the rocks, although the shingle made no sound. They were moving on big stones, he decided, with their boots off. They were being uncommonly crafty. He wondered which of the bailiffs this could be, for he could think of none with such skill in moving. He thrust his hands into the sack so that their color wouldn't show. His jacket was brown, his trousers gray, his hair a tousled mass above his face. He bowed his head to keep his face shadowed and peered through his bushy eyebrows. The moonlight was increasing as clouds slid away to the east and the moon rose in the sky. Suddenly he knew that this wasn't the bailiff at all, but he held his breath and his hands took hold of the sack.

The tiger stood on the rock, its tail drooping like the tail of a wandering cat. It turned its head and looked towards the moonlit sky and as it did so Bob the Cough made a gentle sound that might have been a sigh. He hadn't been able to hold his breath any longer. This was something that made him frightened. What trick of the light made a farm cat look so big? Moonlight, some people swore, did queer things. It drove men out of their minds. It made people see things that weren't there. Did it make small cats look a thousand times their size? Did it? He licked his lip and shivered. The strange thing was that the light of the moon hadn't yet fallen upon the cat, and the rock on which it stood wasn't enlarged by the strange half-light. He knew that rock. It was twelve to fifteen feet long and about four feet from the shingle at the back. It still looked twelve feet long! The cat, however, looked big enough to cover most of the rock. Its head seemed about four feet from the rock. He tried to work out how far away it was, puzzling his mind to recall the lay-out of the scene and every boulder as he knew it by daylight. He caught his breath again and knew that this was no trick of light and no farm cat, nor was it any sort of big dog. He didn't stop to wonder what it was doing here in the silence of the Welsh hills, but he knew it, and remembered it, from the only picture book he had ever possessed. It might be a ghost, but ghost or not, it was the shape of a tiger!

Perhaps a minute passed, perhaps it was much longer before Bob the Cough took his hands gently out of the bag and began to feel for a small pebble on one of the ledges. He wanted to see if this thing, this apparition, would turn its head when he tossed a pebble into the water.

The pebble rolled under his fingers and eluded them for a moment, but he kept his eyes on the tiger and listened until he could have sworn he heard it breathing. When he had the pebble, he gently raised his arm and tossed it as far as he could without making too much violent movement to betray his position. The stone plopped into the water. The head of the beast turned and looked steadily in that direction. Would a ghost have done that? The moon flared like the light of the sun on the far slope and the last of the clouds sailed clear, leaving the sky to the south and west as empty as an inverted bowl. Bob the Cough could see the slope above the rocks now. Only the beast was in shadow as the rocks were. He wondered if it would see him as he started up the moonlit slope and whether it would come after him. He moved clear of the bag, leaving it on the rock, let the line slip and spill into the water and gently began to ease off his boots and then his socks, rolling up the end of his trousers a little so that he could run if he had to. Tigers, he remembered hearing somewhere, come in bounds and strike as a cat strikes at an escaping blackbird, except that a single blow can break the back of a cow.

It had often been said in Pentre Ddu that you had to hand it to old Bob the Cough, for the only thing he was afraid of was work. He might sneak about at night, he might evade trouble when he could, but he was never afraid to stand and make a show when he had to.

He was afraid now, as afraid as he had ever been in his life, but he wasn't too frightened to attempt to escape. He had seen the frightened rabbit before the stoat. His feet gripped the rough surface of the rock and he gently stepped over onto the next. The movement took an age. He fancied at first that nothing had altered, and the beast stood motionless as it had been since the pebble had fallen into the water; but all at once he knew that it had turned its head in his direction. He had gone perhaps forty feet.

Many another man in the same circumstances would have lost his head and begun to scramble over the rocks, slipping and floundering, but Bob the Cough managed to keep his mind clear. He sprang from boulder to boulder with a little more speed, it is true, but even when out of the corner of his eye he saw that the beast was not standing where it had been before, he made sure that he jumped precisely and didn't slip until he was on the grass of the slope. The tiger wasn't bounding or running. It was padding slowly in his direction, like a curious cat. He began to run up the slope, his legs sinking in the soft peat to the calf at times, but he kept on. The moonlight made the scene as bright as day. The tiger seemed to trot after the little man whose breath came in gulps now as he made for the flat ground at the top of the slope. The same distance still separated the pursuer and the pursued as Bob came to the flat where the green tent was pitched. He plodded past no more than ten yards from it, and, as he did so, Willis came out and stopped and stared at him and then, when the tiger appeared, he threw himself down and scrambled into the tent like a frightened rabbit.

"What's up, man?" asked Taffy Davies sleepily.

"My God!" whispered Willis. "I've just seen a man being chased by a tiger!"

"You've what?" said Jimmie Temple, laughing at what he thought he had heard. "You've seen what?"

His words were muffled in his blanket. Flynn knew what he had said. He raised himself on his elbow and peered at Willis.

"Down the slope, wasn't it, Willie?" he asked in a quiet voice.

"Outside," said Willis weakly. "Not five yards away."

Taffy Davies pushed him aside and stuck his head out. He couldn't see Bob the Cough, for Bob was running for his life now. The tiger stood on a mound not far from the tent, staring after him. Taffy fell on his side, for he had lost his balance. His face was in the grass. He inched his body back into the tent.

"Jesu!" he said in a strong Welsh accent that only came to him in moments of excitement. "What'll we do? It's outside there, just standing!"

"Where's the man?" whispered Willis.

"I didn't see a man," said Taffy.

Jimmie Temple didn't know whether he ought to look out or not. He felt, for a minute, that this was all a great leg-pull, hatched up by the other three and worked out in detail to make him believe that there really was a tiger outside.

"Let me see," he whispered.

"Keep still!" pleaded Willis. "For God's sake keep still and keep quiet!"

He gripped Jimmie's arm and the latter knew that this was no joke. Something was outside, something big enough to frighten a man. At that moment the tiger made a rumbling sound in its throat. Perhaps it heard the hated voices of men. Perhaps it smelled their presence or knew that they were in the tent. Flynn put his hand out and touched his friend on the arm.

"It was down by the lake when I went for the water!" he whispered. "I knew there was something there!"

"It must be a tame one," he went on. "What would a tiger be doing here?"

Jimmie Temple almost laughed. It was the sort of remark old Quack might be expected to make. What did it matter whether the tiger was tame or wild? Who was going to find out?

"Shut up!" hissed Taffy Davies. "I think it's coming to the tent."

Why he thought this no one knew, for his face was on the floor of the tent and the flaps had fallen together again. He couldn't see what was happening outside.

"Where's the ax?" whispered the frightened Willis.

"What d'you think you can do with that? Chop its bloody head off?" demanded Taffy, but he wasn't joking. He was shaking in every limb. He was sure that the tiger stood between them and the moonlight and he could see its outline on the green canvas.

Far away across the peat, Bob the Cough floundered in a water-hole, extricated himself, and plunged on. When he glanced back, the roughness of the bog and moorland made him think the tiger was plodding after him.

"Oh God, oh God!" he mumbled. "Get me home. Get me home. Save me."

When he came to the plantation he felt safer and, in spite of the roughness underfoot and the branches that struck him in the face, he rushed on, going downhill and over stones without slowing or considering that if he fell the beast might get him. He came at last to the bottom fence and the village.

CHAPTER 4

Captain Anderson was a young man of great poise. If he quaked a little in his shoes at times he had the gift of being able to control the outward signs of fear or anxiety. Nothing ruffled him in the ordinary course of his duties. He was prepared to go anywhere and do anything the Army might ask of him. He was, in fact, an excellent soldier. A little young, perhaps, to carry the responsibility of leading men after a tiger in the dark, but to be truthful his immediate superiors knew very little about tigers by day or by night. Captain Anderson knew all about patrols, all about movement by night, the use of small arms, scouting and ambush. He had had it all as a cadet, and a tiger is, after all, but a single enemy. It carries no carbine, no grenades. It can be surrounded and riddled with bullets from a Sten gun. This sort of thought had passed through Captain Anderson's mind. He had only one small anxiety. Tigers move as a cat moves. They move naturally as a platoon leader hopes that one day his men may be able to move, in complete silence, as ready for immediate action as the finger of a frightened man holding a gun.

"Look, chaps," he had said to his group of volunteers, "you know as well as I do that a tiger is a pretty big beast. It can kill a man . . ."

"You can say that again," someone mumbled.

"But," went on Captain Anderson, "once we locate it we have only to get in close enough and bring our fire-power to bear . . ."

He smiled a tight little smile that was meant to extend his complete confidence to everyone before him.

"Put it this way," he said; "one good burst would chop down half a dozen tigers. I know that the problem will be to locate the brute, but it must be located and killed before terror runs rife in the village we're going to. It must be killed before it kills again! It has already killed one of its trainers. It has tasted blood. It could conceivably run wild in the mountains and kill again and again. You and I are being sent to stop this beast before it can strike again. We shall have the assistance of the police and men who know the immediate locality. Before morning, certainly before the villagers have had their breakfast, this beast will be accounted for. The police and the public expect it of us."

"Ooh, ah," said one of the men at the back and he began to hum a bar or two of a jazz tune.

"Any questions?" asked Captain Anderson.

His sergeant whispered something and the captain whacked his calf with his cane.

"We'll see," he said. "Certainly they'll need something to fortify them."

They waited for the sergeant formally to take charge and give orders for them to clamber into the trucks.

"When I was out in Poona," said one, "I shot so many tigers my missus refused to have another in the house. We had tiger for breakfast, dinner an' tea. We made rissoles of 'em. We had 'em fried in batter. It put me off 'em for life. I'm still off 'em."

"You suppose Andy's ever seen a flamin' tiger?" someone else enquired.

"I dunno about tigers, but you seen that bit o' fluff he runs around? She's got some claws on her, I can tell ya! Now if we was huntin' somethin' like that . . ."

"That'll do!" said Sergeant Morris. "We're off on ruddy safari. You'll all get a bit of the skin to put your feet on when you get out of bed in the morning. That's a promise. I've notified your next of kin they'll either be getting tiger meat or an invitation to a mass funeral."

They climbed into the trucks, most of them wondering how the Captain proposed to find a tiger in the dark. "Hold that tiger! Hold that tiger!" they sang as they rumbled along. Captain Anderson, sitting up in front, couldn't bring himself to smile. His hands were a little sticky. He wondered how he had ever got himself into this thing.

"I've stalked deer in the Highlands, sir," he had said.

The Colonel had looked him in the eye and said something about deer and tigers being fundamentally different animals. Major Quinn, who really had shot tigers in India, was on leave. It wasn't fair to put old Richardson on a job like this. Carter cracked himself up as a game shot, but he had broken an arm, and besides he was as timid as a shrew. Anderson was the obvious choice, and all he had to do was to ask for volunteers. No doubt the beast would be dead by morning. By all accounts someone had taken a shot at it already and it had gone off into a thicket.

"One thing, Anderson," he had said before he dismissed him. "If possible get that tiger's head. We'll have it mounted and stuck over the bar in the mess!"

"I will, sir!" said Anderson.

"In that case, make it a lung shot," said the colonel. He didn't allow himself to smile until Anderson had gone.

Now, as though tied together by rope, the three trucks trailed each other along the winding roads to Pentre Ddu. The story of the tiger had already got about. People who had stood outside public houses talking about it turned to stare after the Army vehicles as they went rushing through.

"They've sent the troops to get it!" they told each other excitedly. "Wouldn't like the ruddy job meself!"

"They'll get it, though! All you gotta do is give it a good burst with a Bren an' that's the end of the tiger, mate!"

"All you gotta do is get the tiger to show itself and then get it in your sights and then hit it in the right place before it comes right on and butchers you with one clout, right behind your perishing Bren, mate!"

"Anybody'd think it was lit up wi' fairy lights! How you gonna find a tiger in the dark? Shout 'Puss, puss'? Anyhow, they say it's not one tiger, it's a truck full of 'em. Five of the perishin' brutes."

"The bloke what's responsible for lettin' them escape ought to be slung into jail!"

"The bloke what was responsible for lettin' them out, mate, is feedin' the dogs in Pentre Ddu, mate. So they heard over the phone at the Cross Keys. They reckon that dogs is lickin' his blood at Watkins's garage an' nobody's got the guts to go out an' cover the corpse up!"

"I still say he ought to be slung into jail!"

"If he hears you where he is now I'll bet he says amen to that, mate!"

The tiger hadn't started to walk in the villages along the valley. The police cars and the Army trucks hurried through to Pentre Ddu. By daylight the tiger would be everywhere, in the quiet, half-asleep streets of four villages, in the corners of river meadows where the mist still hung, in the shadows of hazel copses, behind ricks, in outhouses, moving across distant slopes, peering out of conifer woods, in a dozen places. If the gallant Captain and his men managed to bring it to bay before daylight its ghost would live for hours.

The forecourt of Watkins's garage was lit now. They were using Watkins's lighting while they examined the truck, the trailer, the gory scene around it. The villagers had gained a little courage because the police were there, and they hung on the fringe, watching all that the representatives of authority did. They were intrigued when a constable laboriously took the number of the trailer and examined the license on the vehicle. A sergeant was sketching the position of the body, the trailer, the open cage. He even got out a tape and began to measure up, although what this could have to do with the death of poor Josef no one could fathom. At length a van arrived and the remains were lifted in a sheet, placed on a stretcher and removed. Some sawdust was obtained from Jack Robert's workshop and sprinkled on the chippings. The police retired to the Horseshoe and the Army trucks arrived. Women rubbed their elbows as they cupped them in the palms of their hands and shivered although it was warm. Men put their hands in their pockets, smoked, spat and talked. The Army peered out of their trucks. Captain Anderson and his sergeant got down and disappeared into the Horseshoe.

"Hold that tiger! Hold that tiger!" chanted some of the men. The villagers didn't smile. They began to retreat to their houses. Such an attitude gave them no sense of safety. A few minutes before, the body of the poor victim had lain exactly on the spot straddled by the wheels of the second truck.

"Well, sir," said Captain Anderson, "I consider that the first thing to do is to warn the people to keep indoors, to make some sort of reconnaissance in the direction in which the tiger was last seen. It may be hiding quite close to us. The Indian wallah may have located it."

Inspector Williams grunted. "The people have been warned to stay indoors and I don't think they're likely to get in the way. You must decide what your men are going to do. My men will stop traffic along the road, such as it may be, and at first light will spread out to warn people in cottages and the hill farms round about. Superintendent Rees is with the Chief Constable now. They should arrive here in an hour or so. Perhaps a joint plan of action can be worked out then. In the meantime, I suggest you take precautions to see that any activity on the part of your men doesn't drive the tiger back into the hills and make the job of locating and destroying it very much more difficult. You realize what it would mean if the tiger got into the hinterland above this place?"

The Captain touched his ginger moustache. "Naturally," he said. "My objective is to get it before it has the chance."

The Inspector turned again to Frank Baker. "And then, sir," he said, dismissing the Captain as pointedly as he could, "you found the door wouldn't open? You tugged at it and it continued to stick?"

"It wouldn't open," said Frank Baker. "He was hammering on the outside and lunging at the door to get in. I was pulling and he couldn't see that the door was being jammed. I heard the shot shortly after that."

"The door opened all right when you tried again."

"I can't remember trying it, but somebody opened it. Bill Evans came in, as far as I can remember."

Inspector Williams went to the door and opened it. It gritted just a little on the tiles but it opened freely enough. He stooped and looked for stones that might have caused the door to stick. He was wondering what had happened to the Indian. One of his men had gone over into the gully and come back again without finding any sign of the man.

It was all very strange. In daylight they would be able to make a proper search of the thicket, the gully and the forestry tract up the hill, but at the moment search with lamps was futile and very dangerous. Let the young fool of an Army officer do what he liked, his men were not going to be sent combing the woods in the dark to be pulled down and slaughtered by the tiger that was hiding, aware of every movement in the undergrowth. It just didn't make sense.

Outside the Horseshoe, Captain Anderson paused for a moment. He felt that he should personally lead a small group of men in the direction the tiger had taken. A tiger's eyes, he felt sure, glowed at night, as did the eyes of a cat. He felt that if he caught the beast in the light of a powerful torch one of his men could shoot it. It was worth trying. Sergeant Morris said very little at any time. He said very little now. Somewhere he had read that a tiger, if followed into cover, simply doubles back and stalks the would-be stalker. Sometimes it turns off at right angles and doubles a short way to make an ambush. He couldn't remember where it was he had heard this and he hadn't paid particular attention.

"Look, sir," he said after a while, "we might do well to wait until first light. It'll be light enough for us to move somewhere after four. We'd stand some chance then."

"We must get cracking now, Sergeant!" said Captain Anderson. "Time is against us already! I'll lead a couple of men into the gully. If I find any sign there I'll come back and we'll organize a movement calculated to encircle the brute."

"Yes, sir," said Morris heavily. It all sounded quite fantastic, mad. To talk of encircling a tiger with perhaps a platoon of men carrying rifles, wearing hobnailed boots in a wood in darkness! He wanted to laugh and then he shivered.

"I think you had better come with me and bring Thompson and Maloney."

"Very good, sir," he replied and went over to the second truck. "Hey, Thompson, Maloney, you want tiger-skin waistcoats for next winter?"

Both men laughed.

"Well, get down here an' get fell in. You an' me an' Captain Anderson's to make the supreme sacrifice."

He didn't make a habit of cracking this sort of joke with his men. It did nothing for morale, but an intelligent order was an intelligent order and a stupid one advertised itself in no time. The two volunteers clattered down from the truck and kicked about in the chippings and sawdust.

"Cripes!" said Maloney. "This stuff's blood!"

"That's probably where the bloke what let the tiger out bought it," said Thompson looking at his companion's sawdust-coated boot. "It wasn't no kitten he was playin' with, mate!"

Captain Anderson put his cane in the truck and unholstered his revolver. He felt just a little ridiculous with a revolver in his hand. Ten yards was no distance to a tiger and would a revolver stop it? He called a corporal to the back of the truck and relieved him of his automatic. Firepower, he decided, was something, even if the weapon was no more accurate and the impact of the bullet no greater. He had heard of an elephant gun. Perhaps there was a tiger rifle, something with the necessary killing power to stop a tiger in its tracks.

"Right," he said. "Follow me."

He held the automatic weapon in one hand and the torch in the other. Morris helped him negotiate the hedge and then the fence as they made their way into the gully. He didn't put the torch on. The midges rose and swarmed on his neck and brow immediately. He could feel them gnawing at his wrists. The noise the party made as they crept forward was unbelievable, but, as always, a man trying to move quietly imagines that it is his companion who is making the noise, or else he fancies that he is moving in complete silence. Behind them, in the truck, the men were silent for a while.

"You gotta hand it to Anderson," one of them whispered. "He may be soft in the nut, but he don't hesitate. He's brave enough."

"He just ain't got a bloody clue, mate! He thinks the tiger's sittin' in there lickin' its end like a tomcat. Wait an' see. He'll come back an' say it's all clear an' then you an' me'll be in there walkin' right into the beggar. Might as well walk right into a bloody express train. You can't stop one o' them with a Army rifle, mate!"

"Why not?" somebody demanded. "Why not?"

"Because unless you hits a vital spot, mate, the bullet goes on through. You've gotta have knock-down power, a big soft bullet what'll turn over an' smash the brute."

"Knock-down power! All you gotta do is wait until you see the whites of its eyes! All you gotta do is hit a vital spot, mate. Say, 'Hold it a minute, tiger'!"

"Hold that tiger! Hold that tiger!"

"Shut up! Shut up!" half a dozen soldiers shouted.

There was silence again. Outside the trucks, moths flew around the bright lights. There was no one on the forecourt now, but down the village every door was open and showed a light. Women peered from windows. Men talked to each other across the street.

In the Horseshoe Betty Collins was explaining to the Inspector how Josef had gone out and how Ram Singh had laughed at her suggestion that the Pole really intended to release one of the tigers.

"And when the tiger was out you went outside and saw . . ."

"The Indian went outside. I thought he was goin' to do something to get the tiger back in the cage. I never saw what happened really. I went to the door, but Mr. Baker was there tryin' to get it open. It was awful, awful! I felt sure the tiger was about to spring, an' then I heard the shot strikin' the wall and the door, I think, an' then it went quiet. I heard feet scufflin' an' somebody shoutin' somethin'. I fainted. Mr. Baker gave me a glass of water and Mrs. Baker came down."

"The Indian shut the door behind him, did he?" asked the Inspector.

"He must have done," she said, looking down at the floor. "I pray God he's all right. They say the gun he took from Jack Roberts wasn't loaded."

"It wasn't loaded," said the Inspector. "Tell me, when this man who let the tiger out first came in, would you say he was already drunk? How many drinks did he have here?"

"I dunno," she said. "Four or five, maybe. I can't remember. So much has happened."

"If the Indian didn't try to stop him, why didn't you call Mr. Baker when you saw him going out?"

"The Indian said he wouldn't do it. He said he'd gone to the 'Gents', an' he always talked like that."

"Had you ever known the door to stick before?"

She looked at Frank Baker. The Inspector was very interested in this business about the door. He liked being cocky, she thought. After all, who was to say whether the Indian had come to any harm or not? He might come knocking at the door at any time.

Inspector Williams waited for her to answer. His mind was coldly dwelling on the fact that from up the village street an old woman, sitting in her doorway in a chair, had seen Betty Collins and the Indian at the doorway of the Horseshoe, and it was a strange thing, he thought, that Betty Collins should have been brought into the story if she hadn't been in the door of the Horseshoe.

"I can't say I have," she said, "but then I never have the occasion to open or shut the door. Mr. Baker opens it in the morning and it generally stays open until closing time when he locks up."

It was only then that she realized the significance of what

she had said. The Inspector's face didn't betray his thought that if the door generally stayed open the Indian must have gone out of his way to close it, a peculiar thing to do when he might find himself confronted by an escaped tiger. A peculiar thing to do if he intended only to look out and see his companion. A peculiar thing altogether. These thoughts added to his suspicion that something odd had happened. If the Indian was all right he might be able to explain it. If he wasn't they might never find out. He sighed heavily. He was weary of a life in which lies and suspicion played such a great part. It wouldn't be long before he took his pension and had done with it and could go to the bowling-green on a summer's evening.

One of the Inspector's men came in and stood waiting to speak to him. He looked at him and asked him what he wanted.

"A woman outside, sir. Her name is Rowlands. She says her brother, a fellow they call Bob the Cough, has gone up fishin' an' will likely be comin' down before daylight. She's terrified anything might happen to him."

"If she knows exactly where he is we might get somebody to go up," said the Inspector doubtfully. "I don't think the beast would attack anyone carrying a lamp, although you never know."

The constable went outside and talked for a few minutes in Welsh with a woman standing in the porch.

"She says she thinks he went to the black lake, sir," he said when he returned. "He generally goes there or over to the lake of the frog."

"And where is that?" the Inspector asked.

"About two miles over the top from the black lake. The black lake's three and a half miles from here."

"Tell her we'll do what we can, but it's a poor chance our finding the man in the hills even by moonlight, if and when the moon comes up."

At that moment Pentre Ddu was in deep shadow, for, although the moon was on the uplands and the top of the conifer ridge, the steep slope beyond the gully and the hill to the east of the village kept the place in darkness.

Could anyone blame him if he didn't send someone up to find this Bob the Cough chap? the Inspector asked himself. Perhaps the bold Captain would jump at the chance of going. It would be one way of occupying him and his men. What in the world did a bunch of Army boys know about hunting a tiger? What, for that matter, did he, as a police officer, know about it either? He called a constable in.

"Look," he said, "contact that Army chap and tell him I'd like to see him. Where is he, by the way?"

"Gone into the bushes, sir, I believe," said the constable. "I'll try and find out if his men have any contact with him. These chaps have walkie-talkie, I think."

Oddly enough, this was one piece of useful equipment that Captain Anderson hadn't thought of. He was out of touch with his men, crawling among hazels, over slimy boulders and along a stream with his sergeant and aides behind him, saying nothing, achieving nothing. Finally, when he could bear the midges no longer and had had his sleeve tugged twice by a long and tough thorn, he laid his automatic on the ground and snapped on his torch. A moth fluttered into his face. He could see nothing but a large mossy stone above him. His knees were being hurt badly by small stones over which he had crawled. He eased himself and removed his hand from the automatic completely. It was only then that he saw that it was red with blood. He stared at it for some moments.

"Sergeant!" he gasped.

It wasn't his blood. It was the blood of the Indian. He knew that he couldn't be mistaken. The tiger had got him right here where he was on his hands and knees. He began to shake, for he had a picture in his mind of the tiger crouching over the body of its victim, its tail moving in the switching fashion of an angry cat.

"What is it, sir?" whispered Sergeant Morris.

Captain Anderson couldn't move. "Get back," he said. "Turn about and get out of here, for God's sake!"

Thompson and Maloney lost no time in retreating. They were well ahead of Sergeant Morris, but Captain Anderson found Sergeant Morris a great obstacle to his own escape.

"For God's sake, man!" he said, "get a move on! That Indian chap has been butchered by the tiger. I crawled right into him!"

They were back on the road before Captain Anderson recovered his nerve. He stood up and handed Morris his automatic.

"Let the men get down and stretch their legs, then tell them to make themselves comfortable until daylight. We can't go in there in the dark, I realize that now. It would be suicide."

He walked over to the Horseshoe and went in. The Inspector didn't look up from the table at which he sat writing.

"Yes?" he said.

"I've found the Indian, sir," said Captain Anderson.

There was ample evidence of the fact. Blood on the Captain's battle-dress, on his knees and on his hands. There was even blood on his face.

"You found him?" asked the Inspector. "And he was dead?"

"I am sure he was," said the Captain. "I didn't stop to bring the body. I thought of my men. Got them out of there. We're going to make a drive at daylight. It can't be done in the dark. I'd like a whisky, if you've got one."

"You didn't stop to see whether the poor beggar was dead or not?" said the Inspector slowly. "You thought of your men."

"I know he was dead," said Captain Anderson.

He was about to say that he knew a dead man when he saw one, but he didn't. He had never seen one.

CHAPTER 5

At one o'clock, when the moon was lighting most of the valley and the roof-tops of Pentre Ddu, the talk of the soldiers in the trucks had subsided to a drowsy murmur. It had been talk of tigers, talk of the behavior of N.C.O.s and officers, talk of beer and women, and wildest fancy, but now most of the men were dozing. The stream that ran through the gully and passed under the road whispered and gurgled through the stones and made a sound designed, it might have been thought, to put villagers to sleep and leave the night to owls and cats, prowling fox and grubbing badgers.

Sergeant Morris, in the second of the two trucks, was wondering once again what it would be like to be going up the gully and into the firs beyond in search of a tiger that had made an end of two men. How would they contain it up there on the rough hill-side? How could they corner and kill it, even in daylight?

"It's bloody well beyond me," he said aloud, and then he heard the faint, slightly muffled sound of a telephone bell ringing in the Horseshoe. For a moment he thought that perhaps someone, somewhere, had killed the brute and the whole thing was being called off. Captain Anderson would be relieved, he knew that, for he wasn't so keen now to go up through the trees. He had run out of all that guff about fire-power and making the villagers safe by breakfast-time. It had all been a load of old malarkey, of course. Captain Anderson's experience of coming face to face with death was nothing beyond the experience of anyone meeting a hearse on the way to a cemetery. He was brave in imagination, a decent, downy-chinned young chap, but without the hardening of reality. Blood on his hands and on his battle-dress gave him the jitters.

"You know, son," Sergeant Morris said to the nearest man to him, "you gotta see a lot of violent death before you know what it's about."

He had seen his share. Killing wasn't just like pouring boiling water on ants at the back door. The enemy could hit back. A tiger was capable of killing, and there was one thing about it—it had no fear of the platoon, the organization behind the individual.

The telephone had stopped ringing. He wondered if someone would come out with a message for them. Captain Anderson stood smoking and looking up at the hills. In the moonlight Sergeant Morris could see the stains of blood on his uniform. The blood wouldn't come out and there was nothing he could do about it, but every so often Anderson went to the bank, got some grass and tried to scrub his blouse or the knees of his trousers. He did it furtively, in the shadow of a bush, as though he might be tying up a boot-lace. Morris smiled sourly about his officer's behavior. If you put up a show you went right on with it for the sake of morale. You went right to the point where the men behind you were ready to run, but hesitated because you were there, even when it seemed madness to go on. You went as far as reason and a little beyond sometimes, and when you turned back you didn't scramble like a scalded cat to get past men you had been leading into danger. You retreated in good order and with dignity and made sense of it, so that if immediately your withdrawal was complete it became necessary for you to attempt another advance, you were capable of even that. Captain Anderson had it all out of the book, but he wasn't carrying any old scars. He had no memories to bolster his courage, only imagination, and that was sharp on both edges, to make a man stupidly brave and terribly frightened. Morris got down from the truck and stretched his legs, finally walking over to Captain Anderson.

"I suppose some arrangement was made about rations, sir?" he enquired.

Captain Anderson puffed at his cigarette. "It's laid on, Sergeant," he said in a voice that was patronizing.

"Just wanted to make sure, sir," he said. "Nothing was said."

That at least was a little dig on the "put-your-men-in-the-picture" line, but, of course, there was no picture. They were like so many truck-loads of sheep. Nothing made sense.

"We'll be lucky to come up with that brute in a week," he observed.

Captain Anderson tried his best to talk down to the gray-haired sergeant. "Mustn't take the black view, you know," he said, but there was no conviction in it. He didn't believe what he was saying. The old badger was cupping his hands about a cigarette as he lit it, and he could see the expression on his face. Morris came from Liverpool and had an odd sort of make-up. He was cynical, contemptuous of anything that didn't lead to or bear upon direct action. You couldn't hope to get his moral support even if you could command his cooperation. He reserved judgment.

The telephone was ringing again.

"Shall I see if anything has come through for us, sir?" Morris asked.

"You can," said Anderson. For his part, he didn't want to go near the place again. The Inspector had said very little, but he had left no doubt about what he thought of them for leaving the gully without bringing back the Indian's body.

Morris knocked on the door of the Horseshoe and let himself in. The Inspector was organizing a party of constables and a sergeant to go with lamps and find the Indian. He looked at Sergeant Morris and grunted.

"Captain Anderson wondered if any message had come through for him, sir," said Morris.

"No message," said the Inspector. "You were with him when he found the Indian?"

"I was with him, sir. He didn't exactly find the Indian. He crawled through some blood, sir, as far as I could make out, and decided that it wasn't wise to remain there."

He knew that anyone who heard him saying this would know exactly what he thought of the whole business.

"Could you locate the place where the blood was?"

"I think so, sir."

"Would you be prepared to show my men?"

Morris hesitated and flushed as he saw that his hesitation was being misunderstood. Very quietly he said, "I'm not afraid of blood or dead men or tigers. If it's my duty to go, I go where I'm told, and I do what I'm told. Captain Anderson decided we should get out of there. I don't argue with my officers!"

"I see," said the Inspector. "You'd want his permission before you went with my men?"

That was partly the point. If he went without it it might seem a criticism of their earlier conduct. If he asked permission, that too could be construed as a reflection on Captain Anderson's judgment.

"All right, sir," he said. "I'll ask permission afterwards, if you like. Could I have a drink? I've a hell of a thirst. My tongue's sticking to my mouth."

Frank Baker, who looked tired and worn out, came forward and offered him a tankard. "On the house," he said.

The telephone rang again and a constable took it.

"You've got a rifle handy?" asked the Inspector.

"I can get one," said Morris, "if you think it's much use."

The Inspector looked him in the eye. "Somebody's going to shoot that tiger some time," he said. "It won't give itself up. In the meantime it may kill other people. Bring your rifle. You don't need to keep your hackles up with me. I know you're not scared. We could all demonstrate that we're brave by going into the gully without a rifle. It would prove that we don't give a damn for our lives. It would also prove that some of us should be in a lunatic asylum. We are supposed to be looking after the innocent and helpless public. You can't do that facing a tiger with your bare hands."

He smiled gently and scratched his head. "I'm not coming with you," he said. "I'm too bloody old and too bloody scared, and besides the Chief expects me to be sitting here seeing that other chaps do this sort of thing."

The police sergeant at his elbow coughed. The constables grinned. They liked the Inspector. He was a fatherly old codger. His face seemed like a carving in old Welsh oak. It had the stamp of the son of the soil upon it. He might have been a hill farmer or a shepherd. His authority was natural and relied not at all upon class and breeding.

"It'll be a help if you can take my men to the place where you found the blood and they can bring the Indian or what's left of him out of there as quickly as possible. The tiger might just be lying there gnawing on his bones. It would be very handy if you had a rifle. I can't promise you'll get any medals."

Sergeant Morris swallowed his beer and grinned. "I'll get one right away," he said.

One of the men in the truck handed out a rifle when Morris shook him and asked for one. Captain Anderson called him over.

"The police are going to search the gully with lamps to help them find the Indian's body, sir," he said. "The Inspector thought it would be a good idea if someone with a rifle covered them. . . ."

He could see Captain Anderson's face in the moonlight and knew what he was thinking.

"Very well, Sergeant," he said after a minute or two. "I

suppose I'd better agree, but they should have come to me about it first."

"Shall I ask the Inspector to have a word with you, sir?"

Captain Anderson looked up at the hills and shifted uncomfortably, hating Morris. He could still feel the thick blood of the Indian on his hands, although he had gone to the water-trough and washed them most thoroughly.

"No need," he said curtly. "Tell him I give permission for you to escort them."

Up on the hill-side in a small field strewn with stones, a black bullock that stood beside a hedge raised its head and bellowed. The sound was deep and it echoed in the nearby trees. Captain Anderson looked in that direction. It had startled him. Sergeant Morris knew it wasn't the escaped tiger, but a second later one of the tigers in the trailer complained angrily. The trailer, with its flat tire, had been hauled away from the garage forecourt and stood beside an old boarded-up building past Jack Roberts's house.

"Did you hear that?" mumbled one of the half-asleep men in the first truck. "You know what I think? That bleeder in the trailer knows the escaped one's somewhere near!"

Those who were awake enough to think this over pondered it for a while, and one got down on his knees and peered out.

"It's in the bloody field!" he gasped. "Just over the hedge!"

There was a scramble to see and to grab for weapons. Someone worked his bolt. Safety-catches clicked. Captain Anderson found himself thinking the same thing. He put his hand on his revolver. He looked over the hedge at the clump of gorse in the center of the field.

"You chaps have got the jitters," he said.

They heard him. The laugh that greeted the remark wasn't friendly. He wondered what they were thinking about him.

"If you ask me," said Maloney, "that brute knows its mate is close at hand."

The tiger growled again. It was a deep, vibrant noise, full of fury. In almost every cottage in the village someone was propped on an elbow staring across a dimly lit bedroom and wondering the same thing. Was the escaped beast walking the shadows of the street? Was it close at hand in the next-door garden? Every sound was considered while hearts thumped. Had the troops gone creeping off to hunt it while the beast came sneaking back? People thought about the strength of bolted and latched doors and a creature like a great cat padding on the flags of paths. Only the very young and the old and deaf slept soundly.

"I think," said Captain Anderson, "you had better detail so many scouts to do a turn and relieve them every hour. Post them at either end of the village, at crossings and corners and along this hedge."

The bleary-eyed corporal got down, swearing under his breath, and began to call a roll, using a pocket flashlight to check the names on his list.

"Maloney!" he hissed, "you irresponsible Irish nut! What you wanna upset the Captain's bowels like that for? You gottim scared stiff now!"

"Sorry, Corp," said Maloney. "What about me bein' posted at the pub?"

"Me for the pub, Corp!" someone else pleaded.

"Look," said the corporal angrily, "you're supposed to be protecting the public. Turn it up or I'll put somebody on a charge!"

"Nuts!" somebody mumbled.

Sergeant Morris was helping three burly policemen over the hedge, holding a lantern and his rifle. They carried a folded stretcher. The lantern was hardly needed, for the scene was almost as brightly lit as it would have been by day, although, like a great black mountain, clouds were building in the northwest, and every so often the leaves of the hedge rustled with a breeze that was far from warm.

"Did you hear the tiger?" Sergeant Morris asked the nearest constable.

"You just keep that ruddy rifle ready," said the policeman. "It might be that the escaped one's on its way back!"

Once they were in the thicket and going towards the gully the swinging lanterns did alarming things with the shadows. The black boulders and crouching bushes sprang forward and receded, and everyone seemed to be a tiger about to spring.

"Cats don't like lights at night, I've been told," said Morris, "and tigers are only big cats."

The police sergeant laughed shortly. "Try feedin' one a saucer of milk," he said. "Big cats, my flamin' foot!"

They went follow-my-leader through the tangle where an hour or two earlier Captain Anderson had led his party. Morris could see the disturbed soil.

"We're nearly there," he said, and then he saw part of Ram Singh's clothing. The gory mess, spread across a fallen tree and a crumpled honeysuckle plant, needed no identification. Hardened as he was, Sergeant Morris wanted to be sick. He lowered his lantern to the ground and crouched with the muzzle of his rifle pointing into the undergrowth ahead.

"This is where it happened," he said tensely. Behind him the police raised their lanterns.

"Shove the stretcher forward, Davies," said one of them.

Morris stood up. He was ashamed of feeling sick. He didn't look at the Indian's face in the broken earth or see the glint of the dead man's teeth between his parted lips. The police did their gruesome work, and they turned about with the stretcher, one lighting the way, two carrying the body and Morris bringing up the rear with his rifle and his lantern. It wasn't until they were out of the moonlight again that Morris realized that he hadn't once looked back and carrying the gun and the lantern he might have been stalked and brought down without warning. They got the stretcher over the hedge. Captain Anderson was not to be seen. He had gone off to inspect the guard that had been posted. At the entrance to the Horseshoe they lowered the stretcher, and one of the men went in to get something to cover the corpse.

"Well, I better report," said Morris, and he went off towards the trucks.

"We found the Indian," he told his men. "Never expected to see him alive in any case, but you should see what the tiger did to him! He was broken up. Just so much bloody meat."

They stared across the moonlit field, and one of them whistled softly, shivering at the same time.

Maloney found himself at the end of the village farthest from the Horseshoe. He stood against a five-barred gate wishing that he had kept his thoughts about the behavior of tigers to himself. It had only put old Anderson in a whirl when the brute was probably miles away up among the fir trees. He stared across the field that stretched behind the gardens and became aware of movement that wasn't a bush swaying in the breeze because something passed from between two lumps of rock and went down along the edge of a fringe of gorse! He slipped his safety-catch. This time he wasn't going to let the whole thing turn into a general panic. He was going to stop whatever it was as soon as he could get it in his sights. The tiger in the trailer growled once more. The movement out on the field ceased. He could picture the escaped tiger standing still, and his anxiety was not what it might do if it came to the gate so much as how he could see clearly enough in the dappled background of bushes and shadows. His sights were non-existent. He put the rifle firmly into his shoulder and squinted along the barrel, laying the muzzle on a moonlit patch of grass across which he hoped the beast would pass. It was coming on. He held his breath. It seemed to stop just beyond the moonlit area and Maloney's pulses throbbed.

"Steady, boy," he whispered to himself. "Steady!"

He was taking up the first pressure and almost ready to squeeze the shot off as the shadow moved into the line of his vision when he heard quite distinctly the sound of a heel-shod on a stone.

"My God!" he gasped. "Some mad beggar creepin' about out there!"

His vision blurred, and by the time he had replaced his safety-catch the limping, doubled figure of a man was almost at the gate.

"A'right!" he said angrily. "Stop there! What the hell you think you're up to?"

"I seen a tiger!" mumbled Bob the Cough. "It chased me!"

Maloney reached out and helped him over the gate.

"You turned your ankle, mate?" he asked.

"I'm lucky t'be home! Lucky t'be alive!" said Bob the Cough. He peered at the uniform. "What's up?" he asked.

"A tiger got out of a trailer here an' killed two chaps," said Maloney. "It's still up there somewhere . . ."

"I know," said Bob the Cough. "It was after me! It chased me from the lake. I ran for me life. There's some chaps campin' up there where I seen it. . . ."

Maloney whistled. "You better come an' see my officer," he said. "The police will want t'know all about this. Where you say these blokes are? Did the tiger go after them too?"

"I'm goin' home," said Bob the Cough. "I'm goin' t'bed."

"Come back!" ordered Maloney. "You can't clear off! What about them chaps you was on about?"

"Up in a tent at the black lake," said Bob, sidling away. He hobbled into a gap and disappeared down a pathway lined on either side by a drystone wall overgrown with moss.

It evidently led to the backs of the cottages. Maloney hesitated and then decided not to give chase, but to report the whole thing at once. He tucked his thumb in the sling of his rifle and went clumping down the road.

"Hey, Maloney! Where you beggarin' off to?"

"I told that perishin' corporal I wanted to be by the pub, an' I'm goin' there," he said. "I'm goin' where the beer is, mate!" He grinned to himself and made the same remark to the others along the road as he passed them, enjoying their astonishment. It was the moon, they said, going to Maloney's head. Fancy him going to get himself posted at the pub! He was asking for it, and no mistake. The corporal met him.

"I told you I bagged first trick at the Horseshoe!" he said.

The corporal almost choked. "You're on a charge! You must be flippin' nuts!" he said.

Maloney laughed. "Take it easy, Corp," he said. "I'm only kiddin'! I got somethin' t'report."

"You ruddy better have! What's up?"

"Thought I seen the tiger comin' across the field," said Maloney. "Turned out t'be a bloke what had a sprained ankle. Said he seen the tiger up by some lake. It chased him. Said there was some blokes where he last seen it. They was campin'."

"Where is this bloke?" asked the corporal.

"He snuck off," said Maloney, "but I reckon I know where he went."

"I hope you're not makin' this lot up," said the corporal. "Come with me!"

Captain Anderson listened, looking up at the hills as he had been doing for hours now. "We'd better see what the police have to say about this," he remarked.

The three men went plodding through the granite chippings to the door of the Horseshoe and Captain Anderson went in.

Inside the Horseshoe Inspector Williams was busy writing a report on the discovery of the body of Ram Singh. He was very tired. The telephone seemed to have punctuated every sentence. A newspaper had rung up. The Superintendent had rung up. The Chief Constable had had a first-hand report and chewed it over to decide that he wouldn't be along until morning. A man from the B.B.C. had asked if the landlord could stand by to give a telephone interview for the news bulletin in the morning.

"That would be a chap known as Bob the Cough," said the Inspector. "Where is he now?"

"My man didn't manage to detain him," said Captain Anderson. "He said he was off to bed."

"He'll just have to get out of bed again!" said the Inspector. "I want a word with him, and I want it now, Sergeant! Get him along here, even if he comes in his underpants! I want to know exactly where he saw the tiger and all about these chaps camping up there. Something will have to be done for their safety!"

The sergeant went off up the village street after finding out from Frank Baker where Bob the Cough lived. Maloney followed him up the street.

"Wouldn't let me stay at the Horseshoe," he told his mates, "but I had a lovely pint. Cool as ice-water, it was."

"You're a ruddy liar, Maloney," they said.

"What can't speak can't lie," he said. "Smell me breath!"

But he didn't wait for them to smell his breath. By the time he reached his position by the five-barred gate he could hear the police-sergeant pounding on Bob the Cough's door.

"Rowlands?" asked the sergeant when the door opened. "Inspector Williams wants to see you!"

"He can see me in the mornin'," said Bob the Cough. "To hell with him an' you!"

The burly sergeant reached in and tugged him out through the door. As the Inspector had thought, Bob the

Cough was half-ready for bed. He had taken off his shirt, but he still had his boots and his tight-legged trousers on.

"You come an' make it snappy!" said the sergeant, "or I'll belt you out from between your ears!"

Bob the Cough went limping along, scowling at the thought of the questions he would have to answer before he had time to collect his thoughts. The police would know everything before they were finished. It wasn't so much telling about the tiger and the campers that bothered him as the implications of his presence at the lake and the certainty of investigation and the discovery of his ottering gear.

"You'll regret this, mate!" he threw over his shoulder at the sergeant. "You think because you got a uniform an' a big backside you can sling your weight about, but you could trip up an' break your neck!"

"So could you, an' a damn sight easier!" said the sergeant. "Get a move on before I put my toe to you!"

"How many men do you think were camping?" asked the Inspector.

"I don't think. I don't know," said Bob the Cough. "Half a dozen. Half a flamin' hundred! I seen one comin' down for some water. I heard somebody playin' a mouth organ or somethin'."

"Did the tiger follow you back down to the village?"

Bob the Cough spat onto the toe of his boot and looked at the Inspector with a grimace that showed one tobacco-stained tooth.

"You think I was runnin' backwards watchin' the bloody thing?"

"For all you know it followed you down?"

"For all I know it stayed up there eatin' those blokes in the tent. You maybe think you'll get me to show you the way I come an' find that tent an' them blokes for you. That'll be the day! Your lot done me so many favors in me time I'm killin' meself to do you one!"

"All right!" said the Inspector. "You can cut it out. I'll see about getting your activities up at the lake checked up. If the bailiffs need a little co-operation to sort you out you can be sure I'll give them all the help I can!"

"You go . . ."

The sergeant gave Bob the Cough an ungentle shove.

"All right," he said. "Get off back to your ferret-box! We've had enough of the smell of you here!"

Bob the Cough staggered into the road, wincing at the pain in his ankle. He hoped that the tiger would get at least two of the police before someone shot it, and he wasn't too particular whether it got some of the campers or not. In a way, he held them responsible for the loss of his fish and his gear, and they probably had attracted the tiger up to the lake with the smell of their cooking! To hell with them. To hell with the police and to hell with the soldier to whom he had so stupidly blurted out his news! He ignored the soldiers as he went up the village, pretending he didn't know they were there.

CHAPTER 6

They wanted to take those tigers out of the village, Jack Roberts thought to himself as he lay abed looking up at the shaft of moonlight that angled across the room and for some reason had become dimmer as the clock ticked the night away. It was bad enough knowing that a tiger was loose, without being frightened every so often by the fierce growling of one of those in the trailer. Some people, like old Kitty Price, poor simple soul, would be out of bed every few minutes to see whether the rest of the brutes were escaping too, and it wasn't so far-fetched, for who would have thought that a tiger would ever be loose in Pentre Ddu before this night? Things had happened here, of course, at various times in the history of the place. A man had murdered his wife in one of the cottages, it was said, although that was so long ago no one could remember when.

They had parked the trailer round by old Tom Potatoes's storehouse. It wouldn't worry Tom Potatoes, either, for he lay quietly in the cemetery, unaware of the tiger or the moonlight or the fact that his old storehouse hadn't been used for twenty years. The rest of the tigers were safely locked up. They had lashed about and growled when the trailer bumped along and turned in beside the boarded-up store. Now they were at peace again, but did a tiger ever sleep at night? The way they whipped themselves into a frenzy showed that if they slept at all it was only for a few minutes. He was sure he could hear them moving about. Once you got the odor of that trailer you could imagine that it filled the room as well. You could imagine that one of the brutes was standing on the stairs and the front door was open with a breeze carrying the odor of the beast up into the top of the cottage.

Jack had never been very good in the small hours. It wasn't that his imagination got lively, he told himself, but his spirits sank and then a dismal fear got hold of him. Nothing seemed any good. It was hard to get to sleep too, once you had awakened in the early hours. There was a lot of activity along the street, and he had jumped out of bed once to try to see who it was went clumping along with somebody else close on his heels, but the angle, and an unusually bulky privet bush, had balked him and he had gone back to bed feeling disgruntled about missing whatever was happening. He was tempted, even now, to dress himself and go out and talk to some of the men who were standing guard. It wouldn't be so bad to be doing a turn himself. He thought about his shot-gun and the Indian running away with it like that. He hoped the mad little so-and-so would bring it back. That was, he added mentally, if the tiger hadn't got him long ago. How many people had really seen that tiger? The Indian had seen it. The chap it had killed had seen it. He had seen it, and, of course, that Collins tart at the Horseshoe had seen it, as he had told the Inspector when he called.

"Oh yes," he had said, "she seen it all right because, when I passed Kitty Price, she said: 'That Collins bit-of-stuff didn't half pop out o' sight fast!' I seen it all. Mind you, I never realized what was happenin' until it was all over, even when the chap got killed it didn't seem real t'me. I seen that the Indian was shut out, but I never remember the door bein' shut before except in winter an' on wet days, even at closin' time durin' the day. They shuts up at night an' opens up in the mornin'."

"Had you ever been asked to mend the door of the Horseshoe? Plane a bit off it, or ease a hinge or anything?"

The Inspector had been making notes at the time. "No," Roberts said. "I never have. You think somebody kept that poor black fella outside?"

There was no answer for a moment. The Inspector put his notebook away. "Oh dear me, no," he said. "Nothing farther from my mind. I was considering why he couldn't get in and why the door was sticking. I know they were trying to get it open from the inside."

It seemed, when he thought about it, that the Inspector had gone right out of his way to answer a question when, of course, he didn't need to. His thoughts and opinions were official and confidential, as they said, but he had been extraordinarily open.

"Well," he had said, "you ain't got a mind like mine, sir. I reckon she's a tart, an' I seen some pretty vicious bits o' stuff when I was in the Army. If you asked me . . ."

He broke off. The Inspector was going out. He hadn't

asked him. He had better keep his tongue between his teeth. It struck him that the old Inspector didn't need to ask. He knew about that sort of woman.

He lay for a while pondering the whole thing and then he began to think of tomorrow, as he often did. Tomorrow in the village would be different. Tomorrow the tiger. . . . Unless they shot the brute it would make tomorrow a different day. What about the kids going to school? What about Ben the postman and his round? What about the shopping the people up back might need? What about them milking their cows and not knowing that a tiger was loose? What about the shepherds and poor old Uncle Will working on his little place where he was never done scaring off pigeons, rooks and daws, hoeing, setting up rows, cutting weeds, feeding his sows? It was time they got this tiger. It had been free far too long already.

When he peered at the clock he found he couldn't discern whether it was half-past two or half-past three. He thought of getting up and using a match to read the time, but then his attention was taken by something else. The faint sound of a car engine had droned into his consciousness and the sound began to grow. When it cut off he knew exactly where it was, passing between two masses of rock on the way to the village. A tiger, he told himself, could be standing on one of those big rocks looking down at the car coming. Maybe it wouldn't make a spring at the car, but he had a vision of it launching itself at a man on a motorcycle, a man on a bike, or a man on foot. He shivered at the thought. The sound of the car came back again. It was much louder now. In a minute it would be at the tail of the village.

"What's up, Jack?" his wife asked.

"Just thinkin'," he said. "We could shut ourselves up until they get this tiger, but it wouldn't look very brave, would it?"

"Who wants to look brave?" she asked. "You been brave

an' it didn't put no money in your pocket, did it? They never even give you a pension!"

"It didn't put no money in nobody's pocket," he said. "An' they never give me a pension because I wasn't entitled to one."

"The tiger's not our concern, Jack," she said. "You didn't let it out an' it ain't for you to get it back. Your job is to look after us! That's what your job is, Jack."

"A'right," he said heavily, "I only thought, well, I don't know I can trust them to get it. We got a nipper what might get killed by it, and if it don't get her it might get somebody else's kid, or some poor old soul . . ."

"Don't talk that way!" she said.

He sighed and listened to the car coming, its exhaust and the sound of its wheels echoing from close-to walls.

"There's a car comin' up the street," he said needlessly, for the driver made a great deal of noise as he changed down to negotiate a bend.

Jack got out of bed and went to the window, standing there in his long nightshirt as he peered down. The car drew in at the forecourt of Watkins's garage. The doors opened and clumped shut as four men got out. Two of them had heavy camera cases which they slung on to their shoulders as they adjusted flashlight reflectors and prepared to take pictures.

"Newspaper chaps," said Jack.

He watched them in the half-light. They were talking to the soldiers in the trucks. There was a sudden flash. One of them had taken the first picture in what was to be a front-page story, the story of the Pentre Ddu tiger and a dead man called Josef. So far it had only been told at second hand, but very soon that would be remedied. The press were due to arrive in full force. Chapters of the story of the tiger were to be written.

"Let's have a drink," said the elder of the two newsmen

as the photographers changed plates and got ready to fire more flash-bulbs. "Let's get a phone booked up and things fixed before the rabble get here."

"Anybody seen the tiger?" his companion asked the men in the second truck. He was stirring the sawdust with his boot, as yet unaware that he stood on the spot where the tiger's first victim had died.

"There's a tiger-lily in the garden over there," said Maloney, newly relieved.

Everybody in the truck laughed.

The reporter ignored the comment and went to the next truck. "Some of you chaps went on the search for the missing man, I believe?" he said, without explaining that he had gathered all this over the telephone. "Who went?"

"Private Maloney," they told him. "Private Thompson an' Sergeant Morris an' the Captain, of course. It was his flippin' idea!"

Maloney was leaning out of the truck. He called to the photographers. "Take me picture an' I'll tell ya all about it."

One of them came over to him. "What's special about you?" he asked.

"Special?" said Maloney. "I reckon I'm special. I was one o' them that went in after the Indian. I was the bloke what seen the last man to see the bleedin' tiger. That's all!"

The photographer stepped back and took a flash-light picture of Maloney. The boys behind him all said "Ooh!" and blinked. The blinking was a reaction, but the shout was derisive.

"A ruddy hero!" somebody exclaimed. "Maloney the tiger-killer! You wanna take his picture standin' with his hand on the head o' one o' them tigers in the trailer up the road!"

"You free to do that?" asked the photographer.

"Free?" said Maloney. "When ya gotta go, ya gotta go!"

He got down and hauled his rifle over the tailboard. Behind him the boys called obscenities.

"So long as ya don't want me t'get in beside the tigers," he said.

They plodded down to the trailer, the photographer bringing up the rear. A policeman stepped out as they came to it.

"What you want?" he asked.

"Mind if the Army stands guard?" asked the photographer.

"They're locked up an' don't need guardin'," said the constable.

"Makes no difference," said the photographer. "The public won't be any the wiser. Stand over there, Mulvaney."

"Maloney," said Maloney. "For cripesake get it right. My old lady would go up the pole if you took me picture an' called it Mulvaney."

"All right, Maloney," said the photographer, who had already fired three sets of bulbs taking pictures of the trailer from different angles.

Maloney stood with his rifle across his chest and looked up the street. The constable snorted and said something about guarding the tigers in case the kids got in and twisted their tails.

"I'm lookin' for the escaped tiger to come back," said Maloney. "You maybe kept somebody from picking the lock, but me, I'm protectin' the village, like this, see?"

The flash-light blinded him. He could see nothing but a vivid red, and he swayed.

"Brave lad," said the constable. "You heard about him goin' in after that poor Indian and comin' out like a scalded cat?"

"A bloody hero in blue," said Maloney. "Solid bone heads these blokes got, makes it easy for them when they gotta batter down a door. Take me at the gate where I seen the fella comin' what had just seen the tiger, eh?"

They went along to the gate.

"Hurry up," urged the photographer. "I want to get some pictures of the people at the pub and I would like a shot of the stretcher on which they carried out the Indian's body."

"You've had it there," said Maloney. "The body's gone, but if you buy us a pint I'll lie on the stretcher an' you can cover me with a sheet, so long as the stretcher ain't all covered wi' blood, like."

"Would you?" asked the photographer.

"Buy us a pint an' gi' me a set o' pictures for my old lady an' I'll do anythin'!"

"It's a bargain," said the man.

Maloney gave him the address and he made a pretense of jotting it down inside the flap of a cigarette packet. For one thing he couldn't see to write the address and for another he hadn't the slightest intention of sending Maloney or his mother any pictures.

"You'll send them to the old lady, all right, some proper decent pictures of me?"

"I never send indecent pictures to anybody's mother," said the photographer, smiling. "That's fixed."

Maloney accompanied him back to the truck and waited for him to go and find the stretcher if he could.

"The pin-up boy," his companions scoffed. "Ole Maloney with the laughin' face, Jeannie wi' the light brown hair, Maloney with the blarney from Killarney, ole Maloney-baloney!"

"Shut up!" he said. "They're goin' t'send my ole lady pictures of me."

Maloney went off by himself, mumbling about them and their stupid talk. It would be different when they saw his picture on the front pages of all the papers tomorrow. Private Maloney, one of the brave lads that went after the tiger. He could imagine what they would say then. "Boy, you look smashin', Maloney." Imagine it, old Churchill himself would see it. He might even ring the War Office. "That boy Maloney ought to have a commission, that's what. You should see to it, Minister. I've always thought so." Of course, Churchill wasn't the top dog now, but he was bound to have a lot to say.

"Maloney," said the corporal. "Captain Anderson wants to see you."

The words broke into his dream and made him suddenly very uncomfortable. What did Anderson want? Somehow he knew it wasn't to tell him he was being recommended for a commission.

He was right.

"Maloney," said Captain Anderson. "I am told you have been getting your picture taken and interviewing reporters. Do you appreciate the fact that you are on duty here and that you have no business to transact with the press? I am going to put you on a charge! If anyone approaches you refer them to me! You understand?"

"They was going to send some pictures of me to my old lady, sir. You couldn't blame me for that, could you?"

Captain Anderson swung about. "Get back to your truck," he said.

The photographer who had been hoping to take a picture of Maloney draped with a sheet and lying on a stretcher had changed his mind.

"Could we have the trailer opened so that we can take a picture of the tigers?" he asked.

"You could not," said the Inspector. "That trailer stays locked until someone competent to handle the tigers arrives. It will then be shifted to the nearest zoo just as soon as the tire can be fixed!"

"You're not going to feed the animals?" asked a reporter.

"They'll be fed, don't worry about that," said the Inspector wearily. "I am afraid that they won't be photographed while I have anything to do with it. They've been shoved about enough. We've had enough trouble with tigers and we're not going to open them up to the press so that they can make a stunt out of it. Two men have been killed in this place. These animals are a threat to public safety. There is enough alarm in this place and I'm damned if the old people and the women are going to be frightened any more than they are by letting a procession of photographers tramp in and out of that stinking trailer to take flashlight pictures. That's my answer and you can pass it on. The place is cluttered up with cars, cameras and . . ."

"Crabby old coppers?" someone suggested.

Inspector Williams took a breath and forced himself to smile. "All right," he said. "See it my way. I'm here, responsible for the safety of the people of this place. I am supposed to prevent more panic than already exists, and there is panic, you can take that from me. The tiger that is out there on the hill doesn't need to come back here to kill people. It can kill some of them by giving them heart failure! I'm here to do a job, not co-operate in producing stunts. Feeding the tigers, seeing them shifted away to somewhere safe, is one thing; letting you boys pose them for pictures is another. I'll have you run to the far end of the valley and right over the top first!"

The telephone rang. He picked it up and growled, "Look, I'll make it plainer. This is the last time you are going to try to have unofficial calls put through here! This line is requisitioned for official purposes. It is commandeered, if you like to call it that, in the public interest. You can check that with the Chief Constable himself, but I warn you that if you don't heed what I say you'll be putting a call through to someone who will take you right out from where you're sitting! I don't care what you thought. The subscriber is here. He knows what I'm saying, and if you have a call for him put it through somewhere else in the village and get him summoned to that place!"

Frank Baker came to the table. He had been drinking solidly for hours now and his eyes were big and bloodshot.

"You want some coffee, Inspector?" he asked.

"With plenty of sugar," said the Inspector. "When you get as weary as I am you need sugar."

Another car was pulling in at Watkins's forecourt. It was some kind of newsreel unit, and the driver, thinking that the Army trucks were in the process of moving, put his finger on the horn indicating that he expected them to make room for him. The sound could be heard all over the village. It wasn't an early morning sound in Pentre Ddu. It was a clamour, harsh and insistent, and it woke the dozing villagers who found their hearts suddenly beating fast.

"What's up?" they mumbled to each other. "Was that that tiger?"

The Inspector dropped his pencil.

"Tell that fellow out there that if he doesn't give that hooter a rest I'll charge him!"

His patience was wearing very thin. Nothing had happened in the past two hours or more that could be said to have advanced the purpose of his stay in Pentre Ddu, nothing at all, and there were complications he hadn't begun to sort out, like the business about those fellows camping up at the lake.

In the tent above the black lake the campers lay in darkness.

"I vote," said Willis, turning over restlessly, "that we get ready and make a dash for it, leaving everything here."

"Not until we can see," objected Flynn.

"And where do we dash to?" asked Temple. "Do you fancy a three-mile dash across a peaty moor? Supposing we do, what can we do then? Dash on down through the trees when we can hardly walk through them? How do we know we're not dashing right into the tiger? It may have followed that chap all the way."

"All right," said Willis, "what do you suggest? Do we sit here until it comes to knock the tent over and drag us out?"

"If they know there's a tiger loose they'll send help," said Flynn, then it struck him that "they" might not know.

"If they don't, the tiger'll have it all its own way."

"It won't come after us when it can get sheep," said Flynn lamely.

"Shut up, Quack! What do you know about what the tiger will do?"

"As much as you do!" he said. "For all we know it may have gone right over the mountain by now. We haven't been outside to look."

"You go and track the tiger, Quack!"

"I suggested that we make a dash for it," said Willis once again.

"The trouble with you lot," said Taffy Davies, "is that you're all too bloody scared. We'll walk back. Do you imagine that if we run we can run faster than a tiger? If we stay here the tent wouldn't stop it killing us, would it? It could strike right through the canvas with as much force as it could if it struck us in the open, couldn't it? We walk back. We pack up our things properly and take them back the way we brought them up. Five minutes isn't going to save our lives. We might just as well behave as if we were packing up in the normal way."

They considered this for some minutes as they had considered what Willis had said in the first place. It seemed sane and logical to Flynn and Temple. Willis had no thoughts to reveal.

"You know, Taffy," said Flynn suddenly, "I think you're the only one among us with any sense at all. You're right. You're absolutely right. It's the only thing to do. We could run, but it wouldn't save us. We could leave our stuff here, but five minutes or even an hour wouldn't make it certain that we'd get down without the tiger catching us, supposing it wanted to."

"Quite," said Taffy Davies. "We wait for daylight and then get our stuff together and go."

"If the tiger isn't out there watching us now," said Willis.

They said no more, but lay waiting for daylight to show. Flynn groped for his mouth organ but couldn't find it. He was thinking that he might as well play it. The tiger would find the tent. It knew where it was, whether he played his mouth organ or not. Perhaps, just perhaps, it might be put off by the strange sound, although he had to admit that it might also be made curious too. He gave up the idea and forgot about the mouth organ after a while. He had a feeling that the tent was stiffening up a little. That meant that a light rain was drifting over. There might be a mist, in which case they wouldn't be able to see very far when they set out. It would be almost as bad as moving in the dark. It might even be worse.

CHAPTER 7

Jim Parry was a man who could never lie long in bed when daylight was at hand. He somehow sensed the day before it came and awoke, stretching his thin body in its gray flannel night-shirt and slowly scratching his head while he pondered the problems of his daily life. When he troubled his mind about how to get his old van started in order to get down to the village he invariably had the other problem involved in reaching the village safely and in one piece without making more of a wreck of his van than it already was. He could push the van on the flat, but the hill down into Pentre Ddu was like a snake climbing a tree and its bends were marked by huge boulders sticking out of the bank as though God Himself had considered that a man with bad brakes might otherwise meet his death in the village below.

"It is not a very good sort of day," Jim said to the reflection of himself in the cracked mirror. The reflection said nothing in reply, but it wavered in the candlelight as he pulled off his nightshirt and began to dress. In the shed at the side of the house three little black calves, peering out between the bars of a hurdle, called for comfort and warmth in the form of milk fresh from the cow.

"A'right, bachs," said Jim, "You'll have it soon only the missus ain't here. Only I'm all by meself, like."

He hobbled through to the kitchen in his stockinged feet. His dog dusted the floor with its tail, flailing three or four downy feathers along the flags. Jim had been preparing a chicken the night before. Today, when he got the calves fed, the hens fed, the van started, he was off to far-away Liverpool to see his wife in hospital. The stock, such as it was, could take care of itself. The cow would be milked, but he was afraid she would have to hold on until he got back at night, whatever the hour. It was like that. Some things in a man's life had to be rated more important than others, although all were crying out to be attended to. The chicken Jim had prepared sat on a dish on the shelf. It was the best bird he had and he hoped that they would let Dilys have it. She had been crying for something from home, some little thing that she liked, prepared at home. Well, the chicken was the best he could do. They would surely cook it for her, and God grant that she would get better soon and come back home. It wasn't a lot to ask when you hadn't asked for anything but daily bread all your life. It wasn't much.

He looked at the dog and the dog somehow knew his thoughts before he spoke them.

"You got to go on the chain today," he told the creature. "I'll be gone a long time."

The tail stopped flailing. The dog sank down onto the flags. Jim fumbled in the pocket of his buttonless waistcoat and brought out his watch, which was fastened to a shoelace. He read the time by the light of the candle. A trickle of hot wax ran over his thumb as he did so, but he didn't feel its heat. As soon as he could he would be off. Let the van take him as far as the station and he would bless it. He looked about for a bit of brown paper and string and made a clumsy parcel of the chicken. He didn't want to have to do that after he had milked, had his breakfast and put on his heavy tweed suit and the dickie and cuffs. Let the fancy folk laugh at him if they liked. There was nothing wrong with clean brown paper tied with binder twine. When he had finished making the parcel he put on his boots and went out to the cow. She stood at the gate waiting to come in. Her coat was damp with the flowing mist. He patted her rump as she ambled past. As always she stood still and didn't even swish her tail while he milked. He went to the well and brought water for her, drinking a little himself at the same time. Shortly after he had herded her back to the field he fed the calves with the milk, fed the dog and had his breakfast. It was day, but a heavily shrouded day of the kind common in the hills between a spell of heat and a spell of rain. Beyond the scrub-fringed fields stretched bracken slopes where, in islands of grass, sheep grazed, but Jim could see nothing of his flock, for everything was hidden in the mist. The world didn't stretch to the bracken above, to the nursery of young trees to his left or to the birch and beech and the thorns that grew to the right of the farm. Everything beyond a distance of fifty yards faded away and the boundary of his world was a wall of moisture. He was living in the heart of a cloud.

If he considered this at all he thought about it only for a moment as he stood in the doorway putting his key in the big mortice lock. "Let the place sleep," he said to himself. Mentally he was locking it all up securely, the fields, the flock, the cow, the calves and the hens that would remain to pick about the yard or huddle from the damp in the shelter of the shed or the crowding nettles near the small rickyard. For once the old van behaved herself. He swung the starting handle. The damp air helped. She fired long before there was sweat on his brow or the slightest sign of a blister on his hand, which was something out of the ordinary.

"There you are!" he said, hurrying to climb in and slam the ill-fitting door behind him.

The van lurched over the ruts, passed through the open gate and trundled on to the slope. Soon he would be going headlong down to Pentre Ddu and on and away from there, down the valley to the railway.

It wasn't often that he met anyone on the road at any time of day, but to meet someone at first light was extraordinary indeed. He slammed his heavy boot on the foot-brake and dragged at the hand-brake, turning his front wheels in towards a stone at the same time.

"Good-day," he said in Welsh.

The policeman put his hand on the window.

"You haven't had the news?" he asked.

For a fearful moment Jim Parry's mind raced. Dilys! Something had happened to her away there in Liverpool. Dilys was dead! But she couldn't be—he would have known that. People who matter to one another aren't parted by death without some message, without some kind of wireless between them. No, it couldn't be!

"What news?" he asked, and he could hear himself asking as though he had been outside his own body.

"About the tiger?"

It was a second or two before the sense of the remark was absorbed. About the tiger? About the tiger? A tiger was something that he had never had news about, ever. It didn't belong to his world at all. The policeman could be mad.

"A tiger has escaped," said the policeman. "I have been sent up to warn you and to ask you to help me warn the rest of the people who live up here. It killed two men down in Pentre Ddu last night."

But he was going to Liverpool; to the big hospital where the smell of things was strange and everything was clean and white, and deathly, somehow; where Dilys lay back on her pillow and tried to squeeze back the tears that came in her eyes. Her face on the pillow wasn't white but a strange yellow colour, like sickness, like death, too.

"I've got a long way to go," he said. "I got no time to stop. You better find them that lives round about an' tell them. I'm goin' to Liverpool where my wife's ill. I got no time."

"It would help if you could tell me where they live," said the policeman.

He put his hand in his pocket and pulled out his watch and looked at it anxiously. There was no time and if he didn't go now and didn't see her today he had a queer feeling he would never see her again in this world.

"I got to go," he said. "You better find them best you can. I'm sorry about it, but I got no time."

The policeman began to protest, but he swung the wheel, released the hand-brake and the van rolled on. He steered with his wits alert, knowing all the way that if he struck the bank and got held up now he wouldn't get the train. The van began to rattle and complain. He was going down faster than he had ever done before. Once a wing dug a strip of turf and moss from the bank. Once the side lurched against a big stone and once the wheel bumped through a pot-hole and rear springs complained and flattened out.

"I got to get there today!" he said as he swept on, reaching forward with one hand to wipe the steam on the windshield. It was while he was doing this a second time that he saw the men on the road. They yelled and threw themselves up into the hedge. He dared not look back because of the bend ahead. The chicken in the brown paper rolled off the seat and bounced about his feet. Grit spurted from his tires as he swung round into the road at Pentre Ddu. He was going to get there now all right even if a policeman was waving at him. He slowed down and stuck his head out of the window.

"You know about the tiger?" he asked.

"I heard about it," he said. "I'm in a hurry. What you want?"

"If you've got anybody at home or any livestock loose you should stay home and look after them, get them locked up. Keep your wife and family indoors. Two men have been killed."

"I heard about it. I got to go to Liverpool. My wife's very ill there. It can have what it takes. I got no time . . ."

The policeman stood back and let him go, sorry for him, for the look of desperation that was on the hill farmer's face. A tiger was nothing in his world and death, more fearful than a tiger could contrive, hung over his head.

"Who was he?" the constable asked Frank Baker.

"That was old Jim Parry. He'll be off to Liverpool, I suppose. They say his wife's dying there."

"I suppose he has livestock?"

"He has a cow and some hens," said Baker. "I suppose he'll be back to milk the cow sometime."

"We'd better see that somebody looks after his stock, I suppose," said the policeman, who was a farmer's son himself.

Frank Baker went back inside. He had worries of his own. The newspaper men and the police were all elbowing for space, the former asking for something to eat and the latter clumping in and out with messages. Betty Collins was cooking breakfasts. In the kitchen they had exchanged a few words in private about the story of Ram Singh and the sticking door. She had a hold over him and somehow he didn't mind very much. He had always been dominated by a woman—his mother, and now Betty Collins, who at least had the shape of a woman.

She had put her hand on his arm and said, "Frank, so long as you an' me stick together they can't get anywhere makin' out we were responsible for him bein' shut outside."

"I don't see that it matters," he had told her, "since he went after the tiger of his own will and accord."

"But it wouldn't sound very good, Frank, would it, if I said you kept him out?"

"And if I said you shut the door?" he had countered.

"Frank!" she had replied, "really you are the limit! I shut the door? I was never near it. It was you what tried to keep it shut!"

Somehow she had made it sound convincing. His own sense of guilt had been enough. It didn't matter what she had done. He had put his foot to the door and stopped it opening because the tiger had been out there and because he hadn't thought about the Indian being in danger, hadn't cared what happened to him.

"Mr. Baker," said one of the newspapermen, "I wonder if my colleague could get a picture of you trying to get the door open?"

He stood still and looked at Betty Collins. She smiled at him.

"Go on!" she said. "Show them. Get your picture in the paper."

He allowed himself to be shepherded to the door and stood in the entrance looking stupidly in front of him, his hand on the door.

"You weren't surely standing like that with the tiger outside, were you, Mr. Baker?"

"No," he said quietly. He swung the door shut and put his hand on the handle and the latch at the same time. It didn't look real, as the photographer pointed out. It didn't look as though he were trying to drag the door open. It didn't look as though the door had stuck.

"Tell you what," suggested the photographer, "put your toe against it, pull from the handle and turn your body, then it won't show how the door is sticking. That way it would look very real, wouldn't it?"

Frank didn't say anything. For a minute or two he thought he was going to lose his head and start shouting.

"Go on," urged Betty Collins, who had come through from the kitchen. "Do it like he wants. It'll look just like the real thing."

He turned and did exactly what he had done when Ram Singh had been outside.

"Hold it!" said the photographer. "That's the ticket!"

At that moment someone began to thump the door from the other side. Frank Baker moved his foot and let the handle slip from his grasp. A policeman came in.

"This is plain stupid," Frank Baker mumbled.

"What's up?" asked the policeman.

Frank Baker said no more. He went through to the bar and got himself a glass of port. The photographer shrugged his shoulders.

"I got one good shot, anyway. Seems to have taken that business about the tiger being out there an' the Indian trying to get in as some personal fault of his. Can't say I understand altogether, but then when a door that has never stuck before suddenly sticks like that, a chap doesn't know what to think."

"There's a first time for everything," said Betty Collins, smiling. By everything she meant certain things in particular, of course. The photographer winked at his companion.

"I'll bet she's forgotten the first time," he whispered.

"I heard you," she said. "You newspaper hounds are like bakers an' printers, always frisky in the mornin's."

They laughed, watching her figure undulating in her tight skirt as she went back to the kitchen. Frank Baker poured himself a second glass of port. It had no taste.

"The Army," said the constable to the sergeant, "are all ready for a big push. That young captain's got his courage back now that daylight has come. He wants to take his men right up through the trees and on across the rough to the lake where the tiger was last seen, they tell me. He's having an inspection now. The newsreel chap wants to go with them and all the press boys are standing by to see them go into the gully."

"Good luck to them," said the sergeant, "but if you ask me they'll change their minds when they get up there in that mist. The tiger could be anywhere. They'd be better going to warn people like our chaps are doing and saving their wind for tiger-hunting when we know where it is!"

Inspector Williams came through. He had just had a breakfast of bacon and eggs.

"They were going to send two helicopters to assist us," he said, "but what use would they be in this?"

He nodded his head towards the window through which a stretch of rough field and the lower part of a wood could be seen. The mist was rolling down through the trees and spreading on the field like the smoke puffed by a beekeeper when handling a swarm.

"We can't do much in this, but the tiger can move where it likes," he said. "No doubt by afternoon people will want to know why we haven't caught it or killed it and if it kills anybody in the meantime somebody will have to be hauled over the coals. The Superintendent is due here at any minute and the Chief with him. Get ready for kicks. You can't have a tiger running loose and sit picking your nose in the mist. Does anybody fancy a game of hide and seek?"

"The Army," said the sergeant, "seem to fancy their chance."

"Somebody should tell that young chap that a tiger doesn't recognize umpires and platoons deployed to out-flank it. It's a tiger and it kills to live or lives to kill. It doesn't care which."

"The big advance is almost ready to kick off," said the sergeant.

"We must make a move ourselves," said the Inspector. "We have to see that those campers are all right. I'll have to send two chaps up there to get them back down."

Outside the Horseshoe Captain Anderson was walking up and down before his men. His uniform was stained and a little crumpled and he looked just a little wild-eyed, although the down on his chin hadn't ripened to anything like a warrior's stubble.

"I want you chaps to understand," he said, "that this isn't a game. This is a matter of life and death. We are going up there to make an end of the tiger if we can. Every minute of the time we are advancing through cover and even in the open you must be alert and ready for immediate action. You will be in constant danger from an enemy that will give no warning of its presence and no warning of its intention to attack! Do you understand that?"

"I understand," muttered Maloney, "that I never volunteered to be dragged through bushes by some bloke what didn't know a ruddy tiger from an overgrown tom-cat!"

"You got some comment, Maloney?" asked the corporal.

Maloney shuffled. "No," he said. "I just said you lead an' I'll follow."

The newspapermen had been taking note of Captain Anderson's address to his men. Sergeant Morris smiled to himself. He could see the mist coming down across the field. They would be a fine old rabble once they got in the thick of that lot, even with walkie-talkie, which they hadn't got. Even walkie-talkie wouldn't be a lot of use. He could imagine the exchanges that would take place while they floundered about peering into tangles looking for a tiger. Captain Anderson was a good boy, but he wasn't a ruddy tiger expert. He looked along the ranks and took note of the different expressions. He knew what Maloney was thinking, for instance, and Maloney wasn't a bad lad either, just full of his own particular brand of malarkey. And then there was Thompson who would follow you there and back and remain as solid as a rock just so long as you didn't tell him what you were thinking. If anybody had to face a tiger and stand and shoot it would be a good thing to have Thompson at his right hand. There were some, of course, who were boldest with a pint in their hands, and some who would sneak off at the slightest provocation, but he felt sure they were all as good men as Anderson, which was a good thing if you believed that links in a chain are important. Here they were, going to play shepherd to a tiger. It was a lark if you liked larks of this sort.

"Remember the women and children," he muttered as he led them along the hedge and Captain Anderson waited to see them spread out and prepare to beat up into the gully and the plantation on either side.

"Here we go," said Maloney. "I wonder what my old lady will say when she sees me picture in the paper tomorrow. I won't half be a lad when I go home." "Was you on that tiger-hunt, Maloney? Was you the bloke that shot it? You never did! I seen your picture in the paper an' all them villagers in that Welsh village huggin' an' kissin' you. You must've felt a bleedin' hero that day, eh?"

"For cripesake, wake up, Maloney! Where you wanderin' to?" asked the corporal.

Maloney came to his wits. The dream was over for the time being. He was compelled to watch where he was going. It wouldn't do to fall over a gorse bush with his safety catch off and a round up the spout. Besides, there was just the chance that the tiger was at hand and his immortal hour had come. He often talked about his immortal hour, although mostly to himself. Thompson, for instance, wouldn't take anything seriously. He said what Maloney thought about was immoral hours and he had had plenty of those.

"Look, Maloney, you heard what Andy said about bein' in continual danger?" said the corporal. "That's twice you wandered across the line of advance! You keep your position!"

"I heard what Andy said! I seen what Andy done last night. Andy may be a big boy to his old lady, but he don't impress me bein' a bloody hero! This isn't the right sort of day t'go tiger-stalkin'. Anybody could tell you that!"

The corporal ignored him. He was thinking much the same thing. They were into the trees now and coming to a standstill because one flank couldn't get through a tangle of undergrowth and rocks and the other had to climb out of a ditch and wade in saplings that were just high enough to make communication impossible. Maloney and the corporal lost touch with each other. Somewhere a whistle was blown. Maloney got down on one knee. They had had the big push. They had lost their escort of newsreel and newspaper photographers. There was nothing to photograph in men getting bogged down in wet undergrowth and a jungle of trees through which the mist trailed.

"You wouldn't believe it," said Maloney aloud, "but there I was, crouchin' in the trees with nobody to back me up when I suddenly heard the branches swishing. It was the tiger passing through, comin' right down the line straight at me. I see the branches moving. I knew what it was.

'Wait,' I says to meself. 'Hold it, boy. It's it or you.' It come right on. I was scared stiff, mate, but I thought about them poor beggars down in the village. . . . When I shot, it stood still an' then it sprung. I shot it again. It fell not three feet from the toe o' me boot. The sergeant an' the captain come runnin'. I got it, I said. They was white in the face, scared stiff, like me. . . ."

It had become quiet. There was no sound of movement to left or to right. The whistle had blown. Captain Anderson was, presumably, working out his next move. Sergeant Morris was waiting, as he always waited, for his officer to decide whether to continue a hopeless advance or to call the movement off and go back and reconsider, as a man always could do when he was playing a game and not fighting an enemy. Maloney wiped moisture from his cheek and looked ahead. The tips of the conifers immediately to his front were swaying. The movement rippled along them following a direct line. Something was passing through them just as he had seen it all a few minutes before. This was it! The tiger was coming down! He found himself working out that it was coming exactly down the line that the poacher chap might have taken. It was probably tracking him! It was going to run straight into him. He put up the gun and waited. The light brown object came into view for a brief second and the young firs swished and screened it again. He held his breath. Its head was just about chest-high. A foot below the head would, he hoped, put the bullet right into its lungs. The trees moved at their tips. He put his cheek to the stock of the rifle and took up the pressure on the trigger. The shot snapped off. He didn't hear the echo. In an instant he had worked his bolt. There was no need to fire again. It was down. It didn't move. A whistle shrilled. Someone shouted. He stood motionless, afraid to go forward. It might suddenly spring up and come charging through the underbrush at him. The corporal was close at hand.

"Maloney!" he shouted. "Was it you that fired? What happened?"

"I'm here!" he croaked. He couldn't take the rifle from his shoulder or take his eyes off the place where the tiger had been.

"What's up?" gasped the corporal.

Now he couldn't say a word. He was rigid and speechless. The corporal stood at his elbow looking in the direction in which he had fired.

"I shot it. . . ." he whispered after a moment or two. "Watch out in case it comes."

They stood together staring at the place. It didn't seem as though either of them would be able to advance, and then Sergeant Morris came scrambling through.

"What is it, Corporal?" he asked breathlessly.

"Maloney says he shot it, Sarge," said the corporal. "It's in there."

CHAPTER 8

The tiger walked in the midst, its coat damp, and its tracks showing where it had crossed rocks and padded through mud. It was hungry and it was cold, for in the years since it had been shipped from India its coat had never once been wet with rain and it had never walked abroad and slept outside a cage. Its movements were graceful and yet it showed that it was unaccustomed to much walking, although hunger urged it to keep moving on. Once, when it cornered three sheep, frantic with terror, in the angle of two drystone walls that were part of an old fold, it might have killed and eaten, but for some reason it changed its mind and let the frenzied sheep leap away, falling over rocks and tumbling down slopes as they bounded to safety. It could have been that something about the powerful smell of these sheep repelled the tiger, but whatever the reason for its allowing them to escape, it did so, and made no attempt to strike them down again.

Instead of turning into the hills beyond the black lake the tiger came back towards Pentre Ddu, following the line that Bob the Cough had taken. Ahead of it in the midst, unaware of its presence, the little party of climbers stumbled along with their gear. It was not long after first light. Had the morning been clear the tiger would have seen them and they might have seen it crossing the peat. As it was they made for the village with all haste and the tiger followed. Neither was aware of the presence of the other, but the party of climbers thought about the tiger while the tiger if it had thoughts at all, concentrated on finding food. It was a hunter unused to the way of hunting, but by instinct it headed in the right direction.

"When I get back," said Flynn, "I'm going to get drunk. I'm going to get so drunk I'll need a stomach pump."

"If you get back," said Temple, jumping from one bit of firm ground to the next and struggling to maintain his balance. "If the tiger doesn't come plundering up out of this blasted mist and knock us all down like helpless sparrows!"

"Save your breath!" said Willis. "Stop talking rot."

"I can smell tiger," said Taffy Davies. "He's right behind us. I can smell it on the wind."

Willis snorted. "Have you ever smelled a tiger in the first place?" he demanded.

Taffy Davies halted for breath and put his hand on Flynn's arm.

"You can smell it, can't you, Quack?"

Flynn was about to say no when his companion nudged him and nodded towards Willis.

"Yes, I can! I can smell it all right. Can't you smell it?"

Temple sniffed and grabbed at his pack. "Let's get to hell out of here," he said, making a desperate effort to run. "You're damn well right!"

They began to trot. Taffy Davies grinned to himself. Flynn thought it funny at first, but when he began to get out of breath he changed his mind. It was all very well making Willis run for his life, but it was killing them. He slowed down.

"Come on, man!" said Taffy. "Don't hang about like that! The ruddy thing's on our track all right. That smell can only be from a tiger!"

Flynn began to walk. He was just about all in. He stopped and gasped for breath and then, as he stood still, he fancied that he really did smell something. How near would a tiger have to be for them to smell the beast? No, it was nonsense, and yet he could swear that he could smell something more than the smell of sheep, the marsh gas and the peat, the damp grass and heather.

"You're right, Taffy!" he said, gathering all his strength and plunging on.

Taffy, who hadn't slowed down, gulped to prevent himself from laughing and looked at Willis.

"You don't smell it, do you?" he asked.

Willis didn't say anything. He considered it not a subject to joke about. They had a long way to go. The tiger had been following the man they had seen at the lake. It could just as easily be stalking them now.

The mist seemed to be clearing for a little while. Once they got a glimpse of the ragged line of trees near the planting of firs and Flynn looked back, but he could see nothing because the mist swirled across the moorland and thickened in the hollows. The tiger was less than a mile away. Flynn began to imagine that it was about a hundred yards behind. They reached firmer ground and clumped on, lumbering like heavy cart-horses with their loads swaying on their backs.

All of them were out of breath and almost exhausted. The last hundred yards to the gray posts of the old fence took them a long time, it seemed. There was barbed wire on the fence, rusty barbed wire that sagged and was not easy to straddle because the fence-posts lay at drunken angles.

"Hurry up!" urged Taffy Davies. "It must be after us. I can smell it stronger than before."

For Temple the joke had gone far enough. He had paid the price for collaborating. He wanted to go down through the trees without falling and breaking his neck. He had had more than enough.

"Shut up!" he said. "Of course you can't smell the tiger! It was funny to begin with, but I've had enough!"

"All right," said Taffy, "I can't smell the tiger. I can see it. Look!"

He pointed back into the mist. Willis, straddling the wire, looked in the direction from which they had come, and he saw the tiger!

"My God!" he said, and fell, his pack tumbling over his head.

Flynn laughed. Taffy Davies stared and saw nothing. The mist rolled on. Temple looked at Willis and reached down to help him to his feet.

"Come on," he said, "we've all had enough. Taffy can't smell the tiger. It's no use you trying to make out you've seen it. It isn't a joke now. We must get on out of this."

Willis, however, turned on his side, wriggled out of his pack, scrambled to his feet and sprang away, crashing into the trees and running like a madman. Taffy Davies stared after him.

"He thinks he's turned the joke on us," he said. "Well, he won't think it so funny when he has to come back up here for his stuff. I'm not carrying it!"

"We'd better carry it," said Temple, "or we'll never see

it again. Nobody's going to come up here for it with a tiger loose."

"They'll have recaptured it long ago," said Taffy. "If we haven't dreamed the whole thing."

They could hear Willis crashing on down through the trees. Flynn and Temple picked up the pack and carried it between them. It made progress difficult, for the space between the trees was small and the wet branches struck them in the face when they tried to walk abreast.

"Willis! Come back, you damned fool! Come back, do you hear?" shouted Taffy, but Willis didn't hear. He was ploughing down through the trees, tripping and stumbling, getting his face lashed with branches and sometimes closing his eyes as he made his escape. He had seen the tiger, he was sure of that, standing on a peat bank out there in the mist, its body at a sort of angle so that he could see the great chest of the beast and its trailing tail. The mist seemed to have made it appear enormous. It was coming after them. There was no doubt of that. As he rushed on he could hear the faint sound of a whistle down below. He didn't think about it, for at every turn some new obstacle loomed in his path, and he had to reach out to save himself from crashing into a mossy rock or falling over a branch tangled in briar and bramble. The whistle sounded again, and this time he wondered about it, for he had fallen headlong, his toe caught in a root. When he tried to get up he found his knee was twisted and the muscles of his thigh stabbed with pain. He tried to run, but he couldn't. He could only stagger along. He put his head down and put his hand to his knee to brace the weight of his body as he went on downhill. He was glad that he was emerging from a belt of tall trees to a section that allowed him to see more of the sky, for this lessened the danger of him stumbling. It couldn't be so far now, he said to himself. He had forgotten about his companions. He didn't hear them coming and he didn't hear the click of

Maloney's safety-catch, nor did he hear the rifle when it fired, but the whistle blew. Faintly and far away, he heard the whistle blow. It was the last thing he heard.

Sergeant Morris took the corporal's automatic.

"Cover me with that rifle," he said.

The corporal stepped to one side and tried to cover the sergeant as he went forward. He found himself thinking that Morris was an unreal sort of man, an inhuman creature who could do this sort of thing without waiting to screw himself up and without making a show of what he was doing. The tiger might be waiting there in the trees, ready to smash Morris down and kill him.

"Steady, Sarge," he muttered, but Morris didn't hear him. He walked through the conifer branches without blinking, without taking his eyes from the place where they said the tiger lay. He looked down when something kicked and moved, his finger ready to press the trigger and make the gun spray the place with lead.

He stopped and let the muzzle of the gun drop.

"Corp!" he said, "Maloney! Quick! Get Anderson, fetch a stretcher. You've shot a bloke!"

Maloney ran a few paces forward.

"No, Sarge!" he said. "I never shot a bloke! It was the tiger!"

Morris was kneeling beside Willis. He had his hand inside the student's shirt, feeling his heart.

"If you'd done it on purpose, Maloney, you couldn't have done a better job. I wouldn't say this bloke has a tuppenny chance. Get a stretcher!"

Maloney stood still. The corporal had gone running for Captain Anderson.

"Maloney's shot a civilian, sir!" he reported.

Captain Anderson groaned. "No," he said to himself. "Oh, no!"

He began to run to the place and the corporal ran on

down through the rough field to the village. The men in extended order stayed where they were. One or two called to each other.

"What's up? What was the shot for? They seen the tiger?"

They were all tense and half-afraid for their own safety as the mist filtered through the trees.

"Is it bad?" asked Captain Anderson, kneeling down beside the wounded man.

Sergeant Morris looked at him. "I'm afraid so, sir. It seems to have gone down through the chest and out through the back. I don't think he can survive it."

The sergeant's hands had blood on them. He wiped them on the grass and held Willis's head up a little. Captain Anderson stared at the man's face. He was wondering if this was the look of death.

"I must see what's keeping the corporal," he said after a minute.

The sergeant said nothing and Captain Anderson turned and looked at Maloney.

"You better get down to the village, Maloney," he said. "There's nothing you can do."

He picked up the rifle and drew the bolt. There was a live round in the breech. Maloney had automatically reloaded, fancying himself confronted with the tiger, he supposed. Suddenly he blinked. A flash had been fired.

"Just a minute!" he said angrily. "Give me that camera!"

The photographer stared at him.

"You'd better think about that again," he said. "I have every right to be here and to take pictures if I like!"

Captain Anderson looked at Maloney.

"Maloney," he said, "take that camera from him!"

Maloney reached out and grabbed the camera by the sling.

"Leave it, sonny," said the photographer, "or you and your officer will wish you'd never been born!"

Maloney held on and looked at Captain Anderson.

"All right," said the Captain. "I'll see your credentials."

The photographer produced a press card. Captain Anderson took careful note.

"I'll make sure you don't use that picture or any others you've taken," he said.

The photographer turned round and went off. Sergeant Morris cleared his throat.

"I think this poor chap's turned it in, sir," he said.

They were looking at one another when they heard the sound in the trees up the slope. Captain Anderson put his hand to his revolver and then picked up Maloney's rifle again. Morris didn't stand up, but glanced over his shoulder. He knew that this wasn't the tiger coming. He could hear the sound of boots on the damp earth, the swishing of branches as several bodies passed through them, and he was on the point of telling Anderson to watch what he was doing when one of the men coming down coughed. They waited for them to appear. Flynn was in the lead and Temple immediately behind them. They reached the spot without first seeing the three men. They had heard the shot and Taffy had grunted and said that somebody had probably shot old Willis, thinking he was a mountain goat.

"What happened?" asked Flynn as Temple crowded him with the pack they carried.

Captain Anderson looked at them.

"Was he with you?" he asked.

Flynn looked down, and for the first time knew that the man lying behind the sergeant's crouching figure was Willis.

"Willis!" he said. "What's happened, Willis?"

"He was shot by accident. One of our chaps mistook him for the tiger."

Taffy Davies came ploughing through at the side of Sergeant Morris.

"Hey, Willis," he said. "Cut it out! Don't put on an act!"

He stared at the blood on Morris's hands and the white face of the shot man.

"Hey, Willis," he said again softly. "Willis, boy."

"I think he's dead," said Morris.

Flynn dropped the pack and went down on his knees beside the body.

"You were all together?" asked Morris.

Flynn nodded. "We were together," he said. "He's dead, poor old Willie. He thought he saw the tiger. We were kidding him. He wouldn't have been rushing down like that if we hadn't kidded him about it."

"It was meant to be a joke," said Temple.

"It was my fault," said Taffy Davies heavily.

"Who shot him?" asked Flynn.

No one said anything. Flynn looked at the Captain who held the rifle and then at the sergeant. Finally he looked at Maloney. Maloney's face told the story. They looked at each other for several seconds.

"I'll find out about the stretcher, sir," said Maloney.

"Do that," said Captain Anderson. When Maloney had lumbered away he looked at Flynn. "It was a pure accident, of course," he said. "There will be an enquiry."

"That will make it right," said Flynn, and Sergeant Morris looked him in the eye.

"Nothing is made right by anything," he said, "even stupid remarks like that, son."

He put Willis's head gently back on the ground and stood up. He could see two policemen coming up. One of them was the Inspector. Two men were bringing the stretcher. He could hear them getting it over a fence. The corporal was hurrying along.

"Better get the chaps back for now," said Captain Anderson. "Have them stand-to down in the road. I'll make arrangements about Maloney in the meantime. No use keeping him here. He'd better be taken back to camp."

In the village a whisper was already going from door to door.

"They had a shot at the tiger! A chap just come down for a stretcher. Looks like the tiger injured one o' them soldiers."

"The tiger's got one o' them soldiers."

At the far end of the village, ten minutes later, an old man sucked on his pipe and told the only person who hadn't had the news. "They wounded the tiger, but it killed one o' the troops. They're off up the slope after it now. You got to hand it to them. They're brave, them lads what goes up there in this mist."

"What has happened?" asked Inspector Williams. "One of your men got shot?"

He paused and looked past Captain Anderson. "One of the campers?" he said. "Is he badly hit?"

"He's dead," said Sergeant Morris. "Never had a chance. If only he had made some sound that would have given warning. If he had whistled."

"Whistled or sung," said Flynn, "like a blackbird."

"All right," said Sergeant Morris, "that's enough."

"He apparently thought he saw the tiger up there and left his companions and started to run," said Captain Anderson. "He must have been running doubled up to get shot as he did. Maloney was convinced it was the tiger."

"He's convinced now," said Flynn.

Taffy Davies put his hand on Flynn's arm. "Come on, Quack," he said. "The chap didn't know it was Willis. It was an accident. If it was anybody's fault it was ours for making him think the tiger was there."

The Inspector looked at Flynn. "I'll want your names and addresses," he said, "and a statement from each of you. Perhaps you'll go down to the Horseshoe and wait for me there?"

The stretcher had arrived. Sergeant Morris helped lift

the dead man onto it. They came out of the trees and onto the field as the corporal emerged with the platoon.

"Who was it done it?" they asked each other.

"Looks as if he's bought it if you ask me."

"Corp says Maloney done it, the silly sod."

"They'll do old Maloney for this."

"Poor old Maloney! What will his old lady say now? Wanted his picture in the paper. He'll get it in the paper now all right!"

"If we go back up there chasin' this tiger, mate, I'm shootin' no matter what. I don't care if I do shoot a ruddy civvy. No tiger's gettin' me! Not much it ain't."

The stretcher and the platoon reached the road at the same time and the activity close to the Horseshoe increased. Pressmen crowded forward, people came out from their houses and joined the throng, forgetting the tiger in the face of new tragedy.

"He's dead, all right," they said to one another, "but the tiger got away."

"Where is it now? Have they forgotten all about it? Is it creepin' down into the back gardens while they all make a fuss here?"

"Search me."

Inspector Williams thrust his way through to the Horseshoe and Captain Anderson followed him. Both of them wanted to telephone. The Inspector got there first. One of his constables handed him the instrument.

"I am afraid there has been a fatal accident here," he said. "One of the men combing the lower plantation shot a chap who was coming down from the mountain," he reported. "One of a party of climbers who were camping up there. Yes, I'm afraid he's dead. The Army will hold an enquiry. Notify the coroner, will you? He's going to have a busy day in Pentre Ddu if he holds them all at once. Yes, perhaps we'd better wait until the end of the week and see what the score is then, but you can't blame anybody. There's a heavy mist coming down into the valley from the mountain. Impossible to get after the tiger in these conditions. We could ask for dogs, but do you think the dogs would be a lot of use? When it clears we might make use of dogs and with a couple of helicopters, some radio vans and the co-operation of the Army we might get on its track, but that won't be today, I'm afraid. Our men are busy warning everybody for miles around. It might have been better to have got the B.B.C. to put out an announcement, but that could create panic. The man's name was Willis. Comes from Cheltenham, I think. His relatives will have to be informed. We'll be on with that information as soon as I've interviewed the rest of the party."

Captain Anderson took the instrument and asked to be put through to his commanding officer. The receiver was hot and sticky and his own hand was perspiring. What would the old man say? "Maloney is a sound chap, sir," he began to explain in thoughts while he waited for the call. "A bit of an exhibitionist in some ways, but as steady as the rest. I warned them about the danger of attack by the tiger. I didn't think they would need to be warned about the presence of anyone in the forest. No, sir, I felt that that was covered by the repeated stressing of the need to advance in line and not to move without knowing just what position the next section was in. Maloney says he was sure it was the tiger. He didn't know otherwise until Sergeant Morris told him what he had done. I'll have him sent back to camp. The police will want a statement. I'm taking his story now. He'll have to be at the inquest of course."

When he finally got put through he said all this to his superior and warned him about the photograph that had been taken. His commanding officer mumbled something about the press and the Press Council.

"It's politics, my boy," he said. "Watch how you shoot that

tiger or you'll have the Women's League for the Protection of Tabby Cats after you."

"I'll watch," he said weakly.

The Inspector was interviewing the three climbers. He stood listening to what they had to say for several minutes before he went outside.

"I believe you are sending this chap Maloney back to camp?" asked a reporter. "Is he under arrest?"

"Under arrest? Of course not! He is being sent back because he is suffering from shock. Do you imagine we'd want him on this job after a thing like this has happened?"

"Have you any comment to make about Maloney's conduct, sir?"

"No comment whatsoever. Maloney is a good soldier. The thing was an accident."

Maloney was sitting in the truck waiting for Captain Anderson.

"Maloney," he said, "I'm sending you back to camp in a few minutes. I want an exact statement of what happened before you are sent back. You are to make no statement to anyone, do you understand, apart from the statement you make to me? You must not give any information to the press. I will give your statement to the police. When you get back you are not to discuss this with anyone in camp."

Maloney slumped in the seat. He was still shaking. He was wondering what the old lady would say now. He had shot a man. The man was dead. Yesterday the only trouble in his life had been how to get an odd pint of beer and wangle a pass, and now the world had changed. Why hadn't he held his fire? Why hadn't he waited as he had when that poacher chap came across the field? What would they do to him now? They couldn't send him to prison for manslaughter, could they? Even if they didn't, there was probably some charge that would put him in the guardhouse for God knew how long, and none of it, none of it at all, could bring back the poor chap who was lying dead in the Horseshoe.

Two old men stood in the road looking at the truck in which Maloney sat. They were talking to each other in Welsh.

"This tiger is responsible for another man being killed, all because it was let out by that chap last night. How many more will be killed here? It has come to Pentre Ddu like a plague sent to punish."

"It hasn't killed anybody from Pentre Ddu yet, just the same. It has killed two foreigners and a soldier, hasn't it? Perhaps they will kill it before it does any harm to anybody here."

"That is the chap who shot the man coming down from the mountain."

"I am sorry for him, poor fellow. Sorry indeed, and for his poor mother."

"I am sorry for the mother of the poor fellow who was shot."

CHAPTER 9

Butter was something he liked with his potatoes. To be completely happy, he liked to have a glass of milk too, when he had salt beef, probably because this had been the habit in his childhood when buttered potatoes, salt beef and buttermilk were often all that was to be had. Betty Collins hadn't forgotten the butter. Inspector Williams reached out with his knife and helped himself to a fairly big knob of it which he applied to his still hot potatoes. He savored the pickled beef in his mouth and chewed it slowly while he stared out of the window at the little garden behind the Horseshoe.

The Horseshoe had more customers in than it usually had on a week-day, but that was no wonder. He could hear the clattering of boots on the flags, the sound of chair legs being roughly drawn across the floor, the clink of glasses and the mumble of voices. He didn't need to guess at what the talk was about, and he was glad to be away from it for half an hour; to forget the dead men and the tiger; to look at the misty hill and think about nothing that was new and dramatic but to slip back in time. The background noise of the Horseshoe was nostalgically familiar. It belonged to a market town inn where he sat with his father at noon and the atmosphere was strong with the smell of sour ale, the sheep smell of shepherds and their cringing collie dogs withdrawn under chairs or settles. He could see his father's hand on his walking-stick as he tapped his hard black boots while he talked.

"Wants to be a policeman," his father had said, "for the sake of the suit of clothes."

The old man hadn't meant to be spiteful about it. He had smiled as he said it so that those listening would know that he didn't want anyone to follow the observation with hurtful remarks. He had looked at the floor and grinned foolishly and his father's audience had smiled at him in return when he looked up again, showing their tobacco-stained teeth, sipping their beer and nodding when one of them said, "Well, good luck to him, isn't it? You have to have policemen with so many wicked people about!"

"It's a long time, a lifetime, boy," he could hear his father saying, "and you should set your feet where you mean them to go from the start."

He had set his feet in that pair of policeman's boots, worn them in villages and towns, clattered over cobbles to part brawlers, and once walked slowly in them to take a knife from a lunatic. Here he was now, almost at the end of the road, and he wasn't sure whether spiritually he wasn't a farmer or a shepherd in spite of everything, for who was able to say that spiritually he was his brother's keeper? Someone in the room beyond raised his voice and said something about fair play, the police weren't paid to hunt tigers, and he found himself done with dreaming. The door behind him was opened abruptly and the sergeant said, "The Chief's arrived." That meant that at last the Chief was coming to look into the thing for himself. He wiped his mouth with the napkin. When he put his cap on, his wife always said, he was official. What she meant was that he discarded sentimentality, and this was almost true. You couldn't be sorry for people who broke the law.

The hubbub in the bar was undiminished. He opened the door and heard someone saying that the big noise had arrived, meaning that the Chief's car was pulling into the garage forecourt.

"Was it all right?" called Betty Collins.

"Thank you very much," he said, and she smiled warmly at him.

He knew the smile and knew her sort, and nothing about her impressed him favorably. Baker was serving behind the bar, too. He looked fuddled, and he probably was. Had they shut that Indian chap outside for some reason he couldn't fathom? The thought had been troubling him for hours. Maybe the tiger's escape was related to both its keepers being shut outside. Certainly both had been inside shortly before the tragedy.

"Have you had lunch, Inspector?" asked the Chief when he met him in the doorway. "Could you fix up some coffee somewhere where we can talk privately about this business?"

He called Betty Collins and asked her to bring some coffee. The room seemed very small and overcrowded with chairs when he and the Chief shared it, and the Chief's bulk blotted out his view of the garden. He felt hemmed in. The story of the tiger didn't seem to belong to a small room with large-patterned wallpaper and a black iron fireplace. The room was real and familiar. The things that had happened in Pentre Ddu weren't real. They would be real one day, when the inquest was over, when the tiger was dead, and he was sitting by the bowling-green smoking his pipe to keep the midges away. They sat not quite opposite each other, for there wasn't much room beneath the table. The Chief cleared his throat.

"Nothing developed since your last report, I suppose?"

"Nothing," he said, "and nothing will, I hope, until this mist has lifted. If something happens it's more likely to be the tiger running into somebody and killing them, than somebody killing the tiger. The sort of gun a hill farmer has wouldn't be any use."

"Much better if people are warned that whatever happens they had better not take a shot at it with a shot-gun."

"We've been warning people all over the place. Some of them are scared stiff and some are surly and think we want to stop them looking after their livestock. You'd never believe the way some of them have taken the news!"

"Did you hear the news on the radio this morning?"

The Inspector shook his head. "I suppose they made the most of it. I told them we had decided not to issue a warning over the radio for fear it would create a panic. I suppose they referred to you?"

"I told them that it would all be over in a matter of hours, we hoped. I didn't say what it would mean if the tiger got well away into the hills in the mist, but it won't be long before that angle is being exploited in the press, and then it won't be long before an outcry starts. You interviewed these climbers or hikers. Did they see the tiger since it was seen by the man Rowlands?"

"The chap who was shot was thought to have seen it. He thought he saw it. That's the only explanation for his mad rush away from his companions, but whether he really saw it or not, I don't know."

"It could be within three miles of the village still or it could be across in the next valley! It could be ten miles up the valley or away down the river. We might hear of it killing somebody miles away and we sit here waiting."

"Not much else we can do, sir, is there? The idea of the troops helping was all right, but honestly, what can they do in this sort of weather? I even wonder how effective they'll be in beating the woods. If the tiger happened to be in front of them and broke through they'd just as likely shoot one another as shoot it. You've got to have experience of driving game. A wounded tiger would be a great deal more dangerous than a half-tame brute trying to get its bearings in unfamiliar surroundings."

"Quite, quite," said the Chief. "The problem at the moment, of course, is to keep people in, to make them stay indoors at least until visibility improves and the beast can be driven or tracked down and killed."

"If anybody gets attacked in the meantime we'll be held responsible. When the Super was on, just before lunch, he said there was a rumor that the tiger had killed another man. The editor of one of the big daily papers had been on to him to ask him if he thought the problem was beyond the police and did he think enough troops had been summoned."

"I'm having a statement drawn up for issue to the press and the radio," the Chief told him, "but we'll hold on a little. The mist may lift yet, and we'll be able to say what we're doing rather than what we propose to do. As it is, even road patrols are useless in parts where the mist is down to the road. It's no use watching on one stretch when the beast can cross in half a dozen places farther on."

"I have a feeling it's up there and not so far away," said the Inspector. "I lived here when I was a small boy. I can almost see the tiger up there among the black willows and the mountain ash trees. It would be seen and reported but for this mist, but we'll maybe have news before it's seen. It'll kill a sheep or a cow or a pig before long, and one of these hill farmers will come belting down to tell us and ask for compensation!"

"I hope you're right. Two Members of Parliament have telephoned me this morning. If the Home Secretary doesn't get on before the afternoon's out it will be most odd. It isn't hard to see just how the wind will blow if the tiger kills again."

Inspector Williams nodded his head gravely. He knew the politicians and their ways.

"Perhaps," he said, "you might invite the two Members to come up and see what is being done? They might help us in the hunt for the tiger. I'd take them up there in the mist myself. They might put in a word about allowance and pensions after that!"

Someone knocked at the door and the Inspector had to get up so that the coffee could be brought in.

"I hope you won't think I'm a pessimist, sir," he said, "but if I remember this valley and this sort of mist, things won't improve for two or three days. It used to happen once or twice in the summer every year. My mother used to say that the hill put its hat on and it wouldn't take it off until it dropped over its eyes, which meant that it would come right down and hang in the valley for two or three days."

"With all respect to your mother, Williams, I hope that that was one of those old wives' tales. If it happens that way we'll all be very sorry for ourselves, I'm afraid, and perhaps one, and maybe two people will fall foul of the tiger."

The Inspector smiled. "She was uncannily good at weather signs," he said, "but times have changed. Perhaps the theory's out of date now, like all the other old things we used to set store by."

"Just in this," said the Chief, "let us hope that signs mean nothing."

They finished their coffee and the Inspector outlined the

routine duties he had allocated to his subordinates. Afterwards they went out onto the road and stood for a few minutes watching Captain Anderson's men being served with a meal.

"Those men will be relieved shortly, I suppose?" asked the Chief.

"I expect so," said the Inspector, wondering when he would be free to get some sleep other than the cat-naps he had taken during the night.

Captain Anderson came over. He looked rough and haggard.

"We'll leave half a dozen men here," he said, "to be called upon if needed while the remainder are taken back to camp and replacements are sent over. I shall return and get some arrangements made to billet the men somewhere close at hand. The C.O. feels that we can only stand by until the weather lifts. After that, of course, we shall be here to fall in with any scheme you put forward. It's your show, of course."

Inspector Williams looked at the Chief and put up a hand to rub his nose and hide a smile. Oh yes, he was thinking, it was the responsibility of the police.

"Quite so," said the Chief. "We can do nothing in this. Unfortunately the same doesn't apply to the tiger. It can do as it pleases. So long as the men you are leaving know how to use a rifle we shall be happy. If the tiger happens to be reported anywhere in the neighborhood we shall have to rush them there. At the moment we have only half a dozen rifles, and they are in the possession of men on patrol on the roads."

Captain Anderson saluted and took his cane under his arm. They watched him detail Sergeant Morris and six men to remain behind and the trucks moved away.

"Where did he get the blood on his uniform?" asked the Chief.

The Inspector told him. "He's young," he said, "and it isn't his fault that he hasn't seen many dead men. Nobody wants to see death or blood, do they?"

The Horseshoe's customers were still tiger-hunting when he went back inside. He stood for a moment listening to them and watching their gestures as they elaborated on how to deal with tigers.

"That's right, isn' it, Inspector?" somebody asked. "In India they ties a goat to a peg an' goes up a tree an' waits for the tiger to come an' eat it, then the bloke up the tree puts on his light an' shoots it."

"That's about right," he said, smiling, "but this tiger doesn't know the rules. It's never seen a tethered goat and there are plenty of sheep and cows for it to feed on without bothering with tethered goats."

"Ah," said the man, "you got somethin' there. That's what I say about it. This tiger isn't a wild tiger what knows what to do. If so you could tell what it would do. This one's like a canary what escapes from a cage. It's gotta find its way about."

"Only it isn't a canary," he said. "It's a cat, a ruddy big cat."

They all laughed and he went through to the other little room that he had turned into an office, made some notes for the coroner's officer and then went out to walk down the road, partly because he felt he needed fresh air to prevent a fit of yawning coming on and partly because he wanted to see the constable who was due down from the hill at any moment. It was quiet on the road. The stream was hushed. There was hardly a sound of life in the village except for the muffled talk back in the Horseshoe and the hollow sound of Jack Roberts's mallet knocking a joint together.

The constable who had gone up to warn people in some outlying cottages came down wheeling his bicycle.

"Have you had any report of the tiger?" he asked him.

The constable shook his head. "One of the kids up there said she had seen something big like a tiger, and I talked to her about it for five minutes before her ma came out of the garden and said I shouldn't pay attention to what she said because she wasn't right at the best of times, and worse about the middle of the month."

"I suppose they all went indoors and locked up?"

"One old chap said he wasn't worried, and in any case if the tiger pushed hard on the door the catch wouldn't hold, but the rest got the kids in and said they'd keep the doors and windows shut."

He walked back along the road with the constable. The mist was coming right down now into Pentre Ddu and he couldn't help thinking about what his mother had said. They wouldn't be able to get after the tiger for days, and in the meantime it would be a miracle if the tiger didn't come up with somebody. The only hope was that it would kill a farm animal and give some sign of its whereabouts. Perhaps it would kill and stay with the kill so that it could be traced and destroyed. That was something he hadn't really thought about, but if it killed a man or a woman or a child the consequences were something he didn't like to think about.

When he got back to the Horseshoe the newspapermen seemed to have taken the place over. They were entertaining Bob the Cough, and Bob the Cough was making the most of it.

"I seen it," he said. "I'm the only damn one that's been close to an' lived! If I hadn't known the road through the trees it'd have had me, but I knew it was after me. I been chased before. I spent my life dodgin' trouble."

"You have," said the Inspector, "but you won't always be able to dodge it, maybe. If the tiger didn't get you it was because it wasn't really after you."

Bob the Cough was making some retort about the police

when the Inspector felt a tug at his sleeve. One of his constables had come in.

"Quick, sir," he urged in a whisper. "The tiger's been seen!"

He turned about and went outside immediately.

"Up on one of the farms, sir. That chap over there came down on his tractor to tell us!"

The farmer came clumping over, shedding mud from his boots as he came.

"You better be quick," he said. "The mist is everywhere."

The Inspector sent one of his men to collect the soldiers.

"Hurry like hell!" he said.

The farmer nodded when he asked if he could take him up on the tractor. They whirled about and the tractor shot forward, leaving a tail of the blue vapor which hung in the damp air. They went up the slope rattling and rocking with the van containing the soldiers and two policeman hurrying behind. When the Inspector glanced over his shoulder he saw that the Horseshoe had emptied too, for two cars were following and beyond them a photographer bobbed along on a motor-scooter.

"My missus was scared out o' her wits!" yelled the farmer. "I hope it don't go for any of my animals."

"Better them than your family," he yelled back.

The man nodded and his face was grim. At a steep bend they got away from the van and the mist swallowed them.

"Steady!" shouted the Inspector. "No good without the rifles."

They slowed down and shortly afterwards the van came grinding up.

"It crossed the hard ground above the midden," shouted the farmer. "It was the dog what made me look. It cowered down and began whimperin'. When I turned me head there it was walkin' over the drystone wall where it's broken by the rickyard gate."

Inspector Williams nodded, but he hadn't been able to follow a word in the din the tractor was creating. He guessed he was being given an account of the tiger's sudden appearance. They came at length to a rickety gate that lay back against a hedge.

"Far now?" he shouted.

The farmer shook his head as they moved in a half circle, bumping and jolting until they reached a whitewashed gable beyond which loomed a big ash tree. Down below the huddle of buildings the Inspector could dimly make out a sprawling elderberry and a trash pile. The tiger by all accounts was somewhere close at hand.

"It went across the top o' the trash pile," the farmer said.

The Inspector hurried round the house and stood peering at the old rickyard where the mist moved round the slumped ruin of a haystack. No dog barked, but a scrawny chicken stood on the wall with its head up and the Inspector wondered if its pose indicated the presence of the tiger or curiosity. It clucked once and stepped along the wall. Inside the house the dog barked for the first time and a face loomed at the window.

"It's a'right," the farmer called. "They brung rifles."

But the door remained closed and barred.

"She's got the wind up proper," he said as the van came to a standstill and the soldiers jumped down.

"Through the rickyard," said the Inspector, "but for heaven's sake watch how you go. It might be that the beast is hanging about waiting to kill a bullock."

Sergeant Morris took charge of his men. They went warily over the wall and two of them went through the rickyard, passing the haystack and going on to a blackthorn tree at the corner of the wall. There was no sign of the tiger. At the end of the rickyard they climbed the wall and advanced into a tangle of blackberry and stunted thorns. The Inspector had taken a sturdy stick which he found leaning against a door, and he carried it as he plodded behind the advancing men. Over the first hillock they found themselves among old oak trees. Sergeant Morris signalled to the man nearest him to stop. It was useless going on. The man beyond couldn't see what the plan was. The Inspector stood leaning on his stick.

"I might have known," he said, speaking his thoughts. "It was a waste of time to come, but if we hadn't come what would they have said about us?"

The farmer, who had remained for a minute or two to talk to his wife, came plodding over the field.

"I thought it wouldn't be no good now," he said. "I better get the things in an' lock them up. I suppose you'll go back?"

"We'll wait until you've locked the stock up and shut yourself in."

"I can't stay in all the time. I got work to do, an' even so, water to draw an' so on."

"I'm sorry," said the Inspector. "We can't stay here. The beast is probably a mile away by now."

"I suppose so. You haven't got a spare rifle you could lend me?"

He shook his head. It might come to something like that even yet. The hill farmers couldn't be expected to carry on without protection of some sort. Perhaps by tomorrow the mist would have lifted. What time was it? He looked at his watch. It was no longer afternoon. The mist would thicken now, and it was useless standing up here on the hillside.

"Call it off," he said to Sergeant Morris. "The thing isn't even remotely logical."

"I know," said the sergeant. "We had to make a show."

He was thinking that he had made more than his share of a show. In a few hours he would have been at this game for a solid day. He was nearly out on his feet, and the six men he had brought with him weren't in any better shape. They trudged back to the farmyard. The two constables came round from the back of the buildings.

"There's the print of what might be the tiger's foot in the mud," said one. "Not that it helps very much."

"Not that it helps," said the Inspector. "We know it's a tiger and we know it was here."

He went and looked at the print. He had never seen one before, but even that didn't signify anything.

"I'd rather see its carcass," he said as he got up.

The farmer came to him. "The missus says if you'll all come in she's got some tea made, but she won't have the door open for more than a minute."

They went over to the farmhouse and the door was opened for them. They crowded the kitchen, standing awkwardly while the farmer's wife gave them tea.

"I feel better," she said in Welsh, "seeing so many brave fellows."

The Inspector laughed and sipped his tea. "We'd stay if we could," he said, "but we haven't enough men to go round, and while we're here the tiger is on its way somewhere else. You saw it too, did you?"

"No," she said, smiling faintly, "and I don't want to see it."

"Neither do I," said the Inspector as he prepared to take his leave, "except with a bullet through its brain. Don't worry, these boys will get it before long. "It's only a mangy old menagerie tiger not used to being out at nights."

But she didn't smile. She looked at her three small, round-eyed children hanging around the door into the bedroom.

"You get it quick as you can," she said to the soldiers, "there's good lads, and I'll give you a dinner like you've never had."

"We will," said Sergeant Morris, "and we'll be up for a feed before you've time to get it cooked."

Outside, when the door had closed firmly behind them and they could hear the bolt being slid, Sergeant Morris looked at the Inspector.

"I'm sorry for these poor devils," he said, "trapped up here in the mist. One of them might go out for a jug of water or to scatter some corn for the hens and the tiger might jump them."

"I'm sorry for them too," said the Inspector, "and they're not the only ones in this fix. That mad Pole has something to answer for."

"All Poles are mad," said the sergeant. "I served with them. I know."

They crowded in the van and started back, and it was only then that the Inspector remembered the cars and the scooter that had been following.

"What happened to the newspaper boys?" he asked.

"Their first car conked on the hill, I think," said the constable who was driving. "They'll probably be coming up now."

A few minutes later they met the press cars and the man with the scooter. They pulled on to the bank to let them pass.

"No good?" one shouted.

"We shot two," said Sergeant Morris. "You should have been there. You missed some lovely pictures."

With that they rolled on down to Pentre Ddu, leaving the reporters to struggle on to the farm and try to get interviews through a closed door.

"They'll make something of it, just the same," observed the Inspector. "Even the absence of news makes news. Say something and that's significant. Say nothing and that's just as significant to the boys of the press."

As he got out of the van at Pentre Ddu someone took his photograph.

"I hope you don't think I'm handsome," he said.

CHAPTER 10

When the tiger was half over the broken fence it stood still and listened. It could hear a calf complaining of its hunger. The sound was faint and muffled. The calf was in a shed, the roof of which consisted of old balks of timber, some sagging iron and a covering of turf. The tiger turned its head in the direction of the sound and slowly moved first one hind leg and then the other over the fence. It began to walk towards the farm which it could not see because it was hidden by a hillock and a scrub of trees. Instinctively the big animal took the easiest way, skirting the first patch of gorse, padding over a depression in which there was a pattern of footprints of a flock of sheep. There were no sheep in the hollow, although a dead and bloated ewe lay beside a large stone.

The tiger went up to the top of a rise, listened to the bellowing of the calf, and changed direction once more, shouldering past a clump of hazels and a birch tree and passing through the bracken. Once in a while a dog barked and a chain rattled. Jim Parry's dog was running up and down a wire to which its chain was fastened by means of a ring. It was restless, wet and miserable, and it was hungry now. At the gate at the end of the yard the cow stood, patiently waiting for someone to come to take her in and relieve her of the burden of her milk. She was still there when the tiger stopped on the slope above the little farm. She couldn't see it, but she could sense some kind of danger and went away from the gate. The dog didn't bark any more, but he ran up and down the length of the wire, his nostrils distended, his hair up and his limbs stiff. He could smell the beast, and it was a strange, forbidding odor.

In a little while the tiger stepped over a small gorse bush and slowly, like an exploring cat, walked down to the farmyard, turning its head to look at the jerking wire. The dog had stopped running to and fro. It was straining to get away and the tiger, as it dropped into the yard, had to pass the dog to get at the calves. Every now and again one of the calves gave tongue. The other one huddled at the back of the shed, its forelegs folded under its body. It was dejected and frightened of whatever it was that was out there in the mist. The dog's ears fell back on its head and its tail curled in until it hung beneath its belly. It trembled as the tiger came. When the tiger reached it it stopped, half crouched and bared its fangs. When it struck the dog it made a single, swift and powerful movement of its foreleg and the dog bounded once and the chain fell. Blood began to trickle from the dog's mouth. Its eyes had rolled back. Its neck was broken. The tiger gave it no more attention. It knew that it had killed. The calf behind the hurdle shivered and stepped back a pace or two from the bars. The tiger reached the shed, turned to stare into it, and then it sprang forward to reach the calves, snapping the binder twine that held up the hurdle. The two calves rushed blindly against the wall. One made a desperate attempt to get away while its counterpart was killed, but got its forefeet in the fallen hurdle. The tiger killed it too, with a slap of its paw that broke the little black animal's back. It dragged the victim out, tugging it away from the entangling hurdle and growling as it did so. When it had it clear it sat down on the rough ground and began to feed, filling the air with the sound of crunching bones.

The cow in the field had gone from the gate, but it need not have. The tiger was hungry and it had come to satisfy its hunger. There was nothing left in the yard to kill except some fowls that huddled, wet and bedraggled, beneath an old broken cart. The fowls stayed where they were. The tiger had no time for them until one, a thin, inquisitive bird, straightened herself and took first one step and then another, towards the feeding beast, cocking her head and advancing with all the curiosity of a barnyard bird, ready to peck or fly up in hysteria at the slightest provocation.

There were bright drops of blood on the damp stones, and a tuft or two of black hair from one of the dead calves. The hen carried her head high, turning first this way and then the other to see all there was to be seen and not be taken unawares. She picked nervously once at a tuft of hair and stood a long time inspecting the strange beast before she stepped nearer. The tiger was feeding and looking straight at the hen. When the hen came within range of its paw it suddenly growled and struck the stupid bird. The feathers drifted down and stuck to the stones. The dead hen lay over among the nettles, its body twitching and convulsing once or twice. The tiger went on feeding as though nothing had happened. The other fowls, huddled under the cart, appeared unaffected by what had happened. In the thicket, just over the hill, a pair of magpies chattered and complained. There were no other sounds but those made by the feeding beast.

In the Horseshoe they were talking about the tiger. There was no other topic of conversation in any public house for miles. News bulletins, broadcast at intervals during the day, had taken care of that.

"You hear what that chap said tonight?" asked one. "Said tigers was natural predacious creatures, which means they kill to live."

"Takes a lot o' brains t' sort that one out, mate. 'Course it'll kill something. It'll kill a sheep, a cow, or maybe a child!"

"This chap had hunted them in India. Said he was willin' to come up an' offer his services in catchin' this one if the police or the authorities needed his assistance."

"Big-headed beggar, I expect. What he think he can do on the mountain with the mist down so you can hardly see five yards? You might have hunted tigers in Timbuctoo. It wouldn't signify nothin' up here!"

Frank Baker wiped the counter. He had had a nap before opening time, but it hadn't done him much good. His hand shook more than ever and his eyes were just as bloodshot. To add to his discomfort his head pounded. He had had enough of tigers and would-be tiger-hunters.

"Give it a rest," he pleaded. "We've heard it all. Everybody knows how to track tigers now."

Betty Collins came through to the bar and looked at herself in the mirror as she straighened her hair.

"I'm sick of it," she said. "I've had tiger for breakfast, dinner and tea. Let's have something else for a change."

She turned on the little radio and music was heard, but before very long a news bulletin was announced.

"In the Welsh village of Pentre Ddu today," said the announcer, "a climber was accidentally shot by a soldier during a search for the tiger that has been terrorizing the locality since it escaped last night. Police and troops are still waiting anxiously for the first clue to the tiger's whereabouts, for further search of the hillside above the village had to be abandoned early today when mist came down. It was, in fact, in the heavy mist that the accident took place, and a student, Vernon Willis, was shot as he came struggling down from a camp in the hills followed by his companions, members of a climbing party spending their holiday in that part of the world. Police officers . . ."

"Shut it off," said Frank Baker. "We know it all."

"None of it would have happened but for that perishing Pole," someone observed.

"I wish I could have stopped him," said Betty Collins, sighing.

"You didn't turn on enough of the old charm, probably," said the same man. "He seems to have thought more of his ruddy tigers."

"He didn't seem to know very much about tigers, if you ask me," said the barmaid. "I think he was wrong in the head."

"What about the Indian? Didn't he try to stop him?"

"He thought too much of Betty's charm to bother about the tigers," a wag laughed.

"Did he, Betty?"

"Did he what?" she asked.

They laughed again, but Frank Baker scowled. "Look," he said, "what happened here is the concern of the police. If you want to know all the ins and outs, you go an' ask them! We been told to attend an inquest. You'll hear it all there!"

He picked up a beer crate and went lumbering through to the back with it. The customers looked at one another.

"He's on the booze again," said one. "Temper like a mean bull when his liver's shrunk up. No harm in talking about the thing, is there? It's all in the paper, anyway."

He produced a paper and spread it on the table. The rest crowded round and studied the pictures of the Horseshoe. There was one of a zoo tiger snarling, some bright pictures of Welsh mountains and two or three flashlights of varying clarity. One showed Betty Collins pointing at something. Her face and figure had been lined in because the print had been so bad.

"Blimey, Betty," said one of the men who saw it, "they built up your bust a bit, as if it needed it!"

"That'll do!" she said. "You get familiar with somebody else."

"Who you gettin' familiar with, eh? Old Frank now?"

She frowned and her little eyes narrowed. "I don't need to tolerate you in here," she said. "All I got to do is to ask the police to shift you out."

"You do, my girl," said the offended one, "an' I'll take you over my knee, take down your . . ."

"All right, all right," said Inspector Williams, who had just come in. "That'll do. We don't want to get indecent, do we?"

"We don't!" said Betty Collins emphatically, and blushed at the laughter her indignation produced.

The Inspector was going home to sleep a night in his own bed and return in the morning. Tomorrow night, he had been told, providing the tiger was still at large, he would be expected to make the Horseshoe his billet. Ah well, he had said to himself, he was missing very little if they kept him in Pentre Ddu while the mist was down. There would be no one on the bowling-green at home. He was about to go out again when the telephone rang and a constable came for him.

"Message I have to give you, sir," he said. "A man named Parry who farms up on the mountain. We're to give him news that since he set out for home his wife has died in hospital. They expect he'll be back here about nine o'clock or shortly after."

"See that he gets the news," said the Inspector heavily. "You can probably get somebody to tell you what he looks like and stop him before he goes up."

The constable nodded. He was new in Pentre Ddu, having arrived that evening. He didn't relish the job of telling the farmer that his wife had died, but it wasn't as frightening a task as hunting a tiger, by any means. Inspector Williams bade him good night and went out to the car, turning up the collar of his raincoat, for it was raining now, a fine rain that chilled the cheek. Some soldiers came past him and he nodded to them. Tomorrow more soldiers were being sent to stand by on the hill farms and help morale in general. Tomorrow the tiger would surely give some indication of its whereabouts, something more positive than a wraith in the mist and a track in the mud.

The soldiers went clattering into the Horseshoe to join the locals and the band of pressmen who were emerging from the back room where they had been holding some sort of meeting.

"Beer for a tiger-hunter," said the first of the soldiers.

George Nesbitt was waiting for his supper and watching the soldiers drifting down the road to the Horseshoe. A great deal was going on down there, and he would have liked to have gone, but his supper wasn't ready and there was always the old lady to put her spoke in, the old battleax. It was a pity, he thought, that the tiger hadn't got her as well as the two men it had killed. That would have been the best thing that could have happened. His thoughts towards her were so violent that he could see Mrs. Coley, his mother-in-law, being torn to pieces by a tiger. "That's it!" he said to himself. "Go it! Tear her to pieces!" He meant every word of it. His loathing and hate choked him. One day he would pick up an ax or a knife or something and kill her on the spot, but, in spite of his desire to see her dead, he shuddered at the thought of committing the deed himself. He had told Flo many times how he felt about her mother, but she did nothing to help get rid of the old woman. She listened, but she seemed to think he suffered from some sort of mental illness. All she ever did to show what she thought was to click her tongue, and he knew then that she had no sympathy for him.

The old lady knew how he felt, well enough. They had had so many public battles that their feud was notorious. People in the village had come to laugh about it and say that Nesbitt worshipped the very ground his mother-in-law would be buried in, and that some people showed a tenderness that came near to the tenderness with which Mrs. Coley would set eyes on Nesbitt's coffin. The feud was good for a laugh at least once every two or three months when the Nesbitt household threatened to come apart at the seams and Nesbitt either left home for an hour or two or shut his mother-in-law out in the street for a similar period.

Now, as he waited, Nesbitt listened to his wife and her mother talking about the tiger.

"What you think, George?" his wife asked. "You think they'll get it?"

"At the quarry," he said, "they reckon it won't take long if the mist clears. Somebody'll shoot it."

"What they know about it at the quarry?" asked Mrs. Coley scornfully.

"As much as you bloody do," he said, kicking out at the leg of the table. "If you ask me, the best way to catch it would be to tether you out for bait, supposing the brute would fancy you, you old goat!"

Flo Nesbitt tugged at her mother's arm and tried to close the door between them, but the old lady's blood was up. She wasn't here to be insulted, she said, her voice rising to a shout.

"Then go somewhere else," said Nesbitt, thumping the top of the table with his fist, "an' I hope the ruddy tiger gets you and spreads you over half the parish. I hope it tears you to bits, you, you . . ."

The old lady was beside herself, and for once words wouldn't come. She turned, picked up a vase of dead flowers and threw the flowers and stinking water over her son-in-law's head. George Nesbitt sat a moment, his jaws working, his face gone white, water flowing down his face, dead and broken flowers strewing his jacket and his shirt front.

"I've had enough!" he yelled.

The dishes rattled. The cat jumped into the garden

through an open window. In the adjoining houses people looked at each other.

"Nesbitt's blowin' his top again," they said. "Only wants the tiger in there with them! Got no shame."

"You're a pig!" yelled the old woman. "You eat like a pig. You behave like a pig. You look like a pig. And you stink!"

Nesbitt wiped the dead flowers from his breast and stood up. He was a tall, balding man, corpulent, with heavy features and eyes that bulged, even when he was not emotionally stimulated.

"Out you go, you narrow-gutted old bitch!" he shouted.

The village cocked its ears. Those who could see the Nesbitts' cottage from their own windows looked expectantly at its door, as though at any moment the old lady might come tumbling out, but the old lady remained and gave as good as she got, and all that happened was that a pane of glass in the front window burst outwards. George Nesbitt, swinging his arm wildly to emphasize some metaphor or underline some insult, had put his fist through the frame.

"One thing," whispered a neighbor who had been holding her breath with excitement, "they got enough police and soldiers here to shut them up this time, even supposin' they murder each other."

Flo Nesbitt had begun to cry. She generally added her wail to the din. It wasn't that she was distressed at such violence, but she felt that it was somehow wrong to sit there dry-eyed, listening to such language, such threats, so many conscience-searing reproaches, without showing emotion and indicating it with a mournful cry.

"If," yelled Nesbitt, "that tiger was in the backyard this minute, I'd throw you to it, and nothing on earth would stop me!"

"That a daughter of mine should've married a big, fat, lazy pig, such a swine . . ."

The neighbors waited, as they had waited before, for a sudden silence and a moan that would indicate that things had come to finality, and Nesbitt had at last struck his mother-in-law and killed her.

"This beats tigers," said one, thrusting his body out of the window to talk to a neighbor who was already halfway out of his window.

"If I had her for a ma-in-law I'd swing for her," said the second man. "You bet I would!"

"If it was me, I'd up-end her in the rain-barrel and forget to pull her out again."

Both gaped when the door was pulled open and Nesbitt, and not his mother-in-law, came out.

"Hello, George," they said sheepishly.

He glared at them and slowly, shamefaced, they ducked back into their respective houses.

Nesbitt stood on the path, trembling with rage. He could hear his mother-in-law going on to Flo as she always did. He had to control himself or he might rush back in and strike her. He turned up his jacket collar and began to walk up the street, aware that half the village watched him furtively from behind curtains. He had gone fifty yards before he thought about the Horseshoe, and then it was too late to go back. Better to let them settle down and mind their own business, if they could. Time enough to go down to the Horseshoe after that. To hell with the nosey-parkers!

At the bend in the road, by the last house, he met the policeman.

"Goin' very far?" he asked.

"Up the road for a walk," he said.

"You haven't forgotten the tiger, have you?"

He frowned. "You haven't forgot it, I hope? I'm goin' this way."

He had had enough battling with words.

"Watch it," said the policeman. "No sense in tempting Providence. You never know where it might be."

"To hell with it and you!" he muttered under his breath, and walked on into the mist.

Before he had gone five yards farther the tiger went out of his thoughts. His mind seethed with rage at his mother-in-law, and he clumped along breathing heavily and talking to himself, swearing and grinding his teeth at times. He had gone more than two miles before he calmed down enough to think again about going to the Horseshoe and having a drink. He turned at last, determined to have more than one drink and then go home and pitch the old lady out on her backside, bag and baggage, once and for all, out into the street, and let it rain like hell on her, he wouldn't let her in!

A car was coming down the road, rattling along. He looked over his shoulder and saw it emerging from the mist. It was Jim Parry in his van. Parry saw him and pulled up.

"You want a lift, Mr. Nesbitt?" he asked.

"Thank you very much," he answered. "I could do with a lift to the Horseshoe."

"Very well," said the old man.

It was only then that Nesbitt remembered that Parry was a devout Baptist.

"You heard about the tiger, Mr. Parry?"

"I heard," said Parry. "Chap at the station told me another man was killed in Pentre Ddu today."

"A soldier shot him," he said. "Poor chap."

They went through the village and Parry slowed down as they came to the Horseshoe.

"Here you are, Mr. Nesbitt," he said.

Nesbitt started to get down, but had to wait because a policeman had his hand on the door of the van.

"Are you Mr. James Parry?" he asked.

The old man nodded.

"I am afraid I have bad news for you, sir. We had a telephone call to say that after you left the hospital this afternoon your wife passed away."

Jim Parry looked at the policeman and then at George Nesbitt. He mumbled something to himself in Welsh and his head fell on his breast. He closed his eyes. After a minute or two the policeman took his hand from the truck door, but Nesbitt made no attempt to get down. He could see the tears on the old man's cheeks.

"Can I do anything for you, Mr. Parry?" he asked softly. "Would you like me to drive you up to your farm?"

The old man said nothing. Nesbitt got down and went around to the other side of the van.

"I'll drive him up," he told the policeman. "He's badly shocked."

When Nesbitt opened the door the old man sat where he was for a minute, and then he moved away from the steering-wheel and let Nesbitt take his place.

"I'm terribly sorry," said Nesbitt.

There was nothing else he could think of to say. Jim Parry didn't seem to have heard. They went jolting and rattling up the lane and began the long climb to his holding. Nesbitt found it hard to negotiate the bends and keep the van going. Once he had to stab at the brakes and felt the van running back when the clutch slipped, but a boulder saved them and they went on, turning into the farm road and bouncing a little because Nesbitt didn't know the contour of the ground and the twists and turns of the ruts they were traversing. He put the lights on, but this didn't help, for the battery was down and the dull yellow glow illuminated only the mist immediately ahead. When they came into the yard Nesbitt brought the truck to a standstill and got out. He stood waiting for the grief-stricken man to join him and then went and helped him to descend. Jim Parry brought his key from his pocket and walked dazedly to the farmhouse door.

"Don't go," he said. "Stop a little while."

Nesbitt hesitated. His foot touched something. He looked down at the dead dog and then in the mist he made out something else, a bulky dark thing that was the body of the second calf which the tiger had trailed out. It seemed to move.

"Mr. Parry!" he called anxiously. "Mr. Parry!"

The old man didn't hear him, but the tiger did. It rose and came toward him. It knocked him from his feet, his body turning over, almost balancing for a moment and then collapsing as though he had tried to stand on his head. The tiger plunged on and was gone. Nesbitt's body jerked once or twice and then he tried to lift his head. Blood was running down his face and across his bald head. His shirt-front had been ripped open, but he knew nothing. His efforts to move were instinctive. He began to crawl, aimlessly, struggling into the nettles like a badly-shot rabbit. He groaned without knowing that he had made any sound. Jim Parry came back to the door and stood looking across the yard for several seconds.

"Come in," he said dully. "It was good of you to bring me up."

He waited and then he stepped out.

"Mr. Nesbitt," he said. "Are you there?"

The stricken man lying among the nettles attempted to rise again. His lower body came up before his head. His shoulders heaved and he tried to get his feet under him and fell against the drystone wall. Jim Parry heard the sound and looked across at the nettles by the wall. He stared for several seconds before he took it in and then he lumbered towards him.

"Are you taken ill, Mr. Nesbitt?" he asked.

He turned Nesbitt over and saw what the tiger had done

to him. At the same time he saw the dead dog and beyond the old van the dark object that was the half-eaten calf. He knew then that the tiger had attacked Nesbitt, and that it had been in the yard before they came.

"Nesbitt," he said, putting his hand gently under the man's shoulders. "I got to lift you up. Tell me if it hurts."

It took all the old man's strength to lift Nesbitt an inch or two.

"Can you crawl a little bit?" he asked, lowering him again.

Nesbitt didn't answer, didn't seem to know where he was, but he crawled and the old man directed him, gently moving his hands towards the van. At length he got him to the step, opened the door and half pushed him up. Nesbitt crawled in. It took a long time to get him wedged against the door in a position where his legs would not interfere with the driver. They began the journey down to Pentre Ddu.

CHAPTER 11

They were lingering in the Horseshoe. Frank Baker had called time and scowled his displeasure, but they were used to his scowl. Even the presence of the police wouldn't make them hurry. Betty Collins wiped over the counter and hung a cloth on the handles of the beer-pumps as though there was something indecent in the sight of them now that time had been called. Jim Parry's boots slipped on the flags at the door as he came in and he shot out a hand to keep his balance. They heard him. He almost collided with a man who was going out.

"God!" said someone. "What's up?"

They stared at the old man, aghast at the blood on his

face and clothes, at the horror in his expression and the way he shook.

"Nesbitt," he said, continuing in Welsh when words at last came. "The beast struck him down."

"What's he say?" asked Betty Collins.

No one bothered to explain. One took the old man's arm and led him to a chair. Frank Baker forgot to call time again, but after a minute he bobbed through from the bar and brought the policeman. The group around old Jim Parry broke up to allow the policeman to hear what he said. Someone rushed outside and came back with the news that Nesbitt was in Parry's van, and from what he could see he was near his end. Frank Baker picked up the telephone and asked for an ambulance. Two men stayed with Jim Parry. The rest rushed outside to see what they could see. George Nesbitt was unconscious, bloody and limp, but he moaned and once an arm moved. The constable who was doing what he could to administer first aid asked someone to bring a stretcher. When Sergeant Wynne arrived at the van they were moving Nesbitt and laying him on the stretcher.

"I'd say his ribs were smashed," said the constable. "He'll be lucky to pull through."

The sergeant, who was in charge because Inspector Williams was home for the night, decided that they couldn't wait for an ambulance.

"Bring the little van," he said. "We'll get him to the hospital in that."

The constable rose and began running up the village, his boots pounding on the road. People who had been sitting quietly in their cottages began to peer out of their windows.

"Something's up," said Jack Roberts. "The tiger's got somebody."

Behind him the radio droned away. The tuned-down voice of the announcer said that in the Welsh village of Pentre Ddu people still waited anxiously for news of the tiger's capture; that it had been seen that afternoon on a hill farm and that efforts to give chase had been frustrated by the gathering mist and the fact that the tiger had apparently gone into a thorn thicket. After the news a Mr. Ponsonby Johnston would give a talk on tigers and the facts concerning the hunt for the one that had escaped.

"Jack," said his wife, "Jack, you watch what you're doin'."

"I'll watch," he said as he went out, closing the door behind him.

On the road he stood for a minute to allow the police van to get past. Shortly afterwards he caught up with it again as they loaded the stretcher.

"Where does he live?" the constable asked him.

"Near the top end," he said. "You want me to get his wife?"

"Tell her she can come with us now. She'll want to be with him."

Jack Roberts hurried up the street, conscious that he, too, was being watched by his neighbors. He knocked on George Nesbitt's door. The house was quiet. He could hear someone moving upstairs. After a minute Mrs. Nesbitt came down.

"It's George," he said gently. "There's been a bit of an accident. The tiger knocked him down. They're takin' him to hospital. You better come."

She stared at him, and he could tell that she was struggling to grasp what he had said.

"Best hurry," he said. "The police told me to come. They're rushin' him to the hospital now. Can't wait for the ambulance to be brought."

She pushed past him and went running down the street in her slippers. He reached to close the door and saw old Mrs. Coley on the stairs.

"What's happened?" she asked.

"The tiger's nearly killed poor George," he said.

She didn't blink. Her mouth seemed to tighten and he could almost read her thoughts. She was hoping that it had killed him; that George would never come back to the cottage. Let her hope. Maybe that was how it would be, but if hope mattered he hoped that George would pull through and come back to throw the old woman out once and for all.

"The police will take her to the hospital with him," he said. "I don't suppose she'll be back tonight, but they say he'll pull through. It takes more than that to kill a chap like George."

Down at the Horseshoe the constable was helping Mrs. Nesbitt into the van. She was weeping bitterly and they had difficulty in persuading her to keep away from her unconscious husband. She crouched in the van and held his limp hand as they set off, swaying and bumping on their way out of the village.

"What happened?" people asked Jack as he went back down the village. He told them what he knew. Four or five soldiers were standing by to go up with Jim Parry when he was fit to make the trip.

"I reckon," said Jack, "they should have a detail of men at every holding, then if the tiger appeared they could at least take a shot at it. The way it is they'll only be going to places after the tiger's been there. It's arse-end-up as usual. Like they say, you've gotta have losses before you learn how to win. Poor George Nesbitt's one o' the losses. I reckon there's nobody in charge of this that knows the first thing about it."

He was speaking to a neighbor who was leaning out of his front room window, his collar off and his braces dangling about his hips.

As Jack went down to the Horseshoe again, he thought more about it. It was easy for the authorities to say that everything that could be done was being done. Who was to say what could be done and who would challenge them until some poor chap got killed by the tiger? Tomorrow, they said, the mist might lift. They know about tomorrow all right. Tomorrow the mist might not lift. That was just as great a truth. Tomorrow his wife or child might be killed.

At the Horseshoe the crowd lingered, although the bar had closed. Betty Collins was doing her best to force them all outside.

"Good at keepin' the door shut against people, aren't ya, Betty?" someone jeered. "Different o' course if it was your bedroom door, eh?"

She swung the door hard and it struck the speaker's ankle.

"A'right, Betty," he said. "I know how ya feels."

Jack Roberts went over and looked at Parry's van. It was a mess of blood.

"Old chap got the news when he come home tonight that Dilys died in hospital after he left."

Trouble, he told himself, wasn't like lightning. It struck in the same place. It struck men when they were down. Maybe there was such a thing as retribution for past sins, but he couldn't believe that there was unless some men's sins were well hidden. The good died young and the innocent seemed to get beaten to their knees while only the evil and the crooked people seemed to get off free. Take Betty Collins at the Horseshoe. By all accounts she was no good, through and through, but did it happen to her? She even won money on the football pools, a goose in a Christmas draw. She slept with everybody and anybody, but some poor stupid kid in the village who went off the rails just once ended up pushing a pram, as sure as fate. What did it prove? It proved that something was written somewhere. You got it rough, you got it smooth, but you had it coming from the kick-off just like George Nesbitt waiting all this time, rejected for the Army, hag-ridden by his mother-in-law, without a child, to be mauled by a tiger.

Jim Parry was helped out to the Army truck and climbed aboard. He didn't really grasp what they were doing with him or where he was going. He sat staring at the young soldiers as the truck started off. They stared back at him and tried to look sympathetic. Once he spoke to them, but either they didn't hear what he said or they didn't understand. They clutched their weapons, licked their lips. One took a cigarette butt from behind his ear and lit it. Sergeant Morris looked back at them from his seat beside the driver and wondered about the old man. He was dazed, poor old soul, and didn't know where he was.

When they came to the farm Sergeant Morris led the old man into the house while his men stood guard, then he went out and looked round. There was no sign of the tiger. On a stone by the wall he came upon a bloody splotch that might have been a print of the tiger's hind foot. Two calves had been chewed up and strewn about the yard. Three hens sat dejectedly on the ridge of an outhouse. He touched the dead dog with his foot. It had been dead for some time. Its blood had started to harden on its nostrils. He went back into the house.

"We'd better leave you some protection," he said to the old man. "Two of my chaps will stay with you. Can you fix them up with a mug o' tea or can they light a fire an' get it for themselves?"

Jim Parry nodded. He put his head in his hands and stared into the dead ashes. It didn't matter very much whether they stayed or not. He wouldn't be here himself, tomorrow. He would wring the necks of the chickens, take the cow over to his neighbor and ask him to take charge of his flock and go away to be with Dilys, to see her decently laid to rest. He had no tears left to cry now, and the fire that had gone out in the morning could stay out for ever but for the fact that these soldiers wanted tea to drink.

"You needn't stop," he said, after a while. "I can shut the door an' sort out what I got to do in the morning. I'm not frightened, you know."

He was speaking the truth. Nothing could frighten him

now. He was past all fear. He had finished shaking. Even the blood on his clothes meant nothing at all, and he had forgotten George Nesbitt and what had happened out there such a short time before.

"We'll stay," said Sergeant Morris. "Wouldn't be right to leave you here, Dad."

One of the soldiers had propped his gun in a corner and came to the fire to get it going. The ashes rose and tumbled and a hen's feather sailed in the draft. It didn't take him long to get dry sticks from the oven and set light to them. In a little while the blackened kettle began to sing. Sergeant Morris, remembering that the old man had lost his wife, frowned when one of the men began to whistle and tap his foot.

"Cut it out, Walker," he hissed.

Walker's foot became still. The whistle died out, but the old man didn't seem to have heard any of it.

"You know," he said in Welsh, "the Rev. Morris Evans married us."

They looked at one another, not understanding what he said. Sergeant Morris raised an eyebrow. That was all, and they stared at the floor. Outside, darkness gathered. A rat ran across the yard and disappeared into a hole in the dry-stone wall. The roosting hens huddled down on the roof looking at the uneven court, at the dead dog and the crumpled nettles where the hen the tiger had struck lay, and where George Nesbitt had crawled in his agony. Out of the mist an owl came flying silently and perched on a post. It remained there as the night lowered. The mist became a low, nearly black cloud. The moon was far away, in a different sky, above a barren wilderness of moist-laden atmosphere.

The doctor who came out of the ward before Mrs. Nesbitt was allowed in had been washing his hands, for he was carrying a hand towel. She wondered about this, for she had always heard that doctors in hospitals wore rubber gloves and masks. He came up to her and smiled.

"You can go in and see him, but only for a minute or two. You must say nothing to him. We have done what we can for the time being. He won't know you. He is suffering from shock as well as the wounds and he has been given injections. I think you might as well go home after you have seen him. There is nothing you can do here."

"He'll live?" she asked, almost pleading.

"I think he'll pull through," he said.

She hurried to go in. The nurse stood a few yards away. She stared at the figure on the bed, sat herself down in the chair, tried to take his hand and found it was inside the sheets. He was white and he hardly seemed to be breathing.

She began to whisper to him, "I'll make it all right for when you come home," she said. "I'll see there never is no more trouble. I'll make her go and she'll never come back, George, I promise."

If he heard he gave no sign. She stood up when the nurse touched her sleeve. She sobbed bitterly as she was led out.

"Would you like a cup of tea?" the nurse asked.

The policeman who had brought her was waiting in the corridor.

"I believe you are going back home?" he asked.

She sipped the tea and nodded without looking at him. Her eyes were red-rimmed and inflamed from so much crying.

The journey back to Pentre Ddu was unreal. The lights of the van showed against an everlasting wall of mist from which emerged a narrow strip of road, the streaming hedges and the lower parts of oaks and elms and ash trees. Mrs. Nesbitt saw these things and yet knew nothing of them. Her thoughts were fixed on the memory of her husband's face as he lay on the bed looking up at the dimly lit ceiling of the ward.

"Well," said the policeman, "here we are, if you'll tell me which cottage you live in."

"Pardon?" she said, and then, guessing what he had said, she told him to pull up. They had just passed her door.

The cottage was in darkness when she got in. She took off her cardigan and stood rubbing her elbows with her palms feeling very alone and afraid. The floor of the room upstairs creaked and her mother came hobbling down.

"He'll live," she said, "if that's what you're thinking."

"Will he?" said the old woman. "That's somethin'."

"Oh, he'll live an' he'll come home," she promised. "He'll be back as soon as they've done what needs to be done. I told him I'd make it all right for him when he come back. I told him."

"What you mean?" asked the old woman.

"I mean you're goin' from here in the mornin' supposin' you go to the workhouse! Supposin' you never get another roof over your head!"

The old woman gripped the stair rail until her knuckles whitened.

"You're worked up," she said. "You're not yourself. You've had a bad shock."

Her daughter rubbed her elbows again and stared into the darkness.

"I've had a shock," she said. "I'm worked up, but I won't think any different in the morning. You better get packed because whatever happens I'm putting you out, Mother. George means more to me than ever you do."

"George!" said the old woman, "the great fat, lazy, no-account. . . ."

"If you don't want to be put out now you'd better stop talkin' like that!" she replied. "I've only got to go down and bring a policeman. This is my house."

Old Mrs. Coley bit back a retort. "Look, girl," she said,

"you better get an aspirin an' a cup o' tea. You're not yourself. You'll feel different in the mornin'."

She tried to get past her to put a kettle on, but the younger woman stayed where she was.

"It's no use," she said. "I mean what I say. You be ready in the morning because when I go to see George that's the news I'm takin' him. That's the thing that'll do more to make him recover than any doctor. Once he knows he's comin' home to be master in his own house."

"Him! Master in his own house! He couldn't be master. He's not worth the name of a man."

Mrs. Nesbitt turned away from her mother and picked up a coat that lay over a chair.

"Here!" she said. "Get your hat. You're finding somewhere else, or walking the road tonight."

She opened the door and waited for the old woman to go out, but Mrs. Coley stood her ground.

"My own daughter!" she said. "My own flesh and blood!"

Sergeant Morris jumped down from the truck in the farmyard at the lower end of Pentre Ddu. They had moved into the farm earlier in the evening and men were billeted in the barn and other out-buildings. He was thinking about the men he had left up on the mountain, about the poor fellow who had run into the tiger, about Maloney and the enquiry yet to come. Anybody with half an eye could see that this whole business was going wrong. You couldn't leave things to the tiger, even if you couldn't hunt it down. The newspaper boys were saying so and asking who advised the shepherds to draw their flocks down off the mountain where they might attract the tiger and certainly keep it near the village. A big shout was coming soon. The evening paper someone had brought up the valley had had the big headlines: THIRD VICTIM IN WELSH TIGER SEARCH. DEATH ROLL WORRIES AUTHORITIES. Now, perhaps, they would scream the news of a fourth victim and someone would scream for something more positive to be done than having men rushing about like scalded cats in the mist, trying to catch a tiger after it had gone.

He went into the barn and sniffed the air to see if anyone had been smoking. A couple of storm lanterns hung from posts. One of them was busily blackening its glass because it was hanging at the wrong angle. There was no smell of tobacco.

"Hello, Sarge," somebody said, rearing on his elbow. "It got another bloke?"

"Knocked him about a bit, too," he replied. "Bowled him arse over tip and left him not knowin' where he was. He's in the hospital. They say he'll live."

"You reckon we're doin' it right, Sarge?"

"What do you mean?" he asked. "Do you see any better way?"

"We haven't stopped it coppin' this bloke, have we? All we done is what Maloney . . ."

"Forget Maloney," he said. "Let it rest. Maloney thought he was shooting the tiger. He's a bit of a silly sod, but I'm sorry for Maloney. We can't look after everybody. We can't be everywhere at once. If you've got any better plan you better tell old Anderson or the police, me lad. If you've any sense you'll keep your trap shut and obey orders. That's what you're here for!"

He turned and went out of the barn, sorry that he had said so much. The boys had a right to their own thoughts and they seemed to see things just as clearly as he did.

At the Horseshoe a single light was burning downstairs where Sergeant Wynne sat beside the telephone making a report. Upstairs Betty Collins was getting ready for bed. Old Mrs. Baker, who had been having one of her turns, was lying in bed in the dark listening to the sounds of the night and wondering how long the whole business would last.

They had let three rooms and had no more accommodation since the police had reserved the others. The mist would keep the tiger safe for at least another day and then they would still have to track it down and shoot it. There was a shilling to be made yet, she hoped, and even when the trouble was over some people might be persuaded to visit the village where the tiger had run loose. She might even get Frank to rent the little field and make a small charge for letting people through to the place where Ram Singh was killed in the gully. There were possibilities, if a person knew how to take advantage of the situation.

Frank Baker was lying on his bed smoking and looking at the stained ceiling. The newspaper boys were off somewhere. He didn't somehow get on very well with them. They thought he might have done something to provide them with a telephone, but what could he do? The police would be there long after the tiger was gone and he had to live with them. He had to watch how he stepped with the police. Soon they would want to hear him say his piece before the Coroner, and that Inspector Williams had an odd way of looking at him. If Betty said her piece as she should they would be all right, but what if she didn't? What if she went back on it and left him to find his own way out of the mess? Was it his fault that the tiger was loose? Was it in any way his fault? Who could have stopped it? The Indian could have done! Betty Collins could have got him to stop the Pole. She could at least have given warning to somebody before things got out of hand. She wasn't guiltless by any means. It squared up to his being so frightened that he shut the Indian out, but who had really shut him out? He reached over to the dressing-table and took the port bottle and a glass. To hell with it! To hell with it all! It had happened a hundred years ago; yesterday, and he had grown old with it in a day. He was on his second glass when the door opened silently. He put the bottle down and looked at Betty Collins. She was wearing a thin nightdress and she filled it in parts with no semblance of modesty.

"Frank," she said softly, "I thought I better come and talk to you. I thought we better talk about the inquest."

"Better let tomorrow wait," he said hoarsely.

She snapped out the light. Neither of them heard the port bottle going over as she collided with the dressing-table. It rolled along and tumbled off onto the floor, but it fell softly on the bedclothes which Frank had thrown back.

Old Mrs. Baker lay listening to the sounds of the night. She had heard Betty Collins walk along the passage. She had heard the light go out. Soon now, she said to herself, they were opening the inquest on the Pole. Soon they would be asking Frank what had happened and they would be asking Betty Collins what her version was. They even wanted to know what she knew about the affair. It was time she began to think what she really knew about it; what she could recall now that she hadn't been able to remember when the Inspector asked. If she could show that baggage up, she would. She would get rid of her before she got her hooks any deeper into poor, stupid Frank. She would get rid of her, even if it left them without help at a time when they could sell twice as much stuff as they had ever sold.

"Inspector," she whispered, "I got something to say that I should have said before. That Collins piece was misbehavin' in here with the Indian when the Polish chap went out to the tigers. When the Indian wanted to go she wouldn't let him. When he tore himself loose an' ran out to stop the tiger bein' let out she fastened the door against him out of spite. She meant him to be caught out there the minute she knew the tiger was loose. Don't take any account of Frank. He's never sober. He's been a trouble to me all my life. It runs in the family. His father was the same. Ask anybody. They'll tell you about him."

She had said it over and over again and the clock had

chimed many times before she heard sounds on the landing again. No light went on. She knew it wasn't the newspaper boys coming back to their rooms. The hinges of Betty Collins's door squealed just a little.

"Tart!" she said. "Cheap bit of fluff! Whore!"

CHAPTER 12

Mist and a summer's morning might sound as though they belonged to each other: mist and a morning in the month of July. Inspector Williams thought about it. A man could think about tomorrow and find that the dream and reality were almost one. He could think about tomorrow and discover, in time, that the new day was no better than the one that had gone and still the lark didn't rise into the clear sky and the swallow sat on the ridge, wretched and miserable as the day. Mist trailed like smoke; it hung about the stream, clothed the hollows where the round rushes grew, shrouded the willows, the hayfield and the tall corn. He sighed as he thought about it, and yet yesterday he had somehow known that today would dawn with no change and the valley would be sitting in mist, damp and sunless as though the equinox had gone and the days of October were marching relentlessly to November.

The tiger was somewhere along there, on the edge of the valley, in the conifer belt, in the scrub, prowling noiselessly about the little fields and the derelict buildings of old steadings where only the blackened chimneys and the hearth stones showed that man had lived and died there and his sons moved on. The tiger had the world to itself, the world of dampness and unreality; the world without the perspective of hilltops and bluffs, crags and peaks and threading streams coming down to the valley. It couldn't be a very comfortable beast nor a very happy one, and the thought of the wretchedness of the tiger made him depressed, for he had a feeling that its misery would make it fierce and more restless. In the sun a cat would lie basking or would move less warily. A restless, uncomfortable and hungry beast was a dangerous thing.

He slowed the car as he came to the village and drove along the street taking his time as though reluctant to reach the Horseshoe. "Today's another yesterday," he muttered to himself.

Today was not exactly yesterday however. Things had happened yesterday that weren't likely to happen again today. Farmer Parry's wife could die but once, and Nesbitt wouldn't meet the tiger again. The soldier, Maloney, and a good enough soldier too, had made sure he wouldn't make the same mistake again by going absent from his unit. They were looking for him. He was to be an important figure at the enquiry, poor fellow. He doubted whether Maloney had ever seemed of any importance to anyone but his mother in all his life before. Maloney's day was dawning too, because a mad Pole had turned a key and let out a tiger.

There was a sour smell about the Horseshoe. He hadn't noticed it before. Perhaps they hadn't been keeping the door open as much as they used to. Perhaps they hadn't let the fresh air in. He didn't blame them. The fresh air was moisture-laden. It made the tiles change their shade and made the wallpaper bulge behind old damp stains. It made the little room he had turned into an office have a damp, sooty smell as though the chimney needed sweeping, which it probably did.

"You've had all the reports, sir," his sergeant said.

He nodded. He had had them all, and even the Chief had read them through by now. What was coming? Would anyone who didn't know the valley and the immediate locality believe that they were helpless to get the tiger because the mist was down? Would the fellow reading the news in London appreciate that here, in the Welsh hills, there was a blanket over everything like a London fog?

"If you had to catch this beast," he said to the sergeant, "what would you do?"

The sergeant rubbed his nose. He knew very well that he wasn't being asked because old Daddy Williams was licked. He was being asked because the old codger really liked to know how a thing looked to the next fellow.

"Honestly," he said, "what I'd do is sit down an' wait until the ruddy mist cleared and I'd get the troops to stand guard and do something useful on as many farms as I could. It's where people are isolated that they're in danger. I don't see it coming to the village. I don't see it walking along the road. In fact, I see it nervous and nearly as frightened as we are."

"That's what I think," the Inspector agreed. "It'll keep out of our way except when it's hungry. If it kills anybody it'll be because they ran into it, but you can't put that across to some people. They think you're making an excuse for letting it run where it will."

"I'd take a bet that if it kills anybody or injures anybody between now and the time it's destroyed it is a case of an accidental encounter, sir."

"I'll ring the Chief and tell him that," he said, smiling. "Maybe after he's read what happened to this Nesbitt chap he'll begin to see the light. It struck down the Pole because he stood between it and freedom. It may have had an intense hatred of the man; of both men. They may have goaded it at different times. In any case it must have known them well by sight if not by smell and it must have associated the two of them with its misery and hunger."

"I believe the brutes were in a shocking state," the constable said. "I was talking to one of the people at the zoo.

They offered the opinion that the one that's loose isn't likely to be easily taken. They say that although they weren't young and in their prime their owner would have had his hands full if he went into the cage with them."

"Peterson's tigers from the Bengal hills," mused the Inspector. "It's a pity Mr. Peterson can't remove his tiger from the Welsh hills."

"We've had another bunch of offers of help since last night," said the sergeant. "One from a woman. She says she was a planter's wife and has shot dozens of tigers. In fact, she mentioned that she had pictures of herself with tigers she had shot to prove her ability."

"Ah," said the Inspector, "maybe I'll get my picture taken with a dead tiger yet, but I hope not. I hope some other clever fellow shoots it. Tell anybody else who gets on we don't so much need tiger-hunters as witch doctors to get rid of the mist. If they can read bones or cast spells tell them to come along!"

He picked up a batch of reports and thumbed them over.

"I doubt whether so much has ever been written about so little before, but I doubt whether anything like this ever happened before in this country. There must be some way of dispersing mist? Didn't they get rid of it on airfields during the war?"

"Setting petrol on fire, sir," said the sergeant. "I don't suppose the tiger would stay to warm itself even if we could disperse the mist, and if we could what a bonfire we'd have in the forest!"

"I see in this morning's paper some lunatic suggests that the tiger should be smoked out of the woods."

"A chap interviewed in the news said he could get it with a net and a spear."

"My grandson could get it with his popgun," said the Inspector. "I was told last night that he had shot five while I'd been away."

Someone knocked at the door and the sergeant answered. "It's Mrs. Baker," he said. "She wants to talk to you, sir."

Old Mrs. Baker hobbled in and waited until the sergeant had left.

"I think I should talk to you about what happened," she said. "About what happened when the tiger got out."

"Oh, yes," he said. "Something happened that I haven't heard about yet?"

She nodded her head, her lips tightening as she thought about Betty Collins. "That tart we've got behind the bar," she said.

"What about her?"

"Well," she said, taking a breath, "when the Pole was here he got drunk. He went out shouting his head off. I could hear the noise and I wondered what was happening down here. I got up and came along to the top of the stair. I could hear him outside. I could hear somebody inside. It was that poor Indian. He was talking to Betty Collins. She was making up to him. They were sky-larking about. I could hear their carry-on. I knew what was happening in there all right."

"What was happening?" the Inspector asked solemnly.

"What always happens with her sort. I heard the Pole shouting. I hear the Indian saying he must go to him. I heard her telling him to stay where he was. I could hear them struggling and the Indian telling her to let him go and then she said, 'Well, go then!' and she rushed after him and slammed the door on him. She held the door while he hammered to get in. The tiger was loose by then. Frank came through. I think he tried to open the door, but he didn't get it open. You can't count very much on poor Frank. He has always been too fond of the bottle. You can't set much store by anything he says or does. I know. I've put up with him ever since his father died. If the Indian had got there the Pole wouldn't have been able to let the tiger out. She stopped him! She's responsible for the Pole being killed as much as anybody. She's responsible for the Indian being killed too."

"I see," said the Inspector. "I missed the point before. She's responsible for the whole thing in your opinion?"

"Who else?" asked Mrs. Baker. "It all lies at her door."

He had been making a few idle notes on his pad. He looked out of the window at the little garden again. Mrs. Baker had seen nothing, he knew that well enough, but she had thought this up since yesterday for some reason and the reason was probably that Frank Baker and Betty Collins had tumbled into bed together. People were always tumbling into bed with Betty Collins, according to rumor, and, of course, the old lady wanted to be rid of her.

"You know," he said, "it's an offense to withhold evidence. It's also an offense to add to it. Of course it isn't an offense to retract a statement before it's made on oath. You have to be very careful. Sometimes people get their heads together to cover something and up pops a third person who has no motive and tells the absolute truth. Generally the truth has something about it that advertizes it. You know it's the truth the minute you hear it."

"That's what I always say," said the old lady as she got up.

He admired the way she said it. He didn't even start to smile, but he was thinking of the old woman who had looked down the village street and would swear that she saw Betty Collins in the porch, outside the door. It sounded like the truth. It was the truth. The lies, however, were thick, like berries on a bush, and maybe none of it mattered very much. No one was going to be charged with anything. Nevertheless, he had found himself deeply intrigued by the business. He wanted to be able to understand a man like Frank Baker and why he did what he did. He knew what made Betty Collins tick. It was that fatal something and the way she filled her clothes. Perhaps, after all, you had to go beyond the turning of a key in a lock to release a tiger. Perhaps the thing that released a tiger and started tragedy was that same old thing that had ruined the life of Adam. How the old deacons would click their tongues and nod their heads in agreement! The demented Pole, the hysterical Indian, poor Willis, poor Nesbitt, all of them depending in some strange way on the smile of a woman of no consequence. He had read it all in history, a score of times, but here, of course, he was judge and jury in his imagination. There was no charge and no case to answer.

The door had hardly closed before it opened again. Frank Baker asked if he could spare him a minute. He nodded.

"My mother has been having a word with you, hasn't she?" he asked. "You know why? You want to know why?"

"Because she wanted to, I suppose."

"Because she thinks Betty Collins was in my bed last night."

"I see," he said. "I suppose she wouldn't like that?"

"She wouldn't like it and she would try to get her out of here."

"Do you think she expects me to get her out of here?"

"I hope you won't try. I hope you won't poke your nose in at all because it's nothing to do with you, or with her."

"It's your affair," said the Inspector, "and nobody's on trial or likely to be."

"That's right, I only wanted to point it out."

"I didn't learn my job last week," he said. "I've been at it a while now. In fact I began when I was a youngster. I'm not concerned with morals. I'm not very concerned with lies either. I'm concerned with what's the truth. The truth protects the innocent and it nearly always convicts the guilty, but here we're not concerned with responsibility for the tiger getting out, or who shut the door and held it shut, or who tried to open it from one side or the other. We're only concerned with putting an end to the tiger when we corner it.

Morals don't come within miles of us. It seems a good thing."

"If she goes from here," said Frank Baker, "I'll probably go with her. I've had about enough anyway. It's a dead and alive little hole and the people are only fit for minding sheep."

"Maybe so," said the Inspector.

He didn't bother to say that he had been brought up in the valley.

Jim Parry took a long time to corner the hens. They flew over the wall and flapped out of reach a dozen times when he nearly had them and they wouldn't come to the corn he had put down. They were terrified, it seemed. They had become jungle birds, perhaps, since the visit of the tiger, and an old instinct had come out in them. At length, however, he grabbed the last of them by the wing and stuffed her into the crate. They were thin, no-account fowls and would hardly fetch five shillings from a dealer, but they were going. He had buried the remains of the calves, regardless of the opinion of the authorities who talked about the tiger returning to the kill. Never once did he look about to see whether or not the tiger was at hand. He loaded the crate in the van, locked the door and went to find the cow. She hadn't come up to be milked. Her udder would be swollen and she would be in a bad way, terrified, as the hens had been, by the sight of the beast. When he found her standing wretchedly at the bottom of the field, he touched her with his stick and she ambled along. He milked her more for the sake of her comfort than for the milk and then drove her on to his neighbor.

"If you will take the cow," he said, "while I get things done it will be a great help to me," he said. "If you would look after my sheep and do what has to be done I will see that everything is all right for you."

His neighbor smiled sympathetically "Any time, Jim," he said. "Anything I can do."

They gripped hands. They had known one another a long time and had that closeness that people in lonely places often have for their nearest neighbor, a fraternity to shame conventions. Jim Parry went away knowing that his stock and his little farm would be looked after as he would have looked after it.

As he went down to the village he thought about his cousin, William Ellis Thomas. He would have to call and give him the news in the proper way. It didn't matter that the village would have told him already. William Ellis would have to be told so that he could express his sympathy and pay his tribute to poor Dilys.

"She has died, William," he said, "and I was not there."

William Ellis sniffed and drew his hand down over his brows.

"You have lost a good woman," he said.

He had been drinking home-made wine. The weakness of William Ellis Thomas was well known. He never went to the Horseshoe. He roundly condemned those who sold their souls to the devil and passed their earnings over the counter in exchange for ale. His conscience would never have allowed him to have done such a thing. Instead, he made a brew and bottled it, kept it, let it mature and brought it out in good time, and as the barley crop had been blessed, so the fermentation and maturing of the wine was blessed and there was no evil in it, only the sun and the ripe grain, the sweet sugar from Demerara, and the yeast. When men stood outside the Horseshoe exchanging oaths and crying their wickedness to the heavens, he sat in his cottage and watched them, warmed by the wine, mellowed to a degree that was never possible by any other means. He felt like God sometimes, so wise he was, so understanding of human frailty. It was a sad thing that this feeling of elevation passed and had to be restored on the following day, sometimes before noon, for on bad days he sank down and felt like the devil in the morning. The remedy was to pop into the press and bring out one of the crocks so that he could restore his spirits and look out at Pentre Ddu again with warmth inside.

"Will you have a little glass of wine, Jim?" he asked before he knew what he was doing.

Old Jim Parry looked at him. He felt very sad and very disappointed that just this once William Ellis couldn't overcome his weakness for drink. He refused to say yes or no. William Ellis knew him too well to ask such a thing. William Ellis was certainly not himself or he would never have suggested it.

"Well, I must go, William Ellis," he said. "I have things to arrange. I will be letting you know when the funeral is to be."

He went out and closed the cottage door behind him. William Ellis reached down for his crock and shook it to see how much of that particular brew remained.

"God rest Dilys Parry," he said, "and God help Jim."

He blinked and wiped his eyes with his hand. "And God help William Ellis Thomas," he added. "God help poor William Ellis Thomas."

He had difficulty balancing the big crock on the lip of his cup while he poured the last of the wine and some of it splashed onto his trousers. "God help George Nesbitt," he said, "and them poor fellows the tiger killed."

The wine went gurgling into the cup. He found another crock under the stair. It was a strange thing how the wicked prospered, he was thinking, and the good were afflicted and destroyed. Look at that Betty Collins at the Horseshoe, for instance, a wicked woman if ever he saw one, and he had seen some wicked women in his time. He hadn't spent all his days in Sunday School, he hadn't. He had seen some wicked ones and he had dallied with some of them too, but that Betty Collins, she was the worst of them all! He had always been going to give her a piece of his mind and he would one day. He would!

After his third cupful he got up and lurched across the room to look along the street. He couldn't see very much because of the mist. He would go down and see what was doing, and have a word with Betty Collins. It was time he said what he had been wanting to say for so long.

The Horseshoe was quiet. The little room occupied by Inspector Williams had its door shut. The newspaper men were having some sort of conference. William Ellis went in. He had never been across the threshold of the Horseshoe in his life before, but there was a first time for everything, he told himself.

"You maybe don't know me, Miss Betty Collins," he said.

Betty Collins looked at him, seeing his little paunch, his florid face, his white moustache and wispy hair, his heavy, rumpled tweed suit and his heavy flannel shirt.

"No," she said stiffly. "I don't."

"You should," he said. "You would know a man worth knowing if you knew me, Thomas, William Ellis Thomas who never stood in a house, in a public house in his life, but who knows a Jezebel when he sees one."

"You're drunk," she said. "Frank, we've got an abusive old man in here."

Frank Baker came through and looked at William Ellis. "Look," he said, "you get out of here!"

William Ellis pulled himself up. "I know the devil when I see it," he said. "I know sin and corruption! I can see where you are going too! You are destroying your soul. Self-destruction!"

Frank Baker stepped around the bar, caught him by the arm, propelled him outside and gave him a good push. He closed the door and went back to the bar and filled a glass of port for himself. He was feeling low. It was strange that the old fool should have said such a thing. He had been thinking about making an end of himself. He had thought about it a lot. What was there in life at all? The sun didn't shine. He wasn't master of himself. He did what his mother wanted and he drank port to forget and it made him feel more low than ever. Nobody believed in him. Nobody wanted him, except, of course, Betty Collins, and he knew that that wouldn't be for long. He had told the Inspector that for two pins he'd pack up and go away with her, but it would never be. She woudn't have him with her. By the time it came to her leaving she would be tired of him. He poured another glass.

"You want to sell the stuff, not drink it, Frank," she said.

"What I want to do isn't clear to me even," he said. "I want to go away from here. I want to begin again somewhere with new people. I want people to believe in me."

"Frank," she said, "you've been takin' too much. Gives me a headache, that stuff. You can't drink it all day!"

He swilled the glass around and swallowed the remains of the port.

"Men who die quick don't know how lucky they are," he said.

She looked at him and smiled. "You don't want to die, Frank," she said. "You got me, Frank, and I can make you live!"

He reached out and they embraced. There was no one to see them. The bar was empty and the place was quiet.

"Careful! Careful!" she pleaded as he fumbled with her blouse. "Somebody might come in!"

He buried his face in her neck. The clock ticked on, but neither of them could hear it for the pounding of their pulses and their labored breathing. Afterwards she looked into the mirror and straightened her hair.

"You want to throw the port bottle away, Frank," she said. "It don't do you any good."

He went out to the back. He felt even gloomier than before and it had nothing to do with the mist being down and the heaviness of the day. Somewhere, out at the back, his father had kept an old revolver and somewhere, in a chest, he had seen some bullets for it. He was going to find the revolver and the bullets and sit down with it and think about himself and his not being wanted and not having anything to show for his life, nothing built, nothing made, nothing achieved. Betty Collins was like a glass of port he could taste on his tongue. Afterwards she didn't mean anything either and he saw her as she was, blowsy, flushed, over-ripe and greedy, like a child who had had too many cream cakes. She had no feeling for him at all. She felt nothing about him, once it was over, any more than he felt any affection or liking for her.

He pulled open a drawer and began to rummage about looking for the gun. Where had he put it? Where had he seen it last? In one of the lower drawers he found an old, faded picture of his father and stared at it for a while. He looked like his father, people said. He had the same sort of eyes, the same mouth, the same lost look. He wondered if that was it. Was he mad?

An old mirror hung from a nail. He turned to it and compared his likeness with that of his father. After a while he dropped the picture into the drawer and went on looking for the gun, but he couldn't find it. Perhaps someone had stolen it.

Betty Collins came through.

"What you looking for, Frank?" she asked.

"I used to have a gun," he said. "I was just wondering where it had got to."

"You worried about the tiger, Frank?" she asked.

He looked out of the window. He was worried about a tiger; about a personal tiger, maybe; a terror in his own life; something that hung over him as fear hung over the village.

"I could shoot the tiger with it," he said soberly. "I could stop it."

She laughed and put her hand on his arm. "You don't want to go playin' the hero now, Frank," she said, "and in any case you might miss it!"

"I wouldn't miss," he replied. "I wouldn't miss!"

He fumbled through the drawer and failed to find what he wanted to find. Someone was in the bar, ringing the bell, and he would have to go, but he would find it yet. He would find it and think about the tiger.

CHAPTER 13

It seemed to Mr. Gerald Ambrose that the time had come to make use of a pith helmet he had bought in a junk shop. He had bought all sorts of things in his time and some of them had become lumber in a real sense. The other day he had found signs that mice were contemplating a family in the pith helmet, but now he had a use for the helmet. The time had come when he might wear it. The time had also come when he should promote himself. The proper rank for a tiger-hunter was major, surely? Colonels were never quite such intrepid fellows in the pursuit of tigers as majors. From this day on he would be Major Gerald Ambrose-Butterfield, the tiger expert, and he wasn't going to telephone the police or write offering his services or advice. He was going to the place with his gear, and he was going to shoot the tiger for them.

He mauled over the contents of his biggest trunk and found some old but well-cut khaki shorts. He found some khaki stockings and a shirt and put these on to see how he looked. His knees were rather knobbly. He filled the shorts too well. The pith helmet had to be adjusted to stop it falling over his eyes, but he had the feeling that he looked something like the thing. It was a pity that he had no binoculars, and the telescope made him feel a little like an admiral, but the rifle was all right. He had a certificate for it too. The Chief Constable had swallowed his story about his expected "return" to parts of India where he would need this weapon and had granted him a permit to have and hold it until such time as he went abroad again. It had a fine leather case and it was an excellent gun in every way, even if he had never fired it. There was a first time for everything, of course, and what better time to use a rifle than when the community stood in peril?

"Have I shot tigers, my dear lady?" he said. "Have I shot tigers? Let me tell you, madam, I have shot more tigers than I have had double whiskies! I have shot four in a single afternoon. Headmen in all parts of India and Africa have reason to thank me for saving them from tigers!"

"Surely," said the old lady, who had read it somewhere, "surely they don't have tigers in Africa?"

"They have no tigers in Africa now," he said brazenly. "I shot the last pair in 1931. You have only to refer to the files of the newspapers of the day."

This was unanswerable. For one thing, the old lady had no newspaper files and was too busy to find time to go off to London to check up.

"Do you think you are wise, Mr. Ambrose?" she said. "The wireless said they have had offers of help from hundreds of people. People keep telephoning and sending telegrams and writing to say they can catch the tiger for them. . . ."

"I shall do none of these things," he told her stiffly. "I shall go there, take a room in the village, study the lie of the land, make my plans and shoot the tiger for them. A tiger, you must understand, is a solitary beast. Shooting it is a one-man job, a job for the lone hunter."

He slapped the pith helmet on his head again and looked at the lone hunter. The lone hunter looked a little over-blown. His face was heavy-jowled and flushed; his arms much too white by contrast. Without the pith helmet he could have passed for the lone grocer bellying up to his counter and blinking behind his spectacles.

"I must get off," he said. "I'll pack a few things and come back in a week or a fortnight. In the meantime you might open the windows and let things air. I feel that the moth is feeding."

He waddled into his room again and began to pack. The pith helmet proved a problem. It simply wouldn't pack and at length he decided to carry it under his arm, which made it a struggle when he had to hump along a heavy gun-case, a telescope which wouldn't pack, and a small suitcase that bulged with second-hand clothes, the wardrobe of the tiger-hunter, Major Gerald Ambrose-Butterfield, D.S.O. He had given himself the D.S.O. while shaving. He felt that he deserved it.

The taxi-driver looked at the gear and wondered what it was all about.

"You wouldn't be a tiger-hunter, would you, sir?" he asked.

The Major smiled and put his pith helmet on the seat.

"Be careful with that rifle," he said.

Major Ambrose-Butterfield knew he was being studied in the mirror and felt for one of the little cigars he carried in a case in his waistcoat pocket. Tiger-hunters, he recollected, invariably had bearers to carry their guns. He would have to see about that. Perhaps he could hire someone to carry his rifle. Some simple village lad. The thing was very heavy. He would leave the case at home, of course, but the lad would carry the rifle and he would carry the telescope. He imagined himself walking the mountain, scanning the hill-side with his telescope and saying over his shoulder, "Give me the rifle, Jones." Jones gave him the rifle. He got down on one knee and took a sight. "Wham!" the rifle echoed across the valley. The tiger bounded and ran and then it dropped, spread-eagled on a rock.

"Gottim, sir!"

He blew down the barrel of the rifle. He had never tried this before and wasn't sure whether the bolt would allow him to do it or not, but for the time being he blew down it nonchalantly and handed it back to the trembling Jones.

"Upwards of a mile, I should say," he said quietly. The glass showed the tiger hadn't moved so much as a hair. He began to walk across the valley to it because he simply had to put his foot on its neck.

The newspaper boys were all around him, their cameras flashing, their notebooks out, and the police were shaking him by the hand while a B.B.C. man thrust a microphone before his face and asked him to say a few words to the listening public. He took off the pith helmet and mopped his brow.

"Nothing very much really," he said. "The beast showed itself and I shot it. Anyone else would have done the same. It was a long shot, I admit, but I knew I had him when he turned and made for the hazel thicket. He hadn't a chance, poor beast."

At Euston he had two porters help him to the train for Wales. They looked at one another as he strode in front with his pith helmet under his arm. The gun-case and the telescope told their own tale. He gave them half a crown each and they beamed at him.

"Good luck, sir," they said. They could put two and two together with the next fellow.

The only other occupant of the first-class carriage was a thin man conventionally dressed in the uniform of a small-town solicitor. He was absorbed in papers which rested on a fat brief-case laid across his knees. He had missed the rifle and the telescope which now rested on the luggage rack, but he couldn't continue to miss the pith helmet. Major Ambrose-Butterfield had placed it where it must be seen, on the seat directly opposite his fellow passenger. The train was steaming out of London before the solicitor looked up and saw the helmet. It seemed a most odd thing to be lying on the seat of a railway compartment. The owner of the thing was obviously a theatrical gentleman hurrying north to take part in a play. He glanced at the rack and saw the old brass telescope and the rifle-case and in spite of himself his curiosity got the better of him.

"Excuse me, sir," he said after a moment, "but I wonder if you are going to Wales in connection with this tiger business?"

Major Ambrose-Butterfield beamed.

"I am going to get the lie of the land and to see what I can do," he said. "I have travelled a great deal in my time and know a little bit about tigers and their ways. I think perhaps I might be able to be of service to the authorities."

He didn't say how.

"You have shot tigers?"

"Indeed I have," said the Major. "I have shot tigers and more fearsome game."

He was relieved when his companion didn't ask what more fearsome game he had shot, because for the moment he could think of no other sort of game, except, perhaps, elephants and lions, and they didn't sound so fearsome.

It was the pith helmet that troubled his companion most. He could see no use for a pith helmet in the Welsh hills where the mist was down, according to the radio. Indeed, he could see no use for a pith helmet on the brightest of summer days in that part of the world. He looked at the cracked patent leather of Major Ambrose-Butterfield's boots and began to wonder about him. He was obviously not a theatrical man. What else could he be but a crank?

The train raced on and the Major dozed. He looked less like a tiger-hunter now than ever, but there was no telling. Perhaps he really was one of the old Indian Army men who came home and yet lived on the plains of India, shooting chukor partridges and more exotic birds, wild duck of every kind and, of course, tigers in the hills. They all seemed to be without roots, these old, sallow-faced warriors. The gentleman with the pith helmet didn't have a sallow face, but his colour might be due to a diet of curry. No, there was something absurd about it all. The telescope, for instance, wasn't a portable instrument. It belonged on some piece of ordnance. It had heavy fittings and it needed a support. Besides, unlike the rifle, it had no case. The rifle might be an imaginary one. There was no telling what the case really contained. He would see a little more in good time, however, for their destination was the same, the valley that contained the village of Pentre Ddu, the place where the tiger walked.

The meal on the train gave Major Ambrose-Butterfield a chance to advertize his mission a little. He talked of tigers and rifles although he knew little about either. Tigers were in the news and his neighbors sipped their soup quietly in order to listen.

Not all of his talk made sense, but not all of his audience knew what a tiger looked like and imagination took hold. They rolled through the Welsh marches into a land of hanging summer mist and by the time they changed trains every one of them could see tigers coming down slopes and emerging from plantations. Major Ambrose-Butterfield, D.S.O. and bar—he had given himself the bar because he felt it befitted such a bold destroyer of tigers—could see tigers on all sides. He had taken a little more whisky to warm him up, for his blood, alas, was thin from foreign service.

The driver of the hire that took him to Pentre Ddu was impressed to say the least. Hadn't he been saying for the past twenty-four hours that what was needed here was someone who could track and shoot a tiger? By all accounts the famous old clubs of London were full of tiger-hunting men. Ordinary people couldn't get in or out without falling over them. They slept all over the place. No one had thought to send for some of them, but here, it seemed, was one who came of his own accord—Major Ambrose-Butterfield, D.S.O. and bar, was being careful now to remove any doubt concerning his free-lance standing. He had not been sent for. He had come.

"Do you happen to know a suitable person in Pentre Ddu who would, for a consideration, be prepared to act as my bearer during the time I am here?" he asked the driver.

"Bearer? I dunno. If it's a easy job you could try Bob the Cough, but if you gotta work for your money it won't do him."

"I must have a young, active, alert fellow to carry my rifle," he said. "I shall be carrying the telescope."

"Ah," said the driver. "You won't need that for a while on account of the mist won't let you see more 'n a coupla yards."

When they reached Pentre Ddu, Major Ambrose-Butterfield took himself to the Horseshoe. He left his rifle and case in the porch and went inside carrying his pith helmet under his arm. The newspaper men nudged each other and came forward in a little group. Here was a story.

"Major Ambrose-Butterfield, D.S.O. and bar," he said. "I've come to see what I can do."

"The pith helmet, sir?" said one innocent-looking newshawk.

"Habit," he said with a smile. "I pick it up as I pick up my rifle when I think about hunting a tiger."

They were taken aback at the cool way he said it.

"You've shot tigers?"

He accepted a drink and began his story. There wasn't a tiger he hadn't shot, it seemed. They began to run off to the telephone to file their stories. Tiger-hunting Major Comes to Welsh Village—the London sub-editors began to think up headlines. "The authorities must face up to it," says Major Ambrose-Butterfield, D.S.O. "Unless something is done quickly the beast will strike again. Once a tiger begins to get a taste for human blood it comes back to make more human kills. . . ." Where Major Gerald Ambrose-Butterfield, D.S.O. got his information from nobody knew, least of all plain Gerald Ambrose, the eccentric son of a deceased tea-taster.

"They gotta white hunter over from Africa," someone up the village told his neighbor. "He's come over special with his rifle and telescope to hunt it down. They say the police are paying him a hundred quid a day while he's doin' it. Come immediate, he did. Still got his helmet in his hand."

The tiger-hunter was coming down the village street now, coming a little unsteadily, but that, perhaps, was because he had so much to carry. Telescopes and rifle-cases, suit-case and pith helmets are cumbersome luggage lumped together.

"Here he comes!" they whispered.

The Major plodded on until he came to a woman at the door of her cottage.

"I'm looking for quarters," he announced. "Somewhere with a good clean bed and simple fare where I can stay until I have done what I came here to do."

"Oh ah," she said, "and what was that?"

"To rid you of your tiger," he said. "Major Gerald Ambrose-Butterfield, D.S.O., at your service."

"I could put you up, sir," she offered. "Bed and breakfast three-ten a week."

It was a lot, he thought, but then the place was swarming with newspaper men, soldiers and police.

"I'll take it," he said. "Thank you very much, and take my word for it, when I go from here that tiger will be dead as many another tiger I set out to shoot is dead!"

"I'm sure it will, sir," she said.

He struggled in with his luggage, feeling he had done enough for one day. The mist was down almost to the tops of the cottages and it was near nightfall.

"Did you know," said the sergeant to Inspector Williams, "that we've got a real live tiger-hunter come to stay in the village?"

Inspector Williams, who had been talking gloomily on the telephone about the prospect of the mist remaining, turned around and look at his sergeant.

"Indeed?" he said. "The first of a wave of cranks, or is he a genuine tiger-hunter? Somebody who knows something about it?"

"Well," said the sergeant, "I couldn't be sure from all the stories he's started, but if it's anything to go by, he brought a pith helmet with him."

Inspector Williams smiled. "A crank," he said. "We must watch out for him. Cranks are the worst nuisance of all. What's his name?"

"Major Gerald Ambrose-Butterfield, D.S.O., sir. He also brought a rifle-case and a telescope."

"Ah," said the Inspector. "We must find out if he has a rifle in his case. If he has we can see whether he has a certificate for it or not. If he has, we can check up where he comes from and whether he knows anything about tigers or not. If he doesn't we'll warn him about obstructing the police in the execution of their duty!"

He laughed as he said it, but he was a little anxious about the first of the would-be tiger-hunters to show face. For several hours now he had been pestered by them from a distance and now one was about to get under his feet.

"Did anyone ask him about the pith helmet?"

"One of the agency boys asked him what it was for and he said he picked it up as naturally as he picked up his rifle when he heard of a tiger to be shot. They had him pose for pictures with it on his head, I'm told. He has gone off to look for a room. He's here to stay, whether he knows how to shoot a tiger or not."

In the cottage of Jenny Jones, Major Gerald Ambrose-Butterfield, D.S.O., arranged his things and asked for a cup of tea. He felt like talking. He was stimulated by the air of the hills, he decided. He could see himself shooting the tiger tomorrow and getting the credit he deserved. This was bigger and better than demonstrating against vivisection in the public gallery of the House as he had done last year, or throwing water over the Japanese Mission as he had tried to do the year before. This was better than all the other causes he had embraced in his day. Let the Bard ask what was in a name, but a name was everything. You called yourself Major Gerald Ambrose-Butterfield, D.S.O. and you were capable of shooting a tiger. He had called himself many names since he had been christened, but here he had stumbled upon a great name and men with great names did great things. They would talk about him in Pentre Ddu long after he had gone, and when he had done his deed he would steal away and change his name so that the legend could go on.

"Do you think your husband would like to be my bearer, Mrs. Jones?" he asked lighting one of his little cigars.

Her face showed alarm.

"I don't think so, sir," she said. "He's uncommon fussy what sort o' work he takes on. You see he's a tiler by trade. Not that he does any tiling, like, but he never does nothing that isn't up to tilin', as it were. It wouldn't do for his dignity, like. Besides, he's not strong. He couldn't carry nobody about on his back."

The problem of the bearer was solved, however, when she talked over the backyard wall with her neighbor. Poor old Jessie Low's boy was cut out for the job. He didn't know over-much about anything. In the words of the village, he did nothing but gawp about, but he could be relied upon to follow where he was led and he could carry things. He carried his mother's shopping basket every Saturday and he had one other advantage, he had no fear. He didn't know what a tiger was.

They were tidying up behind the bar in the Horseshoe.

"I hear," said Betty Collins, "that a tiger-hunter has come to stay with us."

"A crank," said one of the sleepy newspaper men, "a born nut. We'll be hearing more about him yet. There's something familiar about his face. I've seen him somewhere . . ."

"Perhaps he's been in the papers when he shot tigers in India."

"Perhaps," said the newspaper man. "Perhaps he's been in prison or court, or somewhere. Perhaps we'll find out about him before long. Nobody brings a pith helmet to Wales to wear, shooting tigers."

"How do you know?" she asked. "How many tigers have you seen in Wales an' how many tiger-hunters?"

He laughed. "Look, girlie," he said, "come up to my room in half an hour and bring a bottle of gin with you and I'll tell you stories about tigers and tiger-hunters."

She reverently covered the beer pump handles and went off out to the back to see Frank. He was still looking for something, searching at the bottom of a cupboard now.

"You won't need the old gun or the bullets," she said with a laugh. "We got a real tiger-hunter in the village now. Have you heard about him?"

He went on looking. She went over and caught him by the hair of his head.

"Frank!" she said. "Listen to me! I don't like you like this! I like you to be happy. Forget about the tiger. Forget all this nonsense about finding your old gun. Come upstairs, Frank. Leave tigers to them that has nothing better to think about."

He got up off his knees and she embraced him. She was thinking about the newspaper man and his miserable bottle of gin. From now on she was turning over a new leaf and showing some respect for herself.

CHAPTER 14

Jessie Low's boy stood in the yard playing with a willow stick to which he had tied a length of white string. A black-and-white kitten was jumping at the string and each time it sprang up and fell back the boy laughed, a loud guffaw that rumbled in his chest. It was misleading perhaps to call him a boy, but everyone did so although he was a boy no longer and dark whiskers showed on his face. He was twenty-three or four and his body was large although his face and head were small and the co-ordination of his limbs was not much better than that of a babe. His face was innocent except on rare occasions when something flickered in his eyes and his expression held the signs that he was suddenly older, knowing and sad, as though he had become aware that the world judged him and found him lacking in something important. People who talked to him either humored him or talked to him like a baby, for very few indeed are at ease with the so-called simple. They turned upon him a pity that they saved especially for the mentally arrested and the harmless.

"Iss a big tiger," said Jessie Low's boy. "Iss a great big tiger jumpin'!"

His mother, looking out of the window at him, nodded

her head. Sometimes she was unbearably saddened at the sight of him. Sometimes she wiped a tear from her eye at his helplessness and his innocence. Sometimes she saw him as a trial and a burden, it was true, but not often; not for long, for she had a deep and possessive love for him, the love of a mother for an afflicted child.

"Gentleman next door wants you to help him, love," she said. "Wants you to carry something for him when he goes to look for the tiger."

"Ah," he said. "Yes. Iss big tiger."

"You'll go, love, and be a good boy, won't you?"

He didn't look up from the dancing kitten, but he nodded his head and grinned.

"Good boy," he said.

Mrs. Low thought about the money he would get. She would give him something to buy a few sweets. He loved sweets, but he needed a new pair of trousers and his boots were down at the heel.

"Tell Mrs. Jones, love," she said. "Maybe the gentleman's waitin' for you."

He dragged the string from the kitten's mouth and straightened up, rubbing his hand on his brow. He understood what she wanted but he didn't like going next door because Mrs. Jones had told him off so often for throwing things into her yard and batting her cat with a piece of wood. When he eventually went into the next yard he stood a while peering into the kitchen before Mrs. Jones saw him. She came to the door and looked up to him.

"Your mam sent you, Ifor?" she asked.

He nodded and grunted. He very rarely said anything to anyone but his mother although he spoke to cats and dogs and other animals.

"Mrs. Low's boy is here, sir," said Jenny Jones and Major Gerald Ambrose-Butterfield came through. He had dressed himself in his shorts and bush jacket and looked quite absurd with the pith helmet under his arm, but his absurdity was lost upon Mrs. Low's boy and Mrs. Jones expected all foreigners to be absurd, more or less.

"Ah," said the Major, "my bearer. Good! I shall be with you in just a moment."

He put down his helmet and went back for his rifle.

Ifor Low took the gun in his hand and stared at it. He had a vague idea that it was a gun and that it made a noise and this made him a little nervous. He kept the willow stick with the string on it and Major Ambrose-Butterfield frowned.

"You won't want that whip affair, my lad," he said, but the remark was lost upon Mrs. Low's boy. He clutched his stick and held the rifle uncomfortably.

"Better humor him, like, sir," said Mrs. Jones. "He's best if he don't get upset. He's not a bad boy, just a little bit you-know."

Major Ambrose-Butterfield put his helmet on and stepped outside. He was ready to go in search of the tiger.

"This way?" he suggested.

Mrs. Low's boy nodded and seemed to smile. The Major went through the gate and his bearer followed obediently. They were off. Mrs. Jones shook her head. She was beginning to wonder if the tiger-hunter might not be a little more simple in the head than his so-called bearer. They plodded round the passage and across the road. Only Mrs. Low and Mrs. Jones saw them go through the gate and then disappear into the mist that shrouded the field.

"I hope he'll be all right," said Mrs. Low.

"He'll be all right," said Jenny Jones. "The rifle is loaded. I seen him load it before he went out."

"I hope poor Ifor don't take fright if he fires it," said Mrs. Low.

At that moment Inspector Williams, who had had an early breakfast, stepped out of the Horseshoe. He had a feeling that the mist might lift today and that it would be possible to do something about organizing the hunt. Until it did he had a number of things to occupy his mind, among them the formal opening of the inquest and the interviewing of the tiger-hunter. The tiger-hunter was staying with a Mrs. Jenny Jones and the sooner he understood what he was doing in the village the better.

"The gentleman's just gone out," said Mrs. Jenny Jones. "He couldn't wait to get after the tiger, sir."

"Indeed," said the Inspector. "Did he say when he would be back?"

"Lunch-time, sir," she told him. "Didn't want no snack."

"Did he tell you anything about himself?"

"Said when he left the tiger would be dead, sir. Said he'd shot tigers all over the world."

"Did he have a rifle?"

She smiled at him. "Well, wouldn't have gone after a tiger without a rifle, would he? He is a tiger-hunter!"

"Just so," said the Inspector. "I should have known that. He loaded the rifle, I suppose?"

She shook her head at his stupidity.

"He put his helmet on too?"

"Yes," she said. "He put his helmet on. That was the only thing that seemed a bit funny to me. That an' the telescope. Didn't see he needed a telescope when all this mist is hanging about.

"But you're like me," said the Inspector, smiling. "You don't know much about tiger-hunters, do you?"

He was quite convinced now that Major Ambrose-Butterfield was a crank who would have to be locked up or run out of Pentre Ddu.

"He carried the telescope and the rifle?"

"Mrs. Low's poor lad carried the rifle for him, sir."

The Inspector thought about this. He had heard about Mrs. Low's poor lad before.

"Did you see where they went?"

"Across the road, through the gate and up the field," she said.

The Inspector looked into the mist. Two far-from-normal characters walking into the mist and nothing to stop them running into the tiger. Something would have to be done about it. He clumped off back down the village to summon his sergeant and send for the Army representative.

"I want a search party to go up immediately and locate this crank and the poor fellow he's persuaded to go with him. I have an idea that this chap has never seen a tiger in his life and doesn't know what he's doing. He may get himself killed and he may lead the poor half-wit into danger. We can't delay!"

Sergeant Morris adjusted his battle-dress blouse and nodded his head.

"We'll do all we can, sir," he said.

The detail, hurriedly mustered on the road, set out across the field keeping contact with each other as best they could. They reached the young trees without coming up with the tiger-hunter or his bearer and Sergeant Morris stopped and cupped his hands and called as loudly as he could. There was no answer. Up on the rough hill, to the left of the first belt of trees, Major Ambrose-Butterfield, his knees scratched by briars and brambles, panted for breath and peered into the mist. He heard the shouting from below, but it troubled him not at all. He was busy explaining to his bearer what he planned to do and how he proposed to shoot the beast. Mrs. Low's boy cradled the rifle in his arm and flicked the willow-stick whip. He gave no sign that he undersood what was being said to him, but it didn't matter very much. His employer needed no advice or acknowledgement of his wisdom.

"Once we reach soft ground," he said, "I shall cast about for tracks. There are bound to be some tracks somewhere.

When I locate them we shall follow them relentlessly until we come up with the beast."

He rambled on, moving the telescope from one hand to other as his arms became more tired. He was beginning to wish that he had left it behind. When they crossed the second belt of young trees they arrived at the first of the higher fields, the sheep-grazing adjoining Jim Parry's farm. The sheep, of course, had been gathered in and were penned behind hurdles. Major Ambrose-Butterfield raised his helmet, mopped his brow and looked about for the tracks of the tiger. He was doing this when the beast came out of some hazels and walked slowly along a stony ridge, half hidden by bracken. Neither the hunter nor his bearer saw it. It moved sinuously, silently, its long, narrow body barely moving the fronds of bracken through which it passed. It was within five yards of them when it stopped. Major Ambrose-Butterfield was wiping his brow and feeling weary. The midges were devouring him and the telescope had become more than a burden. He was on the point of throwing it away. Ifor Low grunted and his mouth gaped. He saw the beast before his companion was aware that it stood above him on a boulder protruding from the bracken.

"You say something?" he asked heavily.

He looked at the poor fellow's face and followed his stare. The sight he saw made him stiffen so that his neck seemed set. His eyes bulged with fright and his hands gripped the telescope tighter. He wanted to scream his terror, but his throat would emit no sound. A second or two passed. He moved a foot and set it on the ground behind him. The tiger's stance remained unaltered, but its tail flicked slowly from one side to the other, a nervous twitch that fascinated the man with the telescope. It wasn't until he noticed the dull red stain on the brute's chest that he lost control of himself completely and began to shake. It was blood, thick, dark blood, the clotted blood of a victim, beyond all doubt.

Major Ambrose-Butterfield forgot his rifle, forgot everything and began to make his escape. The tiger tensed for an instant as though about to spring, and then it turned its gaze to the son of Mrs. Jessie Low. Major Ambrose-Butterfield collided with him, slipped down, scrambled to his feet, grabbed the rifle, dropped the telescope and began to run. At the hedge he let the rifle fall and threw himself over the thorns. The pith helmet rolled away. The mist covered everything. Gerald Ambrose was making his escape. His dream was over. He was no longer a tiger-hunter.

The tiger stood looking at the helpless man in front of it. Ifor Low twisted the willow twig in his hands and looked at the beast. It was a big cat, he was thinking. It moved its tail like a cat. He moved the stick and its great, fierce cat-eyes followed the movement.

"Iss a big cat," he said. "Iss a big cat, mam."

The string flicked out and swung back. For a moment the cat's reaction seemed to indicate that it would spring, but then it seemed to decide that the man was harmless. He looked unlike the men who had tormented it in the past. He spoke with a soft, hissing voice. There was no threat of violence about him, no telegraphed intention of a desire to kill. After a minute or two it turned to one side, looked back at him and then moved on into the near-by gorse. He swung his willow twig and watched the string going round.

"They've found the so-called tiger-hunter, sir!" said the sergeant.

Inspector Williams hurried out.

"What about the other poor fellow?"

"Says he doesn't know where he is. Left him up there somewhere. Says he just escaped with his life."

"He didn't try to shoot the beast?"

The sergeant shrugged. They were on their way to Mrs. Jones's cottage.

"Where did you leave the man you took with you?" asked the Inspector.

Gerald Ambrose put his head in his hands and sobbed.

"I don't know," he said.

His legs were bleeding, his hands and arms covered with mud. The Inspector looked at him without compassion. "Is your name Ambrose-Butterfield?" he asked.

"Ambrose. Gerald Ambrose."

"The Major?"

He shook his head and looked at the floor. "I'm not a major. I've never fired a rifle except in a fun-fair," he confessed.

"You realize that it is an offense to impersonate and use titles to which you have no right? You understand that a person who does what you have done may be prosecuted for obstructing the police? Have you a certificate for the rifle you were seen to be carrying?"

Gerald Ambrose said nothing.

"You have left this poor simple-minded chap to his fate?"

Somewhere at the back Mrs. Low was crying. She was brought through to confront Gerald Ambrose, who didn't look up.

"Where is he?" she pleaded. "What did you leave him for?"

He had said nothing in reply for several minutes. He looked out of the window and then put his hand across his eyes.

"Don't ask me," he whispered. "Don't ask me. Leave me alone! I ran. I fell. I hurt myself. I don't know how I got back. I don't know where we were. It was standing on a rock above us. I could see its tail moving. I fell over. I got up and I ran."

"Did the tiger attack him? Did you hear him cry out?"

He shook his head. Poor Mrs. Low wailed and Mrs. Jones put her arm around her.

"He isn't a tiger-hunter," she said tonelessly. "He isn't anythin'."

"He's a fake," said the Inspector, "but we'll attend to him before he's much older."

He shook Gerald Ambrose and his fingers dug into the cloth of his bush jacket.

"You're coming back to where you left him. You're going to show us where you left him, do you hear?"

"I won't go!" he sobbed. "You can't make me go!"

The Inspector shrugged his shoulders. He knew he couldn't force the miserable wretch to accompany him back up through the trees to the place where he had left the half-wit.

"I can't make you, but by God I can make things bad for you!"

"Do what you like," said Gerald Ambrose weakly. "I don't care what you do to me. I'm not going back."

Mrs. Low began to cry again. The Inspector put his hand on her arm.

"Don't worry," he said softly. "Don't worry. He'll be all right. We'll find the poor lad."

He tried to make it sound convincing but he couldn't. He looked down at Gerald Ambrose again.

"You'll be wanted. Don't leave here until I've seen you again. You wanted the limelight, my friend, and you shall have it! You'll get publicity before you're finished."

The newspaper men at the gate crowded around him. He stopped for a minute and put on his cap.

"A crank," he said, "a crank and a coward. No more a major than I am. Never saw a tiger in his life, but he left a poor village simpleton up there when the beast crossed his path. I shouldn't wonder if he hasn't been mauled and maybe killed by now."

One of them began to run down the street to the nearest telephone. The rest hesitated and then took to their heels after him. The Inspector found himself alone on the road. Up among the trees someone was blowing a whistle to maintain contact between the advancing men. He couldn't even see the trees. The whistle was strangely hollow and far-off. The fake tiger-hunter had come down the side of the wood, most likely. To the right or left, somewhere up on the waste land where the sheep grazed, Mrs. Low's poor lad, as they called him, was either lying dead or acting as a live bait for a tiger. It was all so foolish and without reason, for he had intended to intercept the crank before he made trouble. He was to blame as much as anyone else for not seeing him and sending him packing first thing in the morning.

When he reached the Horseshoe he dispatched a constable to tell Sergeant Morris and his corporal what had happened and to suggest that they split up and went quickly beyond the second belt of trees to look for Ifor Low.

"Tell them it would be a great relief to me to know that he is safe, and if he would get news to me immediately I would let his mother know."

"You think he's safe?"

He didn't know what to think. A tiger was an alien beast. There was no knowing what it would do. Did it attack and kill every man in its path? He wondered. It had mauled and killed two but only mauled a third and left the farmer, Jim Parry, unmolested. There was a chance that the poor simple Ifor Low might have aroused no savagery in the beast. There was a chance that he was wandering about on the hill carrying the rifle as he had been when the tiger came on the scene. It was a small chance, a small chance, like the chance that the half-wit would know how to use the rifle to defend himself if he had to. A small chance indeed.

The coroner came while he was telephoning for information about a man called Gerald Ambrose with an address in Uxbridge, Middlesex. The inquest was due to open in the back room in half an hour and he had forgotten all about it.

"You may be coming to Pentre Ddu rather a lot, sir," he said. "We seem to be having an epidemic."

The coroner smiled faintly. He didn't blame him. It wasn't funny. There was nothing funny in death and the threat of sudden death hanging over villagers the way it was.

The Inspector told him about the tiger-hunter and Mrs. Low's son as they went through to the back room. Shortly afterwards the witnesses came filing through: Jack Roberts, Betty Collins, Frank Baker, old Mrs. Baker, Kitty Price, Watkins, the garage man, a relative of one of the victims and two police constables. Mrs. Baker was eager for an opportunity to say her piece, but the opportunity never arose. The coroner looked about him, dipped his pen in the inkwell and cleared his throat.

"I propose," he said, "to take evidence of identification only and adjourn this enquiry to a date to be decided upon in due course."

Frank Baker seemed to breathe again. He looked at Betty Collins and she smiled, but Jack Roberts, who had been watching both of them, didn't smile and Kitty Price, who knew what it was all about, didn't smile either. The Inspector kept his thoughts to himself and neither frowned nor smiled, but he missed nothing. The witnesses would have been surprised to know that the coroner was aware of the little inconsistencies of their statements and that the adjournment was partly due to a desire on the part of officialdom to have things tidy and tabulated when the tiger could be entered as deceased, and partly to let truth mature as it usually does when lies are left to ferment.

"You don't want to hear what I got to say?" asked old Mrs. Baker as they left the back room when the court had risen.

The Inspector smiled. "I always listen," he said. "I never refuse to hear what anybody's got to say."

She didn't repeat her piece. She nodded her head. She too

was content to wait if it meant that in the end she could get Betty Collins out of the way.

It was long past noon before they found Ifor Low. He was standing beside a stone wall with his willow twig in his hand. It was obvious that he had had some sort of an ordeal, for his eyes rolled in an odd way and there was froth on his lips, but when they asked him if he had seen the tiger and how he had escaped harm he didn't answer. They led him down the rough road to the village and Sergeant Morris sent word to the Inspector.

"What about the tiger-hunter chap?" asked Sergeant Morris. "Did he leave you and run?"

Ifor Low didn't seem to have heard. He swished his string whip and rolled his eyes. Once he said something that sounded like "cat" but he did not repeat it.

When Inspector Williams came up to meet him he remained as far away from human contact as ever and the word tiger brought no flicker to his eyes nor any change of expression.

"All I know is," said the Inspector, "something looks after the likes of this one, the helpless, the simple and the innocent. It's the same thing that protects a child that walks across a busy road or climbs onto a roof or a bridge. If the tiger didn't strike him down it was because he was what he is, a harmless, simple creature."

Sergeant Morris who heard him say it wasn't inclined to agree. There was something that looked after the young and the innocent, but not when they got in the path of a tiger or a machine-gun. Things were written. The old and the unfit died and the young and healthy survived because they had to survive. A tiger was a wild beast, a savage brute without discrimination, without feeling for weak or strong, just or unjust. Even in war, which was a bloody and brutal thing, the young and the innocent were killed in ratio and as many good men died as bad. Survival was in the seed and destruction in the mouth of the gun or the mouth of the beast and there was no reason in it anywhere.

"It wasn't written," he said, "that's all."

The Inspector looked over his shoulder at the hills and the mist that screened them.

"If it's written there's a lot of it I'd like to read," he said. "The main item would be when this mist will lift, and whether the tiger will do more damage than it has already done before we get him."

Someone had gone running down the village to summon Mrs. Low. She was sobbing when she reached them, but she brushed her hand across her eyes when she saw her son.

"You're safe, love!" she said. "Come home!"

"Iss a big cat, mam," he said. "A great big cat."

They were the first words he had spoken since he had left home. A newspaper man took note of them and read his own meaning into them. A photographer took two flash-light pictures. Inspector Williams raised an eyebrow and asked Mrs. Low to get him to tell her what had happened, but Mrs. Low was too moved to speak. She clung to her son and propelled him towards home.

"Dramatic scenes were witnessed in Pentre Ddu this afternoon," said a reporter talking on the telephone as he stared down the village street, "when Ifor Low was found and brought back from the mountain after hope had almost been abandoned. Low, who had been engaged by a self-styled tiger-hunter to accompany him in search of the escaped tiger, had been left behind by his companion when they were surprised by the beast somewhere on the sheep-grazing far above the village. It was feared that the tiger had mauled and killed Ifor Low. Police and soldiers combed the locality in swirling mist searching for him, while in the village an inquest was opened on the two men killed by the tiger when it made its escape from the trailer. . . ."

They were talking about it all over the village.

"That chap what come here with his rifle an' sun helmet'll probably get took up for false pretences, mark my words. He's responsible. If it hadn't been for him the poor lad wouldn't 'a been there. They say he never saw a tiger before in his life. What you make of it? A crank. A coward, the police inspector says he was. They oughta give him ten years!"

Gerald Ambrose had taken advantage of the hubbub to make himself scarce. In spite of the Inspector's injunction to stay where he was, he had turned his back on Pentre Ddu, leaving behind him a bush jacket, a khaki shirt and a reputation for being a fake, but he wasn't so upset at the thought. It all went with a name, and the fake was Major Gerald Ambrose-Butterfield, D.S.O. and bar. He didn't look like a tiger-hunter as he got back on the London train and he didn't look out at any of his fellow passengers as he hid behind his newspaper. None of them suspected that beyond the sheet carrying the story of his shame and cowardice hid the sometime tiger-hunter, hero of so many imaginary encounters with the beast in stripes.

CHAPTER 15

"Take my word for it," said Bonzo Phillips, "they're lookin' for the tiger everywhere but where it is."

The profundity of the statement needed to be digested, like most of the statements made by Bonzo and prefaced with an injunction to take his word. When his remark about the tiger was found to be nearly as irrefutable as his blue and red nose, a thing not to be denied, and an outstanding truth, they took his word for it and nodded.

"If I wass in Pentre Ddu," he said, "I'd find the ruddy tiger for them!"

"Ah, you would an' all, Bonzo," they said.

Bonzo looked about for a single person who showed by the slightest expression that he doubted his claim, but there was none. No one ever doubted Bonzo, for it didn't pay to doubt him. To doubt Bonzo was to become embroiled in long discussion, in painful hours of prolonged agony that couldn't be lessened by matching him pint for pint, for the more Bonzo swallowed the more certain he became that he heard all, saw all and knew all. It could never be said that he emulated the three wise monkeys. His voice was strident. He spoke his mind. He spoke his thoughts before he considered them. The clientele of The Keys in Newydd, where the bridge after which it had been named was no longer new and no longer mentioned, listened to Bonzo on a variety of topics. He was a man of opinions, and if some of them turned the beer sour, some of them were good for a laugh. He knew about catching tigers, for a man who knows everything knows about tigers.

"Well look, mates," said Bonzo. "Take the way they've set about it. Nothin' done but sittin' on their backsides while the tiger does as it likes. Today a cove from London what don't know the place comes face to face with the tiger!"

"Pure chance!" said somebody at the far end of the bar.

"Pure chance! A'right. He never saw a tiger or Pentre Ddu in his flamin' life before! What about them that knows the district? What about the police and them soldiers what's been hanging about for three days? If it was me in charge I'd have that tiger hanging from a hook by now! They're lookin' where it ain't. That's what. When I was a kid an' my ole man sent me for his belt, you think I looked for it proper? I knew what I was in for if I found it, mate!"

"You mean they ain't lookin' for the tiger, Bonzo?"

Bonzo shook his tousled mop of hair, hunched his heavy

shoulders, looking like the bull of a man he was, and crooked his great hand around his pint glass. His eyes narrowed and he gave a quick, knowing glance from side to side, as though aware of eavesdroppers.

"What's it look like, eh?" he demanded. "What's it look like? You say to a man, a single man, 'Get that tiger,' an' he can't do nothin' else."

"What about the poor ole married man?"

"Shut up!" said Bonzo. "But say it to twenty coppers an' fifty soldiers. They all play about an' wait for the other bloke to step in the way of the tiger's claws! You don't get no medals for gettin' chewed up, see?"

His look was fierce. A tiger might have shrunk from him in that moment. He put his glass down on the bar with a thud.

"Tigers," he said, "are only human. They can be shot or trapped an' strung up by the heels like anybody else. Supposin' that brute was to come down into Newydd tonight. Just supposin'! It could kill me or you or your missus."

"Now you're talkin'," said the humorist.

"It could slaughter us off," continued Bonzo. "It's had time to wander this far, hasn't it? It's had time because they done nothin' at all to stop it, have they? So it comes prowlin' down into Newydd, walkin' up the street like a stray cat, only bigger, an' the first kid it sees it grabs an' carries off an' eats. See what I mean? They got a responsibility to you an' me as well as the people in Pentre Ddu an' round about. If such a thing happens whose fault is it?"

No one could answer. In their minds the tiger came noiselessly down from the grazing above the old quarry workings, walking over the mounds of slate rubble, as unnoticed as one of the ewes that strayed onto the street. They could see it when it struck a pram and the pram smashed like match-wood and its wheels spun as it went over on its side. The tiger carried the mangled child away with a blanket trailing, and in the background children were shouting and screaming in the school yard, but shouting and screaming at play.

Bonzo himself could see the thing as plain as anyone. He shuddered once, for the tiger had sprung at him and ripped his jacket and shirt to shreds as it bore him down. He almost spilled his beer evading the fearful blow it dealt him and quickly removed all danger by drinking the remainder in quick gulps.

"Give us another," he said.

They drew closer together around the bar and no one wanted to laugh or joke. The landlord, a pale-faced little man, found himself incapable of lightening their mood. He, too, could see the tiger in the town, standing on the ledge above his own backyard, getting ready to spring down upon him as he opened the door.

"Bonzo," he said, "there's a good fella, don't keep on about it. Sing us a song or somethin'. They probably got the tiger by now."

"Bet they ain't," said Bonzo. "Turn on the news an' see."

Obediently the landlord turned on the little radio at the back of the bar and they waited for the news.

"The tiger," said the announcer when he reached the lesser items, "continues to elude police and servicemen hunting it in the Welsh hills. Tension increases in the valley as the mist shows no signs of lifting. The question uppermost in the minds of people in the locality is where the beast will go if it moves from the immediate vicinity of the village of Pentre Ddu. In an interview today the Chief Constable said, 'While the mist remains we must be patient. It is almost impossible to see ten yards, and on the slopes visibility is often almost nil, so that any serious attempt to drive the beast or comb the area must be ruled out. It would be foolhardy in the extreme to risk lives under such conditions. Precautions taken ensure that everyone entering the area knows the danger and everyone living in the locality has been urged to keep his or her movements out of doors to a minimum. With the men at our disposal it is impossible to provide protection for every household and every farm and holding, and men must be held in reserve to ensure that if news of the beast is obtained they can be rushed to the scene and endeavour to bring it to bay.' Asked if there was a danger that the tiger might reach adjoining towns and bring life to a standstill in an even larger area, the Chief Constable said it wasn't true to say that life had been brought to a standstill. The possibility of the tiger straying had not been overlooked, but present indications were that it was confined to a certain tract of grazing and woodland and every effort would be made to destroy it inside that territory."

"Ah," said Bonzo. "What you make of that, eh? Don't say it won't stray. Can't say it hasn't strayed. Might be here tonight for all we know. One of us might run into it goin' home. Nobody might know about it until tomorrow mornin', even. What will the police say then? They'll say the tiger ain't where it was. We know where it ain't. Show us where it is."

"You want to go there, Bonzo, and show them how!"

"Ah," he said, pushing away another empty glass. "Wouldn't need to be asked twice, neither. Give me my old shotgun an' my two terriers an' I'll have it, just like I used to get me sack o' rabbits."

"Shotgun ain't much good against a tiger."

"All you know!" said Bonzo. "All you bloody know. I seen a bull shot stone dead with a shotgun! A bull weighs a ton or more. Got a head as thick as this wall, but the old shotgun brought it down on its knees."

"Go on, Bonzo," they said, mouths agape. "You reckon you could stop it with a shotgun?"

"Any day," said Bonzo. "Any day of the week!"

Above the town, in a small field encompassed by a tumbling fence of rusted wire, old Mrs. Carter's donkey grazed. It was a brown donkey, smooth as a worn armchair, old like its owner. The donkey was lonesome in the mist, and the grass was short and damp, and after a while it came to the fence and cropped under the wire. When it lifted its head it found that the wire rose and it had only to walk forward and let it slide over its back to be free. In a minute or two it was free and it stood on the edge of the field with a long scree of old slate at its feet. When it began the journey downhill it set its hind legs and slid a good bit of the way, but when it reached the larger slate it stopped and began to walk daintily along ledges and sheep-tracks that led down to the road. No one noticed the donkey's progress, for no one looked up at the mist-covered hill. It was almost dusk when it stood at length on the road. It began to amble slowly along, travelling as a donkey travels, aimlessly, leisurely. Strangely enough, no one looked out and saw it passing, and no one encountered it as it walked between the first rows of houses. It was quiet in the back streets of Newydd, as still and silent as the inside of a locked chapel. Half the inhabitants of the place were abed and the other half thinking about it, and only one or two hanging about such places as The Keys and the Rising Sun, after closing time.

Bonzo had said all he had to say, but he went on saying it after his usual custom, and his audience dwindled to those who were so far gone in drink that they neither heard nor cared what he said.

"Tigers," said Bonzo, "are foreign to this country, man. Foreign!"

All things foreign were despised by Bonzo. He found it easy to despise tigers, particularly when no one could deny that tigers were destructive, dangerous, and had no business in Pentre Ddu or Newydd.

"That's where it stumps them coppers. They don't know what to do because they don't know nothin' about them!

You gotta remember the tiger don't know his way about here. It don't like the mist or the cold. It don't enjoy bein' free here because it comes from a hot country where there's deer an' things it likes to feed on. Here, what is there? There's nothin', only sheep an' cows an'—an' human bein's. Only you an' me, as helpless as the wild things in the jungle. Helplesser. If it comes what can we do? We got nothin' to defend ourselves with. It could spring among us like a cat among birds!"

The birds nodded their heads solemnly and swayed a little as though the wind was in their tree.

"If I was to look up the street an' see the tiger now, what could I do?" asked Bonzo.

He held out his brawny arms and looked helpless. "What could I do? I couldn't run, could I? A tiger could catch me in a minute! I could only stand and put my flesh an' blood between it an' the place I was born in. That's all! That's all I could do!"

He almost sobbed, but his emotion was wasted on them. In fact, he had lost another of his audience. He rallied his eloquence, putting his thumbs in the armholes of his waistcoat and tipping his great shaggy head back.

"If I wass in charge," he said, "if they wass to put me in charge of it, it would be a different story. Men, women an' children wouldn't be hidin' in terror behind locked doors!"

Although he was quite unaware of the fact, his words were wasted. The last of the nodding, swaying audience had stolen away and he talked to the empty street.

"An' if the tiger come. If the tiger showed face at the end of the street there . . ."

He pointed dramatically and peered along the street in the direction his great forefinger indicated.

"If the tiger come . . ."

The tiger had come! He saw it in the mist, stalking down the center of the road! He quickly rubbed his hand across his eyes and looked again. The beast stood still and seemed to be looking straight at him. He swung about and lurched into a run, his heavy boots clattering on the road. The tiger began to trot after him. He could see it out of the corner of his eye as he ran. At the first turning he threw himself over a wall, ploughed through a garden and came out in another street. He rushed to a door and knocked. A man, in his stockinged feet and wearing vest and trousers, opened the door.

"What's up?" he asked.

"The tiger!" exclaimed Bonzo. "The tiger is here! I seen it in the next street!"

"The tiger's here!" said the man over his shoulder.

"My God!" exclaimed someone behind him.

Bonzo found himself looking at a closed door. He turned and knocked on the next.

"Lock up!" he said. "Keep everybody in. The tiger's here!"

He floundered on.

The second cottager scratched his head. "Bonzo's drunk, I think," he said. "Says the tiger's here."

Nevertheless, he quickly shut the door and drew the bolt across. Bonzo saw his duty plainly. He went from door to door.

"Tell the police, mate!" someone urged.

He stood still, looking up and down the road.

"What can they do? What have they done?" he asked the night.

There was only one thing to do, and that was to get home as quickly as he could and get his shotgun. He stopped knocking on doors and lumbered off to his own house.

The gun was in a closet below the stair. He brought it out and went lurching into the street.

"I'll tell the police when I got the brute," he mumbled.

Where was it now, though? How far had it padded along

the streets? It couldn't be where he had last seen it! He cut through a narrow alley and came out in the main street. In a minute Bonzo, clumping along and looking to right and left, came face to face with the policeman.

"Here," he said, "what you up to?"

"Lookin' for the tiger!" said Bonzo. "I seen it only five minutes ago."

"Oh ah!" said the policeman. "You drunk?"

"I seen it!" insisted Bonzo.

The policeman didn't believe him, but before he could take him by the arm a woman came running around the corner.

"The tiger!" she said. "It's been seen down our road."

"Who seen it?" the policeman asked.

"Everybody! Everybody's talkin' about it. You better get help quick before somebody gets killed."

Bonzo clutched his gun. "What I tell you?" he asked.

The policeman didn't answer. He began to run towards the police station and when he reached it he was out of breath.

"The tiger's in the streets!" he said. "We better do something quick!"

The sergeant stood up and hesitated before reaching for the telephone. When he got through to the Horseshoe at Pentre Ddu he had to wait for Inspector Williams to be summoned.

"Is that you, Inspector?" he asked. "I don't know what the drill is now, but the tiger's here in Newydd by all accounts. There's panic, I'm told. I can hear people runnin' up the street now!"

Inspector Williams put down the telephone. It was nearly dark. He would have to go to Newydd at once and take some men. The tiger had moved, it seemed. Perhaps it would be easier to trap it in the streets of the town, but he prayed it wouldn't kill anyone before his men could give chase.

"Get the van and half a dozen men with rifles. Tell the Captain to follow on as quickly as he can. The tiger's in Newydd!"

The door was closed and before he had gone through it he was joined by two newspaper men who had quite obviously been listening in.

"The tiger's been seen?" they asked.

"There's a report that it's in the streets of Newydd. If it is, we'll stand a chance of getting it."

He was forgetting, of course, that Newydd was an ill-lit town and most of its streets would be in darkness. Perhaps the headlights of a car would be enough, however. He hurried to the van and bundled in. It shot away from the Horseshoe.

Bonzo was no coward. He hurried on down the street, expecting to see the tiger at any minute. He would either wait for it to come at him and give it both barrels or run at it and shoot it when he was close enough to blow its head off. His unsteadiness worried him not at all. He could shoot no matter how unsteady he was. He would show the police! They would have something to talk about for a long time. What had he been saying in The Keys? Wasn't he right, as always? He turned a corner and looked up the street. There it was! He cocked his gun and got down on one knee. Let it come. His heartbeat quickened and his breathing became heavy. The beast came slowly on and he saw its ears. It didn't dawn on him at once that it was old Mrs. Carter's donkey. In fact it didn't change from a tiger to a donkey even when he saw the ears, but it changed as it came and Bonzo began to swear and curse.

"You stupid brute!" he shouted. "You flamin' donkey! You, you . . ."

The point of his gun wavered and dropped. He began to

shake and then he recovered himself, uncocked the gun and stood up. No one had seen him. There was no one at any of the windows as far as he could tell in the gloom, and there was no one on the street. He turned and hurried up the nearest passage, scaled a wall, went down another passage and came at length to his own terrace. No one saw him reach into the letter-box for the key on the string. He went in and put the gun away and fumbled his way up to bed. It was some time before there was a knock at his door. The policeman stood waiting for him.

"Look," he said, "you might tell me where you saw the tiger, if you saw it. I can't find anybody else who actually saw it."

"I saw it all right," he lied. "I saw it in Bryn Terrace. It was comin' down into High Street."

"You sure?" asked the constable.

"Sure?" he said. "Am I sure? You think I'd start a fuss like that if I wassn't sure? What you think I am, mate?"

The constable took his leave. It was no use talking to Bonzo when his monkey was up.

The van and a truck came from Pentre Ddu ten minutes later. Their arrival awoke most of the people who had gone to bed. The story of the tiger began to spread from door to door.

"The tiger's here! Yes, here in Newydd, Mrs. Evans! They seen it tonight. Don't open your door! I knew it would happen. It was bound to happen. They couldn't get it on the mountain an' here it is an' somebody'll be slaughtered in the street!"

"Who seen it?"

"Half a dozen seen it. Everybody up in Bryn Terrace seen it."

It was a long time before they began to compare notes, somewhere long after midnight, and came to the conclusion that the only person who said he had seen it was Bonzo Phillips, and Bonzo Phillips was hardly ever sober.

Inspector Williams deployed his men and they began to search the streets, the passages, the lovers' corners, the alleys and the back entries. It was done with admirable thoroughness. When they had combed the town from end to end the night had almost worn away to daybreak. They found old Mrs. Carter's donkey. It didn't look very much like a tiger. It looked like a donkey and it bared its yellow teeth and made a derisive noise that a donkey loves to make. Inspector Williams took out his watch and saw that it would soon be four o'clock, four o'clock on a summer's morning in a damp, gray slate town.

"You had better call and see this Bonzo Phillips chap," he said, "and tell him from me that if he ever starts a panic like this again he'll end up behind bars! Tell him a donkey has long ears and a tiger has short ears and stripes. Tell him to keep out of the pub if it affects his eyesight so badly!"

The sergeant smiled a sour smile. "If I'd known it was only Bonzo claimed to have seen it, but I didn't," he said.

The newspaper men had all departed to write another scare story and put the donkey in the news.

As he drove back to Pentre Ddu Inspector Williams yawned and wondered about the new day. It had begun early in the streets of Newydd, where they had hunted down a poor little brown donkey with a sad, dejected air about it, but how would it end? Perhaps at last the mist would rise and the tiger would be cornered. It had to happen.

CHAPTER 16

Along the valley they were talking of the tiger being in Newydd. No one mentioned the donkey, for who could positively say that the tiger in Newydd had been a donkey, after all? Bonzo Phillips had sworn to the tiger's stripes and its slinking gait as it had come down the center of the road, and once the imaginary tiger could be credited in Newydd it could be visualized everywhere. When at length the police thought fit to say that it was a donkey, but that Bonzo Phillips had been drunk too often in his time to see anything as harmless as a donkey, people nodded their heads and spoke knowingly about the excuses that officials always made for their own inefficiency.

"Bonzo seen it an' Bonzo ain't no little fella to be scared by a donkey! It takes a lot t'scare Bonzo. I seen him. I know the sort o' bloke Bonzo is. He don't get scared easy. I'd say only a tiger would scare him. The police are all squattin' in Pentre Ddu now. They like it there. They got offices in the pub. Who would want to move? The tiger can go where it likes. Tomorrow, wait an' see, it'll be in your backyard or mine an' they'll be sayin' a donkey bites a man's head off!"

Bonzo Phillips, who now said very little, was rather shaken by his experience, which only made it all sound more plausible.

They talked about the tiger Bonzo had seen, even in Pentre Ddu. It gave them some relief to think that the tiger was ranging farther afield. Bonzo Phillips was known in Pentre Ddu. They knew he liked a pint or two of beer and told some tall tales, but they knew how he looked, and he wasn't a man to be frightened of a donkey or think that a donkey looked like a tiger! They gave him credit for that because they wanted to think that the tiger was somewhere other than in the scrub-oaks and plantings above Pentre Ddu.

Among those who believed that the tiger had been seen in Newydd was Tom Lewis. He had a flock on the far mountain, the common grazing shared with farmers and flock-masters living in the adjoining valley, and he was anxious about the condition of some of his sheep already overdue for inspection. He went out before noon with his two dogs at his heels. The tiger was away along the valley at Newydd. Bonzo Phillips had seen it. Perhaps a misty day wasn't the best time to send dogs over the rough mountain to bring sheep to the old stone folds, but Tom Lewis felt that if he didn't attend to part of his flock very soon the losses would be heavy. He was a good shepherd, used to walking his twenty miles a day and diligently inspecting his flock, but he had been confined to the house for some time and his work had been neglected. It doesn't take a shepherd long to plod uphill and make his way by old and well-known paths. He was gone before the gossip in Pentre Ddu had really warmed up. Not many of the gossipers would have backed their optimism to the extent of accompanying Tom Lewis into the hills. Inspector Williams would have said that he was taking a chance.

Tom's wife watched him go, and although she was a little anxious she comforted herself with the knowledge that no one knew the mountain better and no one had a better pair of dogs. The tiger had never been very real in any case. They lived up from the road and away from the village. They had seen very little of the activity of the police or the army. Even the trailer had gone from the village when Tom and his wife went down to see what was to be seen. The trailer had been removed and only half a bag of sawdust marked the place where the Pole had been killed. What the newspapers said hardly impressed them.

The morning had gone when Ruth Lewis went out to feed her hens, scattering scraps for them from a tin bowl. She scarcely noticed the cat springing onto the wall, and it wasn't until she came back to the house that she saw that it had sprung to the wall for a reason. There were wet pad marks on the tiles in the porch. One of the dogs had come home. Fear and doubt didn't come to her at first. The dog might have been sent home for some reason. It might have taken the sulks. Tom never beat his dogs. He gave them a telling off at times, but he knew too much about them to beat them. They were his eyes and ears, as well as his legs. They used their intelligence when they came upon a stray in some depression or gulley. He relied upon them, and when they misbehaved he contented himself with words that made them put their tails between their legs.

Ruth put her hands on the table and looked beneath it. The bitch had her tail tucked under and lay looking into a corner with the whites of her eyes showing.

"He give you a tellin' off?" she asked. "You done wrong an' he give you a tellin' off, you wicked animal!"

The bitch looked even more wretched and sighed, as a dejected dog will.

"I got a good mind t' put you on the chain!"

On the top of the table was the newspaper. Nearly all of its front page was taken up by a picture, a picture of a slate town on which was imposed another of a tiger, the head of a tiger that was snarling. TERROR STALKS THE VALLEY said the headline. The correspondent of this particular journal had thought it better to keep the donkey in proportion. It wasn't, after all, a very big donkey and only the police seemed to think that the donkey and the tiger were one.

The tiger Ruth Lewis saw had the snarling expression of a wild farm cat, an old, battered tomcat that had fought many battles and was fierce and untrusting. What people like herself read in the newspapers was never quite real. News was limited truth unless it happened right on one's very doorstep, and who had seen the tiger, after all? It was more remote than the sun at that moment, less real than a fly on the ceiling. She reached out and removed it from all semblance of reality by folding the paper and sticking it on the rack above the range.

"Wait 'til Tom comes home!" she said to the dog. "You'll get a tellin' off proper then. You're a disgrace. That's what you are!"

The bitch whimpered. She thought about that for a while and then she began to consider the little gnawing fear that came back even when she had put the tiger away. She saw the tiger stalking Tom and his dogs and the bitch putting her tail between her legs and bolting for home. She saw Tom plodding uphill and on over the moss and the tiger rushing out upon him, knocking him down. Where was the other dog? What had prevented it from coming home? Soon she began to imagine the tiger striking down one of the dogs and the other one getting away. She saw Tom lying on the bracken. The picture of the tiger seemed suddenly real. She grabbed it from the rack and threw it into the fire. Tom would be down somewhere round about five o'clock, tired and hungry and ready to settle in his chair after he had eaten.

The tiger couldn't rest long in one place. It was disturbed by so many things that stimulated instinctive fear. The jay in the conifers seemed to warn it of danger and the magpies' chattering in the thicket was equally a signal to keep on the alert. There was no place where it could lie or sit in comfort, nowhere that wasn't damp and unfriendly. Rocks and slabs of slate were wet and overhanging trees dripped moisture. When it stayed on a knoll above a stream it paced the springy grass because the sound of the stream might have allowed an enemy to steal up. After passing along a ridge it stood a while in a wilderness of mouldering, moss-covered alder stumps where weeds of all kinds sprouted from crevices in the poor soil. Its movements had been almost continuous since its escape and it had gone from place to place, a frightened beast, dangerous because it was frightened and out of its element. Once it came upon an open-fronted building with a heavy slate roof, an old ruin in which a harvest of bracken had once been gathered, and it stood looking at the dry mound of bracken. The building was small, however, and too many things about it reminded the beast of the cage in which it had spent nearly all its life. Had it stayed there it might have been shot, for the building was part of a derelict farm and opened on to a courtyard of ruins half screened by elder bushes, bramble and nettles. In the Horseshoe, Inspector Williams was beginning to think of these derelict places scattered about the uplands. He had marked them with red. Nearly all of them were closely crowded by scrub and tangles, it seemed, and if they were to be surrounded and searched the only chance of success would be to carry out the operation when the mist lifted.

"We perhaps can say where the tiger is not," he said, "but if we've got to swear to it we'll have to say where it is, and prove it. Don't ask me where I think it is. Make your own guess and print that. It's as good as mine."

At that moment, by a strange chance the point of his red pencil was resting upon the dots on the map that indicated the farm where the tiger stood. The tiger had gone before he made his little ring and took note of the Welsh name.

Before the beast came to the first of the sheepfolds, at the foot of the common grazing, it turned its head and stared behind it. The sounds it heard were small and far off, the sounds of a man plodding up through trees and two dogs running before him, sniffing an odor they hadn't known before, the rank odor of the beast. Tom Lewis didn't study his dogs for their reaction to scent. He looked upon them as servants, companions. Let them sniff where they liked. Let them run as they pleased so long as they came immediately when he summoned them to work. Now and again they showed him that a ewe was tethered by a long strand of briar or that a lamb was helpless in a crack between two boulders, but they did such work in the manner of sheep-dogs, stopping, turning, weaving about until they drew attention to whatever it was. They didn't know how to tell him about the strange odor that hung in the wet bracken. They lost a little of their sprightly bearing. They began to run with their noses scenting, their hackles rising. They were nervous.

Tom Lewis thought about the sheep he had between two mountain streams. They wouldn't be hard to round up and bring to the fold even in the mist, if he worked from the high side, because the streams joined just beyond the lower fold. He came to the edge of the scrub and stepped over the stone wall, putting his toe in an aperture in the wall and swinging his other foot down to rest on a well-worn stone. His dogs came over the wall on either side, dropping to the old turf and breaking into a gentle run almost the instant their lean, sinewy bodies struck the ground. He whistled to them. They turned and curled back to his heels and in a little while he let them go on again, losing sight of them in the mist at times and seeing them again as they stopped and checked on his whereabouts. The bitch seemed a little nervous, he thought. She had been at home too long getting fed on the wrong sort of stuff and taking no exercise. He was feeling a little slow himself, in spite of all the years he had walked the hill.

A collie bitch is perhaps the most intelligent sort of dog there is, and Tom's bitch was an exceptional sheepdog, even if she was at times a little too sensitive to the rough edge of his tongue. The bitch was more aware of danger than the dog. The odor was strange, but it also had a message that frightened the bitch. She knew the beast was not far away. When Tom came to the first of the folds he moved his stick from his right hand to his left and stepped up on the wall. He had to pass the fold and skirt his flock so that he could work the ground quickly and save his dogs' as well as his own time and effort. He was swinging over the wall when it happened. One of the large slabs of stone slipped and as he jumped it came down with him. It smashed down on his ankle and the pain made him groan.

The dog had jumped the wall at his side but when he opened his eyes and rubbed the tears from them he couldn't see either the dog or the bitch. He moved his foot and drew breath quickly at the pain that stabbed again. He put his head on the ground and tried to gather his senses and overcome the weakness. When he opened his eyes he was looking along the ground, across muddy stones and sheep trodden soil. At the end of the fold, between the entry walls stood the tiger. He stared at it. It didn't move. It was taller, leaner on the back than he might have expected. It was more sinuous and lean even in the chest, but there was no doubt about it, it was a large beast and he knew it was tense and frightened as he was. The pain in his leg was beginning to take his senses away. He tried not to faint, tried to keep his head and his whole body still; tried not to blink his eyes, feeling that movement would make the tiger spring. Where were the dogs? What had happened to them? He dared not even whistle. His whole leg seemed to have gone dead. In spite of all his efforts he blinked and then closed his eyes and let his head rest on the muddy stones.

There was no telling how many minutes passed. He felt the cold wet stone digging into his cheek. His stick was still in his hand. He had barked his knuckles as he came down. It was funny how the little pain grew as he lost sense of feeling in his injured leg. The tiger was still there.

He knew it hadn't moved. The tiger wasn't in Newydd. It was twenty feet away, standing in the mud, staring at him with those fierce, wild eyes. At any minute the muscles and skin of its shoulders would ripple like the body of a blood horse and it would spring and tear him to pieces!

Where were the dogs? He hoped they were making their way home as fast they could, and then he thought about Ruth and the fright she would get if they came home without him. There was a small sound down the fold. He set his jaws and fear surged stronger than ever. When he opened his eyes he saw the tiger in the act of jumping. It rose and cleared the wall and somehow made no sound as it came down on the other side. He closed his eyes again and began to say prayers in Welsh, hurried, frantic, almost incoherent prayers said in a whisper. The tiger had spared him. It had jumped out of the fold when it could have killed him there in the corner.

After a while he tried to move. The slab of rock slid from his ankle, but he couldn't bear the pain at first and put his brow down on his crooked arm and waited until he had recovered again. He was delighted when he realized that the dog had come back. The bitch hadn't. He knew now why she had looked so odd. She had known the tiger was ahead. She was a clever one. He should have watched her closely and taken heed of her strange nervous way, but until he came to the wall he would have said that the tiger was miles away, along the valley, in the quarries above Newydd.

"Bonzo Phillips seen it."

He spoke the words aloud and repeated the man's name. Would they believe that he had seen the tiger? Did it matter whether they believed him or not? He had still to get home, find out whether he could walk or not, and get home safely, across a wall, through the rough, down through the trees, across two little fields, over a ditch and under a wire. The dog came crawling on its belly to him, its tail beating the muddy ground. He spoke to it, fingered one of its ears, pushed it away when it began to lick his face. He was touched to think it had come back when the smell of the tiger must be there in the fold. He wondered where the tiger was now and thought about the mist and the lie of the land beyond the fold. Somehow he felt it wouldn't molest him unless he came upon it in a place where it was cornered.

He wondered about the whole business. The tiger had killed two men and mauled George Nesbitt. George Nesbitt had come upon it when it was eating and perhaps it had seemed to the beast that he was trying to drive it into the shed where it had found the calves. It had killed the Pole and the Indian because it hated them. Any beast kept shut in a cage, cleaned and prodded by two drunken keepers, must have hated them, and here it was out on the mountain, to be driven into a corner somewhere and butchered.

He licked his knuckle and reached the wall and began to lever himself up without putting weight or any strain upon his injured leg. An oak post with a wire stappled to it made it easier for him to rise and then he lay against the wall, letting his leg hang while he worked the post free of the stones and wiggled it until the wire broke. He had a strong crutch even if it wasn't quite as long as it might have been. He put it under his arm and hobbled a pace or two. The pain made him cry out, but he knew he had to move and start the long journey home before he was in danger of having to spend the night on the hill.

From five o'clock on, Ruth Lewis stood in the window looking up the field into the mist. She wondered whether she shouldn't lock up and go to meet her husband with the bitch. If anything had happened to him the mere fact that she walked in the direction he had gone would be of little use. If anything had happened she would have to get men and somebody with a gun. She thought about this for a while, never taking her eyes off the worn path along the side of the field. If anything had happened would anything be of any use? A tiger, the newspaper said, can kill a man with ease. She hardly needed the newspaper to tell her. Two men had died in Pentre Ddu and the tiger had killed them as quickly as she slapped a mouse dead with her shoe.

"Come here," she said to the bitch.

It came out from under the table where it had lain for a long time and stood licking her hand.

"Go fetch him," she said, but the bitch wouldn't go. Her ears went down and her tail curled under again.

The sight made Ruth Lewis wring her hands. She knew that something terrible had happened. They had come upon the tiger somewhere. Bonzo Phillips was a liar. They should lock him up. He was a drunken good-for-nothing!

The clock chimed the half hour and she looked at it and knew that Tom wasn't still working with the flock. He had had ample time to look them and come down. She came away from the window and put on her raincoat, running back as she pulled it on to see again whether or not her husband was coming down the path.

"There's a woman wants to see you, Inspector," said the sergeant.

"What's it about?"

"Her husband went up to look his sheep and he hasn't come back."

"In the mist?" he said, raising his eyebrows. "When everybody knows the tiger is most likely between Pentre Ddu and the mountain?"

"She says he hadn't been able to get up there because he hadn't been well and he couldn't wait any longer. The tiger, she says, was supposed to be at Newydd."

"They're all as stupid as Bonzo Phillips!" exclaimed the

Inspector. "You give them credit for more, but they don't deserve it! The tiger was supposed to be at Newydd!"

He got up and opened the door.

"You wanted to see me?" he asked.

"My husband," she said, holding back her tears. "He's got sheep on the hill. He went up to see to them. He hasn't come back."

"He hasn't heard about the tiger?" asked the Inspector heavily, but he was sorry he had said it. "When did he go?" When was he expecting to get back?"

She told him. He watched her twisting a handkerchief into a rope. It was an old grimy handkerchief as unlovely as her work-spoiled hands with their over-large knuckles.

"The bitch came back," she said.

The Inspector nodded his head. That made it sound a little frightening. The bitch had come back.

"You know where he had gone exactly?" he asked.

She nodded. "Bob Jones could lead you there," she said. "He used to have sheep there."

"Get a couple of men with rifles," he told the sergeant. "We'll find this Bob Jones and see if he'll lead us up there."

The sergeant went off to carry out his instructions.

"You think he'll be all right?" Ruth Lewis asked, her mouth trembling pathetically.

It didn't sound very promising. It sounded very like a tragedy to the Inspector, but he took out his pipe and lit it and said, "I'm sure he'll be all right. The bitch may have had a thrashing and deserted him. He may have had more to do than he expected. He may even be home by now and wondering where you've got to!"

He did his best to make it sound convincing. The smile was a grimace about the stem of his pipe. He wasn't very good at pretending, when in a matter of an hour or two he might have the job of breaking the news to the woman that she was no longer a wife but a widow.

"No use looking on the black side," he said. "The tiger could be miles away. Bonzo Phillips claimed he had seen it in Newydd as you know; even if he was mistaken it doesn't mean it hasn't gone from here. It could be miles away."

She didn't brighten and he hardly expected her to. "Bonzo Phillips," she said, heavily.

There is nowhere that news, good or bad, travels faster than in a village. They were talking about Tom Lewis being lost on the mountain even while Ruth Lewis was asking the Inspector's help.

"So much for what Bonzo Phillips said!" they exclaimed. "Knew the brute was here all the time. It come to Pentre Ddu like a visitation. Poor Tom Lewis! He was headstrong, obstinate too. You can see him goin' up even if he had no call to go."

"You reckon it's gottim then?"

"What else?"

"You hear what they're saying? The tiger got Tom Lewis. His dog's come back. Ruth Lewis had it with her when she come down to report to the police just now."

"New development here," said the newsman talking to Fleet Street. "A shepherd went up into the hills at noon today it seems. His dog has come back but he hasn't. Looks as if the beast has struck again. Hold on for a fill-in. I'm going to try to get hold of his wife. Might be useful to dig out a few pictures of sheepdogs, but we'll see what we can do here."

The Inspector patted Ruth Lewis's arm and suggested that she go back home immediately. As soon as possible men would be going up to make a search for Tom. She might let him know if the other dog came back, but it was likely that the dog was still with him wherever he was.

She nodded her head when the reporter began to ask her questions.

"Yes, sir," she said. "The bitch came back. No, sir, the

dog didn't. Tom knows the mountain. He never gets lost. He never comes down any other way. He should know the mountain. He's lived beside it since he was a baby."

The flashlight made her blink. The photographer and reporter followed her up the road to take her picture standing at her own door. They took pictures of the bitch too.

"No news of Tom?" people asked as she went home.

She shook her head, too preoccupied to wonder how they knew that he hadn't come back.

Bob Jones came stumping along the road. He stopped to take her by the elbow.

"Don't worry, girl," he said. "You an' me know ole Tom. He can look after hisself. If he hasn't come down it's because he's slipped an' fell or something, like I done once, remember?"

"Maybe he has," she said. "I pray he has."

She didn't think it odd to pray that he had hurt himself. She prayed that he had so that she could take comfort against the awful fear that the tiger had killed him.

"We'll soon find him," said Bob Jones as he hurried away. "I'll tell him you're worryin' an' he better hurry."

She choked with emotion and put her face in her hands for a moment. The photographer used his camera and mentally gave the picture a caption—SHEPHERD'S WIFE WEEPS. She began to walk on. The bitch stayed at her heel.

After they had taken their pictures and departed she stood in the yard waiting for something to happen. The world was hushed and still. Down in Pentre Ddu it was almost as quiet as it was on the hill. The police and soldiers clumped up through the scrub beside Bob Jones. It took them longer than it had taken the shepherd because they waited for each other and crowded each other on the narrow path. It was nearly nine o'clock when they started across the open ground to the first sheepfold. They found Tom

Lewis on a bank. He had fallen across his wooden crutch. The dog crouched at his side.

"He ain't dead!" said Bob Jones.

"Did the tiger get him?" asked one of the soldiers as he lumbered forward to see.

"Don't look like it," said the policeman, "but we'll need that stretcher. If you ask me he's been walkin' on a broken ankle if that's possible."

Someone produced a small bottle of brandy. Tom Lewis's head rolled and he opened his eyes.

"I seen the tiger," he said weakly. "It never came for me."

"Take it easy," said the policeman. "Take it easy now. You seen the tiger. Fair enough. So long as you ain't mauled by it."

They lifted him on to the stretcher and carried him back. The dog ran behind. It was dark before they came to the farmhouse, but Ruth Lewis met them in the yard.

"Tom! Tom!" she called hysterically.

"All right, all right!" he said feebly. "Don't fret, girl. I only hurt my leg."

She dropped on her knees beside the stretcher, keeping the bearers standing while she laughed and cried.

"Look," said the policeman, "we better get him fixed up until the doctor sees him an' says what's to be done. You can laugh an' cry to your heart's content indoors."

They carried him into the house. An hour later they moved him to hospital to have his leg X-rayed and set.

Pentre Ddu was asleep when the newspaper men telephoned their stories. SHEPHERD RETURNS FROM THE DEAD, said one.

Inspector Williams had had no comment to make. He was busy now on the telephone himself and at the end of his conversation he made his daily wish, "I hope that tomorrow things will improve and the mist will lift."

CHAPTER 17

As he came awake he wondered about the sound that had disturbed him and brought him out of his sleep, and it was a little while before he knew it to be the drone of subdued conversation somewhere down below. He turned over and looked at his watch and then looked out of the window at the adjoining roof where the slates were damp and moss-encrusted. It was just daylight, but no sparrow twittered as yet in the eaves and no birds sang in the apple tree. It was a hushed morning as it always is when day is not much more than a widening streak of light. The only sound was the endless murmur of the stream among the stones, a sound that hardly altered from noon until dead of night except with the progress of drought or spate. Almost as soon as he had identified the voices as those of a man and a woman the voices died away. The stair creaked; an outside door squealed on its hinges; a footfall sounded on a flag. He looked up at the sloping ceiling. It was too early by more than an hour for anyone in the Horseshoe to be stirring unless the newspaper men were up to something. When his curiosity finally got the better of him he rose and sat on the edge of his bed and began to dress, peering at the stubble of his beard as he struggled into his uniform. The mirror was old and streaked with the ravages of damp so that his face seemed elongated and shadowed, a great deal uglier than he thought it was.

"Hey ho!" he said softly. "Tomorrow's here."

Sometimes he varied this remark by saying that here was another yesterday. It was a habit, like fingering the stubble on his chin and weighing his watch in his palm while he considered what he would do with the hours ahead.

Going downstairs he decided that he would see who was about, go back and shave and make himself presentable, and then go out before he took his breakfast. Almost before he had eaten his breakfast the telephone would be ringing again and people would be asking what was the news of the tiger. Had it been reported in the night?

"Every incident," the Superintendent had said just before he took his leave, "is being magnified out of all proportion. Panic becomes scandal. The tiger is our fault, you can be sure of that. Its freedom to come and go is our fault in spite of the mist; in spite of everything, including the fact that no one knows how it is to be caught while the mist lasts. You might say we are like an army in war. They don't care what we're up against. They don't want to hear that it is impossible. They want a result, one sort of result. Excuses only increase their irritation."

He smiled at the recollection. A man became responsible by delegating responsibility. There was no doubt of that. The man at the end of the line must get results or take the kicks. The tiger had to be nailed when the mist lifted.

At the door of the kitchen he halted. A suitcase was on the table and on the top of a chest he saw an old revolver and three rounds of blackened ammunition. He stood taking things in, as he always did. The suitcase had been hurriedly packed. Part of its contents bulged out from beneath the lid. The revolver meant something too. It was an old service revolver and it looked as though it had been lying in the bottom of a drawer for a long time. He went in and picked it up and he was still examining it when the door opened. He had somehow expected to see Frank Baker, but Frank Baker hadn't expected to see him.

"Good morning," he said. "I heard noises down here. I thought I had better come and investigate."

Frank Baker looked at the revolver and made no answer.

"This belong to you?" the Inspector asked.

"It belonged to my father," he said heavily.

"You haven't a certificate for it?"

"I only found it yesterday."

"I suppose you'll be going to hand it in, or do you propose to apply for a certificate for it?"

"I've got no use for it," said the other.

"No," he agreed, "I can't imagine you would have. It wouldn't be much use against a tiger. I doubt whether the ammunition is any good even if you could use it."

"You'd better take charge of it."

He looked at the gun and then at Frank Baker. On the table, beside the suitcase, was a bottle of port. It was odd, but the whole thing told a particular story. Even the suitcase bulging there on the table. Frank Baker looked at it and then at the gun. A sort of telepathy seemed to be passing between them.

"I'm going," he said, his gaze shifting to the floor. "I've had enough, enough of everything. I can't stand it any more."

"I know," said the Inspector. "Things sometimes get beyond all of us, the best of us. Nearly beyond us, that is, otherwise we'd commit suicide with things like this, or take to the bottle."

"I'll write when I know where I'm going. You'll want that because of the inquest."

"That's right," he said. "You mustn't go to ground. We'll need your evidence. Everything that happened here is tied up with somebody in some way. They'll want to know your version."

"Well," he said, "I'll let you know."

He took hold of the suitcase and as he did so it slipped and knocked the port bottle to the floor. The red wine flowed over the tiles. He stared at it.

"Pity," said the Inspector. "Good stuff wasted."

Baker was still looking at the mess on the floor when the door opened and Betty Collins came in.

"What's keeping you, Frank?" she asked.

It was only after she had spoken that she saw the Inspector.

"You're going too?" he asked.

"It looks like it, doesn't it?" she replied.

It looked like it, that was true. She looked what she was, a fly-by-night, with a soft-topped, shabby case, an overlarge, overstuffed handbag. Everything about her shouted that she was a slut. Either she had grown to overfill her clothes or she bought them tight, but the Inspector didn't need to know the answer. It was written on her face.

"And I won't be back," she added and smiled. "Come on, Frank, for crying out loud!"

"I'll want your address too," said the Inspector.

"You can have it, dear, just as soon as I know it myself! Don't worry about me. I'll be all right!"

"I won't worry," he said. "I know you'll be all right. Just you be there when we want you. It wouldn't be dignified if we had to come looking for you."

"You could come yourself," she said. "Couldn't he, Frank?"

Frank Baker swung the suitcase round the edge of the table and jostled against her.

"Let's go," he said. "I've told the Inspector what's what."

"You've never eloped before?" asked the Inspector as Frank Baker went through the door. He didn't answer, but Betty Collins smiled over her shoulder.

"There's always a first time, dear," she said. "For everybody and everything."

The door remained ajar. He heard them putting their things into the car and the whirr of the starter. Frank Baker was running away, but it wasn't the first time, in spite of what Betty Collins might think. He had been running away almost since the day he had been born. He had been running away with the bottle in his hand, with the gun in his hand, and now he was running away, or trying to, by putting distance between himself and the Horseshoe, but he would find that the thing he was running away from was with him and when he did Betty Collins wouldn't smile. She would reveal the bitter truth that such a woman held for such a man. It was something she couldn't keep to herself. Before very long he would find that he wasn't with her but with himself, as he had always been, with the makings of his own hell.

He turned around and went back through the hall and upstairs again. The sound of the car going off through the village had died away.

"Well?" said old Mrs. Baker.

"Your son has just left," he said. "Not that it's really any of my business so long as I can get hold of him when he's needed."

"I know," she said, "and that tart's gone with him, hasn't she?"

"She has, but I shouldn't worry about that."

The old lady's knuckles whitened as she clutched the stair-rail.

"It's not as if he couldn't have got himself a woman, married or not. It's not as if she meant anything at all. She doesn't. He's trying to escape, that's all. I know him. She's the port bottle. She's . . ."

She saw the old revolver in his hand. "She's that gun, if you like. It won't be long before he's free of her and looking for some other way."

"This was your husband's gun, I believe."

"It was," she agreed. "He once tried to shoot himself with it. I didn't try to stop him. I knew he wouldn't. I suppose Frank found it and tried too?"

"I couldn't say. It was there. It and the port bottle."

"Well, he could have picked a better time to leave me in the lurch, but he'll be back. I am sure of that."

He went past her to his room. The revolver and the ammunition, when he put it on the dressing-table, seemed strangely out of place. He began to shave, hoping that somebody in the place would do something about breakfast when the time came. He was always hungry when he went out before breakfast.

The soldier he stopped to speak to at the top of the village was eager for conversation. It was a tedious job standing in the damp street, peering into the mist, seeing nothing, hearing nothing except the occasional lowing of a beast.

"I'd swear there was a little bit of a breeze a little while back," he said. "I'd almost swear I couldn't see that bush when I first came on. I think there's a change in the air, sir."

"Maybe you're right," the Inspector agreed. "The mountain has had its hat on long enough. It could clear up later in the day. Can't expect the mist to lift early in the morning, but if it is to lift there will be a breeze and the sun will begin to break through. When that happens we'll be able to talk about tigers."

"Ah," said the soldier, "as if we hadn't been talking about them for days."

He laughed and looked across the field.

"Don't let that bush creep up on you," he said, "but for heaven's sake don't shoot it unless you count its stripes first."

"Like Maloney should have done, eh?"

He walked on, thinking about Maloney, the climbers, Nesbitt, Lewis, and the two tiger men. How long ago was it since the nightmare began? It seemed a summer ago, an endless number of days, one like another, with mist on the hill and the telephone ringing and endless questions. The Home Secretary had been enquiring, they said. Politicians had been making statements about civil and military jurisdiction, about helicopters and radio communications, about experts being consulted. They were always hot on experts. They never spoke to anyone who wasn't an expert on something, and even the Chief was beginning to talk about experts. What was needed wasn't an expert tiger-hunter, for who knew how to hunt an invisible tiger? What was needed was a public relations officer to tell the public just what had been done and what the problem was. Track it with dogs, someone had been telling the Chief, and he had almost fallen for the idea of getting a leash of hounds and starting a John Peel sort of rampage across boulders, through gullies and thickets, uphill and down dale among thorns and over slabs. No one had considered what the real progress was bound to be, and what the ultimate result might be. The tiger in Newydd had turned out to be a donkey, but a half-baked stunt with hounds might make the phantom tiger more real in places where it had never been thought of before!

"Well, Williams, you may have a point there," he had said. "My plan is to encompass a big enough area to be sure of having it encircled and to hunt it down within that area as soon as conditions permit and I rather feel that any attempt to track it might make the possibility of containing it in its present territory much more difficult."

His Superintendent had smiled faintly, recalling, perhaps, another point of view the Chief had been putting earlier.

"I am sure, sir, with all respect," he had said, "that if we do as little as possible to disturb it it will be where we look for it when the mist lifts, or at least within a reasonable distance of its present location. I am even reluctant to follow up the reports we have of its probable whereabouts for fear of spoiling our chances. It's a big beast and it can move fast by day or by night, if all they say of tigers is true. It wouldn't look very good if we were responsible for it being flushed right out of the area and even over the marches, would it?"

The Chief tugged at his gloves.

"Come, come, Williams," he said. "Let us preserve some sense of morale. The thing is to face the job in hand and do what we have to do without indulging in flights of fancy. Immediately the mist begins to lift and it seems possible to move, ring through and give me the news. Let us be ready without delay. I'll have everything co-ordinated at once. They promise to begin flights over the territory the minute I give the word. The Army is waiting to move men to agreed places, radio operators have been given references, our own communications are planned, and if you have any report of the beast's movement when the mist begins to lift that will be of vital importance."

He didn't need to be told. He knew it all. The whole thing depended on the mist rising, but sometimes he thought his own sanity depended on being able to handle the newspaper crowd and answer their foolish questions or stop their equally foolish schemes for making a stunt of some aspect of the business. Yesterday someone had put a newspaper down in front of him and asked him what he thought about his rise to stardom. THE MAN WHO WAITS, the headline had said, and his own picture had occupied half the page. Grizzled Inspector Williams, they had called him, the policeman who stands guard in a Welsh village waiting for the mist to rise. They had started to call the beast the Phantom Tiger of Pentre Ddu. The Sunday newspapers were going to make a great splash, by all accounts.

There wasn't so much to be learned walking up or down the village. The soldier at the gate swore he could see three or four yards farther than he could earlier on, but no matter how he peered at the mist he couldn't see the forestry plantings, the little fields and the higher slopes where the bracken grew. He couldn't see the crag that stood at the bend in the valley. The other side of the valley didn't exist. Out there, beyond the water meadows and the rushes, beyond the river and the groves of alders and sallows was the towering height of the mountains that formed the other side of the valley, almost a replica of the country above Pentre Ddu, a country of little farms and stunted trees, of ravens' crags and haunts of buzzards, of huddling cottages and narrow, winding lanes leading up into the wilderness. When he could see all that, there would be no time to look. The hunt would be on.

Although he had expected to have to wait for his breakfast he was delighted to find that somehow the problem had been solved. He went into the little dining-room and a plump woman who lived in the village came bustling in to serve him.

"Ah," she said, "you been lookin' at the mist, Inspector Williams, haven't you?"

He nodded his head. "I looked hard at it. If looking at it would shift it, it would be gone by now."

"It'll all be gone by tomorrow," she assured him. "Mark what I say. The mist won't be with us tomorrow. It'll be as clear as any summer day when the sun comes up. My ole dad says so an' he knows. He's never wrong, sir. He gets a feelin' about the weather."

The Inspector didn't laugh. He didn't even smile. He believed this sort of thing. He had lived too long to laugh. A man who lived among mountains knew very well that mist ran like a wind-blown cloud or hung like a browsing beast, gathered and dispersed in minutes, lifted and dropped again. Now there was a small sign that the mist might be about to rise. It could happen in the midafternoon, he judged. It might gather heavily at the fall of night. It could run before a wind coming up the valley before tomorrow and, as the old man said, tomorrow's dawn could be bright and clear.

"Have you seen the tiger, sir?" she asked as she put down his piping hot plate.

He shook his head. He hadn't seen it. In a way it was

like fishing in a muddy hole. He didn't know the tiger. He only knew it was there. He had seen the bodies of the Pole and the Indian. He had seen what it had done to George Nesbitt. Apart from the injuries, all he had seen of the tiger's existence was a single wet print on a stone.

"I haven't seen it," he said soberly. "There are a lot of things I haven't seen that I have to believe in. I've seen enough of the tiger to know it's real."

"The papers talk about the phantom tiger," she observed. "My ole dad said they wouldn't talk about phantoms if one o' their lot had been slaughtered like the Indian chap or hurt like poor George Nesbitt."

"The papers," he said, "have nothing better to do until the mist lifts. Once the tiger's killed they'll write their bits, take their pictures and hurry off to some other place where there's misery or fear."

"Ah," she said. "That's just what I say."

He munched his toast and drank his tea. Someone had come in through the back door, for the door into the dining-room swung with the closing of the outer door. He looked to see who it was. It was Frank Baker.

"Well," he said. "You changed your mind?"

"I changed my mind," he replied. "I came back."

He pushed through the door and sat down at the table opposite the Inspector.

"You think I'm a coward?" he asked.

"I don't think anything at all about you," the Inspector said. "I don't think very much about people whose affairs don't concern me, but, if you want to know, I'm sorry for you."

"I gave it up," he said. "I changed my mind. She swore and cursed and called me everything, but I walked away and left her to catch the train. She caught it. I didn't drive away until she had gone. I sat thinking about it all. I came back. There isn't anything else to do. You know, I didn't tell you right about the door. It never stuck."

"I didn't think it did," said the Inspector, "but that doesn't matter. Even if it had stuck it wouldn't have made you a different man. Nobody can be charged with causing the Indian's death. He was killed because he went after the tiger."

"You see, when I came, the door was shut. I suppose she shut the door because she wanted to be safe when she discovered the tiger was loose. I knew the tiger was loose and I knew the Indian wanted to get in. I didn't even try to open the door. I held it against him. I pulled on the latch, but I kept my foot against the door. It wouldn't open. It couldn't open so long as I held it shut!"

"And he banged on the door?"

"He banged on the door. I've heard him banging on the door a hundred times since."

"What do you want me to do? Do you want to make a statement about it?"

"Will it make any difference?"

"I don't know that it will, but it's evidence, even if it has no bearing on the coroner's verdict. You can make yourself out to be responsible for the Indian's death in an indirect way. Why did you hold the door shut? Somebody will want to know that."

"Because I was afraid," he said heavily. "Because I was frightened. I held the door shut for the same reason that she shut it. I was looking after my own skin."

"It doesn't sound very nice, but it won't change the coroner's verdict. In fact, it might almost be argued that the Indian wasn't involved with the tiger until he met it in the gully. It could have turned on Jack Roberts when he shot at it."

"It could have stayed where it was, standing over the Pole if the Indian had got in."

"That, like a lot of other things, comes under 'if', and

when we talk about 'if' we can talk about anything. If you hadn't survived the war. If I hadn't been a policeman. If a gun was fired or a tire hadn't burst."

"Do you want me to write it all down?"

"I'll think about it. You've come back and you've told me about the door, but I might say I expected you to do both. I thought you'd be back, and I knew you had something to say about the door. I knew she never would tell me exactly what happened."

"You think you know it all?"

The Inspector's gray eyes looked into Frank Baker's bloodshot brown eyes.

"No," he said. "Nobody knows it all. You don't, and I know I don't. You've told me the truth about the door. You've got a lot of truth to face up to, Mr. Baker, unpleasant truth that concerns yourself when you reach for the bottle or even a sleeping pill. It's too easy to escape from yourself. Too many people do it. You look a gloomy, miserable sort of a chap, but in that one thing you're an optimist for too long. The only thing that matters in life is that a man should win the battle for mastery of himself. I'm a policeman. I'm not even a church-going man. I shouldn't be giving anybody a sermon. I've got other things to do."

He got up and left Frank Baker sitting at the table. Baker sat for several minutes and then went through to the bar. He looked at the whorls of the window for a while and then he took down a glass and a bottle of port and poured himself a measure. He lifted it to his lips and sniffed at it and stared across the room for a while. He could hear the Indian hammering on the door again and the tiger growling. Quickly he put the glass to his lips and downed its contents.

"To hell with the sermon," he said. "To hell with Betty Collins and to hell with the Horseshoe!"

When he had considered this toast for a moment he filled his glass again.

The Inspector passed through the hall. He saw him with the glass and the bottle in his hand, but he didn't turn his head or give the slightest indication that he had seen him. He went outside and looked up the road, thinking about the weather signs and the forecast that the mist might rise. He also thought about Frank Baker and the door. That was clear enough now. The picture of what had happened was complete. He could see the Indian, although he had never seen him alive, talking to Betty Collins. He could see the Pole outside behaving like a demented being and letting the tiger loose. He could see it all, the beginning of the nightmare of days. Like Frank Baker inside, he could hear the little man beating on the door too, and see the white face of Betty Collins underneath her lipstick and rouge, a woman frightened out of her sex, frightened out of all semblance of womanhood, saving her own life by pure instinct, closing the door against the frightened little man and the tiger behind him. He thought about it all without any particular emotion. None of it apparently mattered. If none of it had happened the tiger would still have gone free and might even have killed someone else in the village, Jack Roberts, for instance.

"How do you think it looks, sir?" asked the sergeant.

He hadn't been giving his attention to what he was looking at for some time.

"I'm told that tomorrow will be bright and clear," he said. "Today I wouldn't swear to."

CHAPTER 18

In spite of predictions, the change that had been in the air became more positive before eleven o'clock had chimed in the Horseshoe. It had been a subtle, insignificant sign at first, but then a gorse bush that had loomed in the middle of a field proved to have a background of rock, thistles showed, and docks around which cattle had grazed, and out of the background emerged the hedge and an ash tree. Above the roofs of the village the mist lifted, clearing a tall yew tree, exposing the crag on the hill beyond the road. A heron that rose by the stream went out across the valley into the mist, but remained visible until it dropped in the reed-fringed pools that were part of the river. The sky, too, began to brighten as the sun radiated above the clouds. A score of small birds began to twitter and the whitewashed walls of the old cottages brightened a shade as the moisture in the air diminished. The magpies became more insistent and their pill-box rattle increased as the light improved.

Inspector Williams knew the change without looking at the hill. He could tell by the whiter glare of the papers on his table. It was time to check his opinion of the day ahead.

He picked up the telephone and made a call.

"It's lifting here, sir," he said. "We should be ready to move quite soon."

When he put the instrument down he sat still, thinking about the conversation he had had. He sighed and wondered about the ability of the tiger to cause more misery and suffering, up there on the hill, when they began their methodical combing of the ridges and gullies, plantings and scrub woods; when they searched the bracken and the derelict farms.

"In about half an hour, Sergeant," he said, "we'll be invaded by the Army, the Navy and the Air Force. They are even bringing along searchlight units. The helicopters will begin traversing the hill as soon as the mist lifts sufficiently to allow accurate observation. Mind you, I doubt whether they'll see much of the beast. I fancy it'll lie low with that noise overhead, but even if it lies low, that should confine it while the search closes in."

The telephone rang again. This time it was his immediate superior.

"Yes, sir," he said, "I'll stand by until you get here. I hope that when you arrive I can get outside. I was born down here and I know the hills."

He was thinking that most people would agree that he was no longer a young man, and perhaps he wasn't even fit and active enough to keep pace with the men who would be out on this job, but he didn't want it said that he sat on his backside and let the youngsters do it all. When it was all over somebody would remember who sat in the comparative comfort of the Horseshoe drinking a glass of bitter, and who climbed until he was all in, and out of breath. They weren't going to say that about him when he retired! They were going to say that he had always been game, even when a tiger was at large and he was past his prime.

Beyond the apple tree he could see the hill, the little fields, the fringes of bracken by the hedge-side banks, a grazing sheep, as unconcerned as could be, and a rusty trough cocked up on end. Beyond all that was the orderliness of the plantings, the nursery ranks of seeding trees, the symmetry of innumerable Norway spruce trees. They were like a dark green carpet, covering the tunnels and rides and cobwebbed caverns stretching endlessly up and across the hillside, where anything that moved on foot saw very little of the sky and walked silently on a deep layer of needles as brown as the coat of a vole. Such places would be hard to search, and down or across the network might come the tiger, silent but fast. Up there at this very moment it might be walking, but perhaps it was miles away, standing near the stream in a place where every tree was moss-hung and ivy-twined, and fungus hung on stumps looking like molten cheese. It could be anywhere, in the marshy hollow where the air was full of the smell of wild garlic, or on the stony hillocks that belonged to hares and their cunningly dispersed leverets.

"You know," he said, "this is going to take it out of those who aren't fit. Even if the tiger isn't seen it isn't going to be a picnic."

"Not seeing it will be the biggest worry," said the sergeant. "Not seeing it will wear the best man down unless, of course, some young serviceman is lucky, sees it, and shoots it within the first half-hour. Once all the activity gets started it seems to me the beast will slowly retreat into the hills."

The Inspector thought a great deal about this. The cordon idea was sound enough, but there was a lot of territory to be encompassed, a lot of rough country that couldn't be left outside the perimeter because the tiger would have an exit. The wild rough country was the nearest thing to a jungle that the beast could hope to find, and there were dozens of places where it would take a brave man to venture knowing that the advantage lay with the beast on higher levels with a jumble of rocks nearly as big as some of the cottages in the village.

"There's a lot to be written," he said. "I hope we're not going to add some fatalities to our list. We've no excuse left now. If we run into the beast on the lower hills here somebody may be mauled, but if we don't we'll certainly end up in one of those cwms, far up in the heart of the mountain. It'll be hide-and-seek then all right, but the tiger is a hundred times better at it than we are!"

It struck him as he finished speaking that it all sounded pretty hopeless and negative. There was one way of spoiling any effort and that was to see the snags and see no advantages. He tried very hard to see the tiger being eliminated. Perhaps he wasn't the man for the job at all? Perhaps his place was in the Horseshoe, keeping a seat warm and accompanying the Super or the Chief when they made a tour of inspection?

"An ounce of lead isn't very much," said the sergeant, smiling, "but we always reckoned that if you put it in the right place it would stop a man and they say it's the same with tigers, not that I've ever shot one!"

The Inspector rubbed his hand across his face and said, "You'll be a Superintendent one day, son. Maybe you'll even rise to be a Chief Constable. You'll never be a mere Inspector. Make sure you don't get in the way of the tiger, that's all. Its heart may stand your ounce of lead long enough to interfere with your rise in the Force. I'm giving you my very best advice. I want to be sure it doesn't get me either. I don't want to be a Super now. I just want to retire when my time comes so that I can play bowls."

They smiled at each other.

"You were saying something about going out?"

He pulled at his nose. "Not if they'll let me sit on my backside," he said, but neither of them considered this a serious statement. The old bulldog would be there with the rest. The sergeant suddenly felt very warm and comradely towards him.

"I want to see that Morris chap," said the Inspector. "I think he's about the most likely fellow I've come across. I've got a feeling that where he is it's going to be safe."

He went outside and met Sergeant Morris on the forecourt of the garage.

"It looks as though we're going to have to put on a show," said Morris. "The newspaper boys are getting impatient for pictures and blood. You've got to give it to them. They get morbid. Did you see they had a picture of poor Maloney being taken under escort? That's one picture his old ma won't be proud to see."

The Inspector smiled. "There's only one picture we want to see and that's the picture of a dead tiger! Somebody might not see it. That's what worries me!"

"Meaning you?"

"Of course," he said, smiling. "Who else?"

"Well, I got some clods in my lot that might be better chased up a tree by a tiger! In fact if the tiger likes to chase us all up a tree I'll be glad to go just to see the others scuttle!"

"They are ready to start the big push any minute," he said. "The High Command have been busy with their paper tiger-hunt. Now they want to see it work out. Your move."

"Yours," said Sergeant Morris. "I'm only a ruddy soldier. I didn't sign for tiger-hunts."

"They never asked me whether I did or not, but if you're going up I'll attach myself."

"You're welcome," said the sergeant, "only where I am there's never a medal to be had."

"We'll try to keep out of the tiger's way, eh?"

"Too true," said the sergeant.

He had come to like the old Inspector, he was thinking. Everybody liked him. He was like somebody's old white-haired father; not a policeman at all, but he had guts.

A line of trucks was coming slowly down the village. The radio communications mob had arrived. All this for one outsize cat, and searchlights too! He smiled. It was an expensive tiger. If only there had been a policeman in the village to take charge of the Pole and the Indian before they got up to their fun and games!

"Hey, you!" he called to a soldier who was shepherding a stray chicken into a corner. "What the hell you think you're up to?"

"Taking it back to where it come from," said the private.

"Where'd it come from?"

"Don't know, Sarge."

"Well, you won't be interested in where it came from or who'll have it for lunch. You're going on a nice little tiger-hunt, my lad. You can have tiger for dinner or the tiger can have you for dinner. Take your pick."

They both looked up. A helicopter came swinging out over the side of the valley and dropped down until it was no more than a hundred feet above the road. They could see the pilot.

"That's a cushy way to hunt a tiger, eh, Sarge?"

It was too, he was thinking, the right way for an old codger like himself, or the Inspector. The Inspector was standing on the road watching the plane. It swung in towards the hill and the first belt of scrub. It didn't seem to him as though the use of helicopters would help a great deal at this stage. Let the drive begin and then if the tiger seemed to be breaking cover anywhere or leaving the immediate area they could give warning. They might even drop a man with a telescopic rifle to pick it off if it crossed open ground.

A car came swishing in to the front door of the Horseshoe. The big noises had arrived to give the enterprise their blessing. Down the road, beyond Pentre Ddu, several hundred troops were being debussed and prepared for the moment when they would begin the drive. An officer came down the road in a little truck. He was talking into a hand microphone. It looked like a full-scale Army exercise if you forgot about the tiger, and for a minute or two he could believe that no one was thinking about the tiger at all, except, perhaps, the pilot of the plane up there. He had nothing to do but to fly over the territory and scan the fields and woods.

Reinforcements had arrived from distant places. He watched policemen getting out of vans and cars. There would be a traffic problem, even when all civilian vehicles were stopped for miles on either side of the village. The maps were being studied by soldiers and police alike. It reminded him of a hunt for an escaped convict during the war.

"You'd better begin by loosening your tunic and seeing your boots aren't tied too tightly if you're going to do much climbing," he told a young constable who stood stiffly as though about to take part in some civic function.

The Super greeted him at the door of the Horseshoe.

"This is it, Williams," he said. "I hope we get the brute quickly and before there are any more casualties. Did you see the paper this morning? They had a cartoon of a policeman asleep in a public house with a tiger looking round the door. I suppose we offended one of them and this was his idea of a joke, but the Chief didn't think it was a joke, and apparently others didn't think it very funny either."

"We can't shoot the tiger to please the newspapers, can we?" he asked soberly.

"Anyhow, we stand a chance at last."

"I was hoping to go up with one of the groups," he said. "I know the hills well."

"So you said, Williams, but do you think you'd be any good? You're not a youngster, you know."

He looked down the street and then at the road between his feet.

"I think I can keep up," he said. "I was walking these hills after sheep when I was a small boy. A man born to the hills is always better at walking and climbing than anybody who isn't, and not one in fifty of these troops or our own chaps is from the mountains. I'll be climbing when they've all lost their wind. I'll have the breath to keep a gun steady and shoot if the occasion arises!"

The Super hesitated. "All right," he said, "but I shall tell your wife you asked to go."

The man with the binoculars scanned the open ground below his position for the thousandth time. He could see the bog-cotton swaying and a small bird perched on a fence post. He could see a kestrel hovering and the shadows behind boulders two or three miles from him. When he grew weary of this inspection he could see his counterparts sitting in other posts with radio operators at their elbows. He could even see their lip movements. He hardly needed to be able to lip-read to know what was being said. The tiger was nowhere to be seen and perhaps it didn't exist. The helicopters droned to and fro and within the boundary of the forestry plantations the drive was slowing down.

"You'd think it was bound to happen soon," said the observer. "The bloody beast hasn't come out, so it must be in there. If we haven't seen it and those bods in that flapping contraption haven't spotted it, it must be in the flamin' woods and it'll break cover!"

The radio operator reported and then made himself more comfortable on the box that served for a seat.

"For my part," he said, "I don't give a damn. I like it up here. It's a doddle. Bring me up a few pints an' I'll make it a picnic."

"Me too," said the man with the binoculars. "They can make it an all summer job if they like."

He began to use his glasses to track a butterfly that went floating past.

"I wonder," he said, "if there are any fish in that lake over there? You could make yourself comfortable and fish . . ."

The tiger could have bounded out of the wood and found cover in the minutes that passed, but the tiger wasn't in the woods any more. It had left the trees almost as soon as the hunt had begun, coming out from a gap in the wire fence and standing in the shelter of a thorn, a deformed thorn bush that lay pointing into the hills and overhanging a little patch of bracken. The shadow of that thorn lay across the beast and while it stood there one of the two helicopters being used swung and swayed on its way overhead like some queer prehistoric creature. Its crew looked down, their eyes strained for a sign of the tiger. The machine passed less than eighty feet above it. Five minutes later the tiger moved across a gap and stood beside a long rock that stuck out of the side of a small knoll. One of the watchers on the higher ground to the east scanned that area and looked at the rock and the tiger for a minute, but the faint shadow of a wisp of cloud passing before the sun ran over the rock, blurring the image and producing an illusion that made the beast part of its background. When the tiger slipped away the watcher was studying the ground far beyond it where a bullock, a lean, rangy animal, rubbed its flank against a stump. The tiger went into a depression in the ground and stopped beside another rock while it listened to the myriad confused sounds of the hunt. The sun was high at the time, a breeze was blowing, rippling the dead grass and the bracken. Slowly the tiger moved along the depression among the little thorn trees and the round boulders.

"Have you kept that area under continual observation?" asked the Captain on his tour of inspection.

He pointed with his stick at the tops of the little thorn trees and the boulders flanking the depression along which the tiger was moving.

"Yes, sir," said the observer. "There's a short stretch along which the tiger would have to pass in full view. I've checked that area continually since I took over."

"Good man," said the Captain. "I want you to keep doing that and alternately turn your glasses on the top area by the fence, a hundred yards nearer the trees."

The tiger stood motionless now, half a mile along the depression, and it listened and watched before sidling past a small holly tree at the side of a sheep track. The helicopter came back again. Observers on both sides, and back on the higher parts of the mountains, watched the machine and its shadow following it on the rough moorland. None could have seen the beast, for it was screened by the holly bush and a large rock that stood in the marshy ground like an elephant at a drinking hole. The tiger remained unseen because, even when it passed from solid cover, its movements were slow and sporadic, and because its coloring matched the old, bleached round rushes and the light and shade of ground bathed in warm sunshine. It wasn't an extraordinary thing, for the watchers were trained in a different sort of observation. They were unused to the ways of the beast and they expected it to move as a hunted man might move, while it escaped unhurriedly, cautiously and travelled, as yet, without fear.

Inspector Williams was taking his food with the detachment in charge of Sergeant Morris when this happened. He was bothered by flies, as they all were, for a million flies had come from the trees and the undergrowth beyond the plantings. The warm sun, hastening decomposition in the damp earth, incubated and hatched countless insects and they emerged to fly about the heads of the men.

"If the tiger doesn't get us, the flies will!" said Sergeant Morris.

The Inspector smiled. "I begin to have a feeling it isn't here."

"Don't say it," protested Morris. "Not all this for nothing."

"I see the brute slipping back into the hills in spite of us, and all this."

He waved a hand upwards in the direction of one of the helicopters that came sailing back. The men about him looked up wearily and struck out at the flies. They, too, no longer believed in the tiger's presence. Some of them no longer believed in the tiger at all. It was all a figment of someone's imagination—that nut Maloney, for instance!

An hour and a half later, when the flanks were ahead of them and they were driving up a gully, they had to struggle to keep their footing on steep slopes where the ground was covered with slimy, wet soil. The heart had gone out of the best of them.

"This is being old," panted the Inspector. "Even the youngsters know the feeling now."

"They'll recover," said Morris, "and you and me should

think of the advice the old bull gave to the young bull!"

It seemed an eternity before they started up the last stretch where they could see a faint white background that meant the edge of the wood. No one said that the tiger had slipped out, but it had, and the observers on the mountain and the men posted at intervals along the fence had missed it. It was long afterwards that someone concluded that the tiger had slipped through at the moment a helicopter was passing overhead. At the same moment the men along the top boundary must have been looking up at the machine.

"It never was there!" exclaimed the fence-line men.

"No tiger could have slipped through!" said the crews of the helicopters when interviewed.

"Perhaps," said someone, "there never was a bloody tiger!"

They didn't laugh. No one laughed, least of all the worn-out police Inspector and his companion, Sergeant Morris.

Down in Pentre Ddu the news spread quickly.

"There ain't no bloody tiger, mate. It's beat 'em. They just don't know where it bloody is!"

"Bonzo Phillips saw it in Newydd, mate; Bonzo knows a tiger from a bloody donkey, mate!"

"What you reckon this lot's cost today—ten thousand quid?"

"The papers called it the phantom tiger. They wasn't far wrong!"

They looked up at the hills again, wondering about all the men and vehicles that had been trunding up the narrow, stone-walled roads and what would be done about the tiger when night came.

"Reckon they're goin' t' floodlight miles up there to try keep the tiger inside a ring."

"Oh ah, they reckon so, but how you think they can do it at night when they can't keep track of the bloody thing in daylight?"

"It's a ruddy phantom tiger, mate! Next thing you'll hear it's done for somebody. Wait an' see. They want to pack this lark up an' shut the whole area off while they get a big game hunter to set about it!"

A procession of trucks came through carrying men to relieve those who had combed the forestry areas. Shortly after eight o'clock Inspector Williams came down. He was worn out and looked much older. He dismounted at the Horseshoe and was accosted by a newspaperman who knew him. He sighed wearily and mopped his face with his handkerchief.

"Well," he said, "it's not within two miles of Pentre Ddu. You can say it's into the National Park if you want to make headlines! Tomorrow you might hear of it if it doesn't slip across the high peaks before we come up with it. When we used to hunt hill foxes, when I was a boy, we used to arrange things with farmers and people over the other side of the mountain. It looks to me as though we may be doing that again. The beast will get so far away that we'll have to wait for a report that it has killed somebody."

"You look all in, Williams," said the Super.

He looked down at his soiled boots and the mud on his uniform. He was nearly done. All he wanted was a good draught of cold ale and a place to rest his legs.

"I used to have an instinct for a place a fox would run to," he said. "We used to work it out between us. I was nearly always right. There are natural ways up into the hills. You'd need to have been a shepherd to know them. I'll be glad to carry on tomorrow. If the tiger doesn't get too far tonight perhaps we'll cut across its line of escape tomorrow."

The Super shook his head. "You'll be stiff and sore tomorrow. Better leave it to the Army boys."

Up in the hills there was some debate about the effectiveness of floodlighting the length of the woodland and the adjoining high ground inside which it was hoped to confine the beast. The tiger was far up a long boulder-strewn valley, moving in cover and at times in deep shadow. The sun dropped behind the high shoulder to the west and the wind began to blow. A curlew cried and a mallard that had a brood beside a lake rose in the air and went quickly off to some boggy ground to feed. A cuckoo perched on a rock, attended by a pipit, and night settled in the hills as the stars began to show.

In the cottages of Pentre Ddu they talked about the day. It seemed a long, long time since the blue trailer had come lurching into Bill Watkins's garage and the Pole had been killed.

"You know," said Kitty Price, "my ole dad would never believe what's happened here! He never would! Soldiers everywhere. The noise they make! Them lights up in the hills. You'd think we was somewhere foreign, like. A tiger on the mountain!"

George Nesbitt, in his bed in hospital, thought about Pentre Ddu and what his wife had told him. He shuddered when he thought of the tiger and they had to give him drugs to quiet him in the night, but the tiger had done one good thing. It had made him master in his own house. Jim Parry, coming home from the funeral of his wife, looked at the glare of lights in the hills, but his heart was weary and heavy and he had no thought for the tiger.

CHAPTER 19

A little before noon a heat haze could be seen across the moorland and beyond the fir plantings. The outlines of rocks and the undulations of the ground itself blurred and shimmered. Soon the water in the pools of streams would begin to dry and stagnate and the peat morass at the tail of the lake would harden on the surface to trap the unwary.

The weather was the sort beloved of basking adders and singing grasshoppers and the big flies that live on rotting carrion. No climbers or walkers were in the hills and the solitude of the place was broken only rarely by the blowing of a whistle as the troops did their work. The helicopters had been sent off to the perimeter. It was becoming more certain that the tiger had eluded the search and the news was on the front pages of the papers as well as on the radio bulletins.

WHERE IS THE TIGER? asked the morning headlines and a dozen answers were given. The tiger was twenty miles away. It was close at hand, much closer to Pentre Ddu than anyone imagined, because it wasn't in the hills at all, but in the swampy ground by the river, among the reeds and rushes beyond the water meadows. An intrepid reporter and cameraman had set themselves to keep watch down there. This, their editor suggested, was the real jungle, and the paper carried a picture of a tiger against a background of tall reeds. A rival journal saw the tiger far beyond the village of Pentre Ddu and displayed a great aerial picture of the National Park upon which it had superimposed a giant tiger. The beast straddled the hills, the lakes and forest. THE JUNGLE, said the caption, AND THE KILLER.

Inspector Williams had seen the newspapers. He had read the allegation that the tiger's escape into the National Park was due to the initial slowness of the police who had arrived on the scene of its escape in time to light up the forecourt of the garage, two or three hours after the beast had slipped into the depths of the forestry tract. A young lady named Betty Collins had been interviewed in Liverpool. "Me?" she had said, "I wouldn't stay another night in the place! People there know the police are beat. They were beat from the start! What can the Army do? They only scare it farther away. No, I never seen the tiger, to say I really seen it, and I don't want to. That's why I came away.

Anybody who sticks their neck out gets what they deserve." The Inspector grunted at this piece of effrontery. Anything passed for wisdom, logic, so long as the tiger lived. It was the giant that the papers made it out to be. It straddled the village. It dominated the mountains, at least, in imaginations worked upon by the stories in the press. People began to see it as something more than a beast with the odor of the cage about it, a frightened if dangerous beast, going aimlessly from cover to cover, slinking from tree to tree, rock to rock, with the danger that at any moment one of the hunters would spot it and lay his cheek along the stock of a rifle to put it down with a bullet through the heart or lungs. From that moment the phantom would walk no more. The flesh and blood tiger would kick and convulse, its coat stained with blood, and the whole legend would collapse with it in a certain anti-climax.

"When I used to come up here with the fox-hunters, long ago—shotguns fired black powder—you had to let the stuff clear before you saw whether you had shot a fox or not. . . ."

Sergeant Morris grinned. "A hundred years ago," he said.

"When I was a lad," said the Inspector, smiling, "we reckoned this cwm on our right was a bad run-out over the mountain. Anything that got up it might be shifted with dogs and there was a chance of a shot. If we divide here we can make sure of this area being clear and come out at the top, climbing the slope to bring us on the flank while they are working along the next cwm which runs much deeper into the mountain."

"Look," said the sergeant, "I'll take one of the lads and the radioman, and the corporal can carry on across the open into the next valley if you come through here with us. We can cut over at the top as you suggest."

"If it's up there we'll have a good chance. If it isn't, well, we can stop the top end and keep some sort of order in the thing. If you ask me, the whole scheme looks like breaking up. If we don't make some contact soon we'll have to be ready to have our heads on the block. That's after some bigger heads have been chopped, of course."

Sergeant Morris blew his whistle and summoned the corporal, who came plodding across a great expanse of heather.

"We're going to search the cwm on the right, independent of your movement," he said. "Use the walkie-talkie on your left flank and send this lanky bloke over to us."

He pointed at the radio operator who was standing on a hillock watching a buzzard sailing over the moor.

"Come on, you!" he shouted. "Hey, nature boy! Yes, you! You, day-dream! We're looking for a perishing cat, not a bird."

The tall soldier lumbered over. He was feeling the weight of his load in the broiling heat.

"If we watched what the birds are doing," he said soberly, "we might detect where the tiger is."

"Quite so," said Sergeant Morris. "Since we can only see three birds at the moment and they're all behaving normally we'd be as well tossing a penny."

"I meant, Sergeant, the reaction of a particular bird might be due to the presence of the tiger."

"I know," said Morris. "I know, boy. We haven't got the time and the C.O. wouldn't like it if we hung about. Now don't you go getting sunstroke, just keep your box of tricks in order and look for tigers. They're bigger than birds."

He came back and fell in with the Inspector, who had opened the neck of his shirt and slackened the sling of the rifle he carried, to make himself more comfortable.

"This is the way it can be up in the hills in midsummer," he said, "either too cold or too hot. Your tall lad might be right about looking for signs. Those sheep grazing on the far slope, for instance. Now I think if the tiger had passed through the cwm the sheep wouldn't be evenly distributed and grazing where they are. They'd be bunched in places the way they would be if a dog had been sent up through them."

"It could have passed through here in the night," said his companion.

"Not if it knew what all the fuss with lights and flares was for."

He laughed at this.

"Do you think it has gone on right over the mountain?" asked Morris.

The Inspector screwed up his eyes and looked at the hills. He was using intuition when he answered. "I think it's up this cwm," he said. "I'm not much of a hand as an optimist, and I couldn't tell you why I think so, but I feel it will either run out at the top as we aproach or we'll meet it in here."

"You want to bet?"

"No," he said. "I'm not much of a betting man either, but if it isn't here it's outside the scope of my imagination. I see it here. I shot a fox here once when I was sixteen. It came out from underneath a rock I was standing on. Some of the holes are like caves running a long way under the slabs."

"Could a tiger hide in one?"

"It could easily shelter in the mouth of one. I think we'll come face to face with it all at once."

"I suppose you've got second sight?" said the sergeant.

He was grinning. It amused the Inspector, for his grandmother had always talked about corpse candles and such things. No, he didn't believe that anyone could see the future, but once in a while there was something like a signal a man had, and he applied his brakes to save himself, although at that instant there was no apparent danger. It was the atmosphere of the cwm that made him feel as he did. It was baked by the sun and its shadows were black by contrast with the dried surfaces of the rocks. An odd dead tree stuck out of the higher slope, little streams ran down in different places, like trailing hair. They whispered like the whispering of hidden men, a ghostly sound that was endless and distorted in echo. Here one day and another had no significance and the place belonged to the mysterious atmosphere of the remote mountain. It is true that someone had built those sky-line drystone walls, but whoever had built them, they had been dead so long that no one knew their names, the villages they had lived in, or where their bones mouldered. Once a lead miner had prospected the cwm and left his mark in broken quartz, and once someone had lived down there by the stream, a hermit or a holy man who had cultivated a little patch and baked his stone bread on a hearth now buried in rubble and clothed in gray lichen. Once an enterprising farmer or villager had come up to make flags from a slab of easily-split slate, but all had lived their time and gone a hundred years before the tiger.

They moved in line, splitting the width of the cwm between them and watching the steep sides as well as the slope at the far end. Up the sides of the cwm or the slope at the end the tiger would have to run to escape. It was a slow, fatiguing job, more dangerous than anything they had yet attempted. As their progress slowed down they found the effort of clambering over and around rocks more and more wearying and at length Sergeant Morris signalled a halt. He was watching a point where a great stone almost blocked the cwm. It jutted over the stream and behind it there was obviously a passage-way to a cleft and a chimney that would have been an irresistible challenge to any climber. The great slabs of rock all around the place had a dozen sheltering places for a tiger.

"Inspector," called the sergeant, pointing, "that seems a dangerous corner ahead."

They all looked in the direction of the big rock. The sun glared from its smooth white surface. It suddenly seemed a milestone on the way, something to be approached warily.

Their shirts were sticking to their backs and they could still hear the pounding of their blood.

"When we move I'll take you with me, Barney, and search that place on its own," said Morris.

The Inspector looked at the place and wondered. They had three rifles and the means of calling help if the tiger happened to be in the cleft. He put his rifle down and began to wipe his head and neck with his handkerchief. It was an odd thing, there wasn't a bird of any kind to be seen in the cwm, no dipper on the stream, no pipit up in the grass, no ousel on the high slope. There was no kind of life except the sheep and they were small, far-away and unreal, perhaps three hundred feet above them. The lanky radio operator began to climb across the rocks, coming down to Morris.

"What's up?" the sergeant called.

The operator came on. He seemed a very stolid sort of young man in spite of his thin frame and his rusty hair. He was determined to cover the distance between himself and the sergeant before he answered. When he reached the rock on which the sergeant rested he took a breath and spoke.

"I think you better know, Sarge," he said. "I'm getting nothing through."

"Well, get cracking and get something through!" said the sergeant. "You're a trained man, aren't you? You know what's in the box, eh?"

"It's not that, Sergeant," he said, "we've got in a dead spot or something. We may be in a depression."

"Depression? Depression? You don't get in a depression going uphill! You give that box a bang, boy, kick it around a bit and make it talk! We want a contact down here. How far away is the truck?"

"I'll have to check the map reference. . . ."

"This is rich," said Sergeant Morris when the Inspector struggled over to him. "What do you think? This box of tricks here doesn't work now! We're up the creek. We're out of touch. We're not in the game any more!"

"Does it matter?" asked the Inspector.

They looked at each other and the sergeant grinned again.

"Well, so long as the tiger isn't here it doesn't matter a damn, I suppose. You still got that feeling about the place?"

The Inspector glanced at the radio operator and nodded slowly.

"But don't take my feeling as being anything worth considering. I feel that way because I'm just about all in. If the tiger's not up here I've had my lot!"

"You see that rock up there?" asked Sergeant Morris.

The radio operator nodded.

"You think if you climbed up there you could get some signal?"

The rock was at least four hundred feet up, high on the rim of the cwm, away beyond a dozen obstacles and hazards that would take an age to scale or clamber through.

"Should pick up something up there," he said without enthusiasm.

"Well, I'm not asking you to go, but if the tiger happens to show before we get to the end and we can't shoot it, you should be somewhere where you can send out a warning, so I leave it to you now. As far as the search is concerned I don't think you can be any use from here on, anyway. The place narrows from the big rock on."

"I'll start up there," said the lanky soldier, "but don't change your mind and want me back."

They watched him go. Sergeant Morris shrugged his shoulders. He was sorry for the man, but the equipment was useless in the cwm and there was nothing else that could be done.

"Hey, Barney," he called. "You got your second wind yet?"

Barney struggled to his feet and came hopping over the rocks, his hobnails scoring them as he slipped and slid.

"They say the modern generation is not much good," said Morris, "but this kid is me when I first signed on. They're just the same sort, some willing, some lazy, some no good."

They stood together by the rock for a little while. Morris took a drink from his water bottle and wiped his mouth with the back of his hand.

"Wish it was a nice pint of bitter," he said. "I could just do with a cool pint now."

Barney licked his lips and winked at the Inspector. "I could drink a barrel, couldn't you, sir?"

"I could take a good pint and sleep," said the Inspector, "but I'm old enough to be your dad, your granddad, nearly."

"But you don't get any thirstier, do you?"

"Only wearier," he said. "You've got to let the old horse rest oftener, son. A mountain goat might go springing over the rocks, but not me. I've got to take my time."

"You take your time," said Morris. "If you'll keep the rest of the ground under observation while we go over the big rock that'll keep tabs on anything that happens while we're not able to give a hand."

The Inspector picked up his rifle and looked at it. It was a long time since he had fired one, but a tiger was like a man, surely. You took care not to aim high, you picked a vital spot, behind the shoulder, if you could, and you restrained your breathing. . . .

"All right," said Morris. "If you've nothing else to do, Barney, we'll take a look-see."

"No time for a smoke?" asked Barney, who had just fished a crumpled packet out of his pocket.

"All right! Have your smoke! I never knew a craftier old sweat than you are! Time for a smoke, Sergeant? You should be on a charge!"

Barney lit his cigarette. The Inspector and the sergeant watched him smoking. He took his time, but when he had

had enough he pinched out the cigarette and put it in his pocket.

"Ready, Sergeant," he said, his grin making him look more like a schoolboy than a soldier.

They stood up. The Inspector watched them hopping from rock to rock until they came to the end of the huge stone. They scrambled round the end of it and disappeared from sight. He suddenly felt his scalp tingling and he gripped the rifle and began to clamber over the rocks.

At the end of the big rock there was a patch of small stones that had been washed there in some long-ago flood. They scrambled through the stones and turned up in the direction of the chimney. They could see rock face above the great stones, but the way to the chimney was barred and obstructed by countless slabs. Sergeant Morris grunted as he heaved himself up on one huge slab to walk three paces and drop down again trailing his gun with him. Barney stood on the next obstruction, looking down at the way he had to go and glancing nervously from side to side. For a minute or two he consoled himself by thinking that it was too difficult, even for a tiger, but when he considered a minute he wasn't sure. He could imagine the beast springing across most of those places where he and the sergeant had scrambled up and down.

"Take it easy now," gasped the sergeant as he sprang across from one rock to the next and found himself slithering dangerously over the edge. Barney forgot the tiger in that moment and dropped on all fours to save himself. His rifle slipped from his hand and skidded over the rock to crash down into a crevice. He was stooping to look for it when Morris himself slipped and fell back.

"This is murder!" he said and got back to his feet. Barney carefully lowered himself down, crossed the rough jumble of rocks to the next big obstacle, laid his rifle up on it and began to pull himself up. He looked right up into the sun.

It made everything seem black for a minute after and he began to feel dizzy.

"Sarge," he said, "Sarge. . . ."

The black shadows disappeared. He opened his mouth to say that he was all in, and in that moment he knew that the tiger was there. It came from the right while he was getting the toes of his boots on the edge of the rock and drawing himself upright. It struck him and sprang over him. He made no sound but turned over on his back, rolled towards the edge of the rock, and lay on the breadth of his back. His neck was broken. He stared up at the heavens, slowly a knee that had been bent straightened as his heel-shod slipped on the rock. He was lying quite flat.

"Hey, kid," said Morris. "What's up? You all right?"

The tiger was no more than three yards away. It sprang at Morris before he knew it was there, but he slipped as it was in mid-spring and only its hind feet made contact. A second later it was gathering its bulk on the rock and turning about. Morris lay below the rock, his face bloody, his eyes closed. The rifle he had been carrying was shattered. The tiger sprang back in the direction from which it had come, slid over another rock and went out of sight. When Inspector Williams was at last able to see past the great rock in the middle of the cwm there was no sign of either man. He had heard no sound. It seemed as though they had vanished.

"Morris!" he called. "You there, Morris?"

There was a faint echo from the chimney, up among the stones in the cleft where the tiger had taken refuge. He pulled himself up onto the first of the obstructions and tried to see what lay ahead.

"Morris!"

It was hard to believe that they had both managed to get out of sight and out of earshot. He pushed off his safety catch and then made the gun safe again. If the tiger had been there one of the two would surely have fired. Could they both have slipped off a rock? Wouldn't one of them have managed to cry out even if one had been knocked unconscious?

"Morris!" he said once again. "Where are you, Morris?"

He made his way forward with great difficulty. On the second or third great slab of rock he almost slipped as Morris had done. He was half-way to where the two men had been attacked when he stopped. The sun was glinting on something just on the edge of one of the rocks above his eye-level. He stared at it. It was a hell-shod, the heel-shod of an Army boot. It didn't somehow mean anything until he had stared at it for several seconds and then he knew that someone was lying on his back up there with his toes towards the sky.

"Morris!" he shouted. "Barney! What has happened?"

Only the echoes answered. He put his rifle on the next rock and dragged himself up onto it, hurriedly scrambled over it, crossed the gap to the next, found a foot-hold ascended again, lowered himself once more and went on without trying to see the heel-shod but knowing that he would soon come to it. At last he reached the rock. He was too occupied with climbing onto it to see the broken rifle that had gone over the edge with Morris and he didn't see the sergeant whose body lay crumpled behind the adjoining shelf of stone.

"What's happened, son?" he asked as he crawled over to Barney. "What's happened?" he asked again.

He had seen the look before, even in faces that were wide-eyed. Barney had died very quickly. There didn't seem to be a mark on him. He was looking up at the sun. His rifle wasn't beside him. The Inspector knelt and took hold of his hand. He knew now that Morris was close and that the tiger had struck silently and swiftly. It was very near, too. He turned and stared at the chimney of rock and the slabs between. The rifle was across his chest. He was ready to shoot and then he heard a faint sound to his left, over the edge of the rock. He looked down and saw Sergeant Morris lying below. There was a great deal of blood about his head. His body was twitching. He was breathing.,

It took the Inspector a minute to lower himself into the crevice in which Morris lay. He took his rifle with him and laid it against the rock close at hand while he slid his arm under the sergeant and lifted him.

"Are you going to try to carry me?" Morris said.

He was surprised to find that he was conscious.

"I'd better," he said. "I can't leave you here."

"Get the walkie-talkie chap to contact. . . . Get them to converge. . . . Send up a stretcher. . . . Barney. . . . What happened to Barney?"

"Barney's dead," he said. "I don't think he knew a thing about it."

"It's close. . . . Not far. . . . Thought it might be up in here. . . . Should have got in a position to cover Barney. . . . Should have gone up myself first. Poor Barney. He was a good lad."

The Inspector took Morris's water-bottle and used the contents to bathe his face. Morris groaned. The lacerations were deep. His cheek-bone was exposed. One eye was mutilated.

"Call them up. . . ." he mumbled. "Get them to stop it in this place. . . . You got to get reinforcements as quick as you can. . . ."

"Lie quiet, Morris," he said. "Take it easy. Don't talk. You can't do any good. We'll get you out of here. I'll get help. Don't worry."

Morris lay still and closed his one remaining eye. He was breathing heavily, suffering from shock and loss of blood. The Inspector looked at the other side of the cwm. He could see the maze of rock on the lower levels, the stunted trees here and there, a green area and then the scree and boulders leading up to the top. Half-way up, like a mountain goat, and seeming as small, was the radio operator. He had evidently made every effort to do as suggested, but did he know what had happened down here? Would he do anything but make contact once his set was capable of receiving a signal? He fumbled in the sergeant's pockets and at last found his whistle. It would surely enable him to bring the chap back if nothing else. He put it to his lips and blew. The sound of the first blast echoed. He watched the man climbing. He hadn't stopped but went steadily on, a sheep scrambling ahead of him fancying he was a shepherd. The Inspector blew again, once, twice, three times. It seemed impossible that the man couldn't hear.

"Look round," he said. "For heaven's sake look round!"

The sunlight and the heat combined to spoil visibility. Once he thought the man had heard. In fact, he had stood still, but soon it became obvious that he had only stopped to get his breath. He kept his face turned towards the steep slope. Even if he had turned the Inspector wasn't sure that he would have been able to see him where he crouched behind Morris. He stood up and went back up on to the rock in order to be seen better if the man did hear the whistle. He blew with all his might and waved his arms. Finally he cupped his hands to his mouth and began to call "Cooeee! Coooeee!" It all seemed quite hopeless and he put his fingers to his lips in a last desperate attempt and whistled as a shepherd sometimes does to recall his dog. The sheep on the far slope of the cwm heard him. He could tell. They stopped grazing, but the sound hadn't reached the man and the sheep in front of him gave no sign that they had heard it. The only chance that remained was that he might halt at the top and look down when he got his set working once more. The climb remaining would take him perhaps half an hour. The Inspector went to the edge of the rock and got down again.

"I couldn't make him hear," he said to Morris.

It was a little while before Morris gave any sign that he understood what had been said.

"You go back and get help. . . ." he said. "Shift some of the stones that are hurting me and go."

He stood up and looked again at the boots of the dead soldier. It didn't seem right to leave him lying there staring at the sky. It didn't seem right to leave Morris, either. He climbed once again on to the rock, removed his tunic and used it to cover the boy's face. When he got down again he made Morris comfortable and wiped the blood from his wounds as gently as he could.

"I'll give him a little time to get to the top," he said to himself.

It was as he said this that he knew how stupid he was. He could have fired the rifle to attract the man's attention. The sound of the shot was bound to carry. He picked up the rifle, aimed it at the sky and pulled the trigger. He saw the radio operator stop and turn round. He began to wave and then he fired another shot. The tiger was at that moment below the chimney. It was padding to and fro as it had done once in its cage.

CHAPTER 20

From the steep slope the great rock seemed quite small. The soldier with the field set looked at the rock and began to orient the source of the rifle report. It was a minute or two before he was able to see the Inspector, who stood waving his arms, a small, doll-like figure on a flat slab of stone. The shots were an alarm, that was plain. They had come upon the tiger. He stared intently but failed to see the sergeant or Barney and then, beyond the figure of the Inspector, he saw the black tunic, a tiny blob from which protruded the legs of a man. One of them had run into trouble. The rifle was being fired because they had cornered the tiger. He would have to hurry to the top and see if he could call up help. He was turning away when he saw movement beyond the figure on the rock. Something had crossed a slab high up near the chimney. The tiger was there! He could hardly take his eyes from the place! Did the man on the rock below know just where it was? He had his back to it! Unless he got to the top and made contact at once the tiger would break out and hide again somewhere else. He turned and began the climb with frantic haste. There was no time to look again. He prayed that the set would work when he got up on the high rocks. Where were the helicopters? Where were they now, when they were needed?

Inspector Williams stopped waving. What was the use? The chap was going to the top. If he hadn't understood there was nothing he could do now but wait for help and look after Morris, or abandon him and go for help himself. If he left the place the tiger might come down and escape and even kill Morris on its way. If he stayed he could keep it where it was or perhaps shoot it. . . . It was the only thing to do. He must take the rifle and go up until he met the tiger.

"Morris," he whispered. "Morris, can you hear me?"

Morris had drifted into semi-consciousness. His sound eye remained closed, his head lolled. The Inspector brushed a fly from his cheek.

"Morris," he repeated, "I'm going to go up and try to shoot it."

There was no sign that Morris had heard. He made him as comfortable as he could and reached for the rifle. It needed reloading, for he had fired several rounds, and, there was no telling, his life might depend on a full magazine.

He began to put extra rounds into the magazine. Morris moved a little and groaned and he went back to him.

"Morris," he said, "I'm going to go up and shoot it if I can."

"Stand by," said Morris dazedly. "Keep it where it is."

He began to have doubts about the wisdom of trying to shoot the beast and failing. If it broke through it could go up or down the cwm and no one would know where to look for it. Morris didn't speak again and he doubted whether his remark had been any sort of reply to his own. If the tiger broke away they wouldn't be any farther forward. Let the radio operator call up some help if he could, if he knew that help was needed! He had heard the shots but he had gone on. Now he was lost under the shadow of a large rock. He was perhaps sixty or seventy feet from the top, but the climb that remained would tax his strength and take time.

Below the chimney the tiger moved from one large rock to another as though looking for a way out. On either side the way was too difficult, steep rocks confronted it and the way back was the only way. It prowled from one rock to another, padding about restlessly, its ears down. Once, when he looked up past the body of the young soldier, Inspector Williams caught a glimpse of it, and when it went out of sight he began to wonder whether it was on its way down. Time passed. High above, a raven sailed over and called to another that came out from the cliff. The soldier climbing on the far side of the cwm reached a bank of grass and stood at last beneath the rock he had made his objective. He began to call up base. Faintly he could hear a conversation at the control. He checked the map reference and prepared to give it.

"The tiger," he said, "the tiger has been seen. Send help immediately to . . ."

Down below a rifle shot echoed from the far cliff.

Inspector Williams was sitting on the rock on which

Barney's body lay when he saw the tiger coming. It was in view for a second, disappeared, and then showed itself for an instant as it plunged over a ledge. It was coming down and now it didn't matter what resulted, he had to do what he could to stop it. He slipped the safety catch, waited for it to show again.

"Hold on," he cautioned himself. "Give it time to come. Don't shoot before you're sure!"

He also began to have thoughts about the safe distance to shoot, allowing for the chance that he might fail and the tiger would come for him as fast as it could run. It showed again as he was pondering. He put up the rifle, took careful aim and fired. It seemed to be motionless behind the foresight, but he knew it was moving. It came on, flashing down across the next rock. He worked the bolt and steadied the rifle once again. When it showed this time it was at an angle, slipping incredibly fast past a rock and coming down like a snake. He judged that he was thirty yards from death and it might not show until it was five yards away.

It showed much sooner. It came down on a ledge and gathered itself to spring forward. He fired his second shot and it seemed to hesitate and then was out of sight. There was no time left to think. The empty cartridge bounced on the rock. He held the gun up. The tiger was there in front of him, five yards off. He fired and it sailed forward, its legs at full stretch, its fangs bared, its ears back, a fearful thing coming right down upon him. He staggered back, slipped and went over the rock, his head striking the slab behind him and his rifle falling. The tiger smashed down where he had been standing. He knew nothing about it until he opened his eyes several seconds later and saw its foreleg on the rock. It had dropped on all fours and collapsed. He didn't know whether it was dead or not, in spite of the blood that ran over the stone. He turned his head stiffly and slowly reached out for the rifle. Lying where he was, he couldn't hope to kill it, and if he stood up it had only to strike once to make an end of him. He looked at Morris. Morris's eye was open. He was staring up at the rock, but he made no sign that he knew what he was looking at until the Inspector whispered his name and then he spoke.

Like a man in a trance he said, "You've stopped it, Inspector."

Inspector Williams stood up and saw the tiger's head lying on the rock. The eyes were fixed. It was quite dead. He began to shake and let the rifle slip out of his hand. All at once his legs weakened and he had to get down on his knees. He felt sick.

"Help immediately," said the radio operator on the hill. "More shots down below me. The tiger must be trying to break away. Three shots. No more. I can't see any sign of movement. Can't see anything at all. No, I can't see the tiger."

The radio network began to operate. Both helicopters swung up from their routine flights, away beyond the far ridge, and converged on the cwm. In the adjoining cwm whistles stopped the advance and signals to wheel and file over the slope began to be given. Men hastened to scale the intervening height and reach the place where the tiger was reported to be. The helicopters droned overhead and dropped into the cwm. Inspector Williams heard them and got to his feet. He got up on to the rock beside the dead tiger and the body of the soldier and, taking off his shirt, began to wave it. They saw him and dropped towards him. One of them let down a rope ladder. A man descended and hung overhead, like a spider, signalling him to be ready to be lifted. He caught the arm that was extended to him and was grateful for the help the man gave him as he climbed into the machine.

"The tiger," he said, out of breath. "You'll have seen it

on the rock. It killed one of us and struck down the sergeant. He's badly in need of medical attention."

"You shot it?"

He nodded, finding the effort to make himself heard above the sound of the engine more than he could stand.

"It won't do any more damage."

The man who had helped him into the machine went down again with a stretcher and first-aid kit. When he decended the helicopter swung away and made room for its counterpart.

"What about Morris?" he asked.

The pilot gave him the thumbs-up sign and the machine gathered speed.

The news that the tiger had been killed was in Pentre Ddu long before the Inspector was being seen by a doctor or Morris was half-way across the mountain in the machine which was transporting him to hospital.

"The tiger's dead," they said. "They say a police inspector shot it after it had killed a soldier somewhere up in the black cwm."

"Ah well, they was bound to get it, wasn't they?"

"Should never have happened, mate! It was their fault in the first place, wa'n't it?"

The telephone lines to Fleet Street were heavily booked, while up in the hills Captain Anderson prodded the body of the dead tiger with his boot and wondered how it was to be moved. His C.O. had said something about getting the head for the mess. A photographer stood on an adjoining rock.

"Hold it there, sir," he said, "you'd like your picture in the *Sunday News,* wouldn't you?"

He straightened up, touched his moustache and looked as ferocious as he could, and the tiger, staring at the cloudless summer sky above the cwm, matched his formidable grimace. Bluebottles were gathering on its congealed blood.